MAKE YOUR MOVE

HEATHER GARVIN

Editor: See acknowledgments
Cover Design: Sam Palencia, Ink and Laurel
Publisher: Tuskan Publishing LLC

MAKE YOUR MOVE

TUSKAN PUBLISHING LLC

To my husband, Dustin
Here's to you, for always knowing how to dance
And for keeping life a little bit country

AUTHOR'S NOTE

Abbie and Carson's story may be sweet in many ways, but this book contains on-page intimate scenes and assault. Make Your Move is intended for mature audiences only.

ONE

Sometimes living here feels like nature's joke, and sweating your ass off is the punchline. Florida's scorching summers may be hell for everyone, but when you have a barn full of stalls to muck, the phrase *hot as hell* just doesn't cut it.

Horseback riding fuels my soul, but as I run my hands through my sweat-soaked hair, I can't help envying those with cooler passions—physically cooler. There are endless hobbies I could have chosen. Not something like cliff diving or wakeboarding. And I'm down for the count when it comes to anything that requires me throwing a ball, but I'm sure with a little time I could have found *something*.

Who am I kidding? Riding is in my blood. It's what I live and breathe, and even though I spend most of my days drenched in sweat, I wouldn't have it any other way.

This doesn't stop me from imagining how nice it would be to

have joined the swim team instead. At the end of practice, all I would have to worry about is washing the chlorine out of my blonde hair before it turns green.

Piece of cake.

But as someone who jumps horses, after practice comes barn work—at least for me, anyway.

George, one of the horses, bobs his head over his stall door as I pass. He belongs to my friend, Sarah, and stopping to give him a scratch on the nose is all it takes for me to forget about the suffocating Florida heat for a moment.

A smile comes to my lips as I rub my hand down his face, but there's a twinge of sadness behind it. Almost a month has passed since Sarah left for college. She got into the University of South Florida like she wanted, but under one condition: starting in the summer instead of the fall.

So much for one more summer with my best friend.

I'm happy for her, but I wish our plans weren't derailed. We were looking forward to one more summer of sleepovers and riding together. She was always here, so her absence doesn't go unnoticed. I think George misses her, too.

"Don't worry," I say to him quietly. "She'll be back."

I swear he gives me a dubious look, but I might be projecting my own concerns.

Part of me wonders if I would have gotten into USF. My

grades are average—nothing bad, but nothing to get overly excited about. I still plan on going to college. It feels like the expected *next step*. But I think the local community college is a better fit. It wouldn't feel right to leave my mom alone to take care of the horses.

I'm forever grateful to her for bringing me up around these animals. Even my dad, a city-slicker from Chicago, would admit there's something calming about being around a horse. He was a good sport for a while. He played the part even though horses were never really his thing. Living a life you aren't suited for eventually catches up with you, though. It didn't matter how much he loved my mom and me. One day, he said he needed to move back, and that was it. The loving parents I idolized as one, split and became two.

I've only visited Chicago a few times, but I don't belong there. Even with my father by my side, the bustle of those crowded streets felt like a driving force to get me out of the city. Dad and I used to be closer, but the longer he's been gone, the less I hear from him.

Shaking the thought from my mind, my eyes fall on the clock hanging a few feet away. It's just after 10 a.m., but by the end of my ride with Sully, my riding pants were glued to my legs, soaked in sweat. As soon as I had untacked my partner in crime, hosed him off, and turned him out, I practically ran to the tack room to change into shorts. Now I can at least feel the fresh air on my legs, but my tank top still clings to me, reminding me that even a 9 a.m.

ride is too late in the peak of summer. It gets way too hot way too early.

I've just started mucking the first stall when I look up to find my boyfriend's Mustang—the car, not the horse—creeping along to avoid stone chips from the crushed gravel. Being a proud member of the neighboring barn, Spring Oaks Stables, Seth doesn't exactly need a barn-capable vehicle. When he goes to ride his horse, Valor is brought out already groomed and tacked. I may be jealous of the gorgeous arena and freshly painted stable at Spring Oaks, but I'm not envious of hands-off horsemanship. Grooming, tacking, bathing, and overall care for the animal are what make me love the sport. I don't ride to compete. I ride for the bond I have with Sully—competing is just a perk.

I drop what I'm doing and head to the front of the barn as he parks his red Mustang with white racing stripes in our grassy field. When he steps out, he's wearing pristine riding attire: cream-colored riding pants free of any and all stains, a black polo shirt, and black tall boots that are probably more expensive than my saddle—which should not be the case. Don't even get me started on how much *his* saddle cost.

"Hey, gorgeous," he says with an impressive flash of white teeth. Come to think of it, everything about Seth is impressive. He's tall with a strong but slender build, eyes that could knock you off your feet, and chestnut brown hair that seems to always have the perfect wave.

My eyes drop to my sweat and dirt-covered body in my still-damp tank top, faded denim shorts, and muck boots before crinkling my nose at him. I don't care that he sees me this way. I think it may be one of the reasons he took notice of me in the beginning. Most of the girls he rides with at Spring Oaks are as pristine as him. Who knows, maybe he found my lack of put-togetherness endearing.

For the record, I *do* care about my appearance, sometimes—when I'm not shoveling shit.

He laughs at my expression. "What? Can't a guy think his girlfriend is gorgeous?" Walking up to me, he adds under his breath, "Even if she smells like a horse's ass," with a grin.

I playfully shove his shoulder. "You know, it wouldn't kill you to pick up a shovel."

His hand dusts off the sleeve I touched, and my eyes go wide. "You did not just do that."

"Do what?" he asks, still brushing the apparent dirt off his shirt.

"You did not just *brush off* where I touched you." The laughter bubbles in my voice as I say it, and I can't fight my smile.

Those sparkling blue eyes look up at me, mischief pulling at the corner of his mouth. "And what if I did?"

I fling my arms around him, squeezing him as tightly as I can. He smells like soap and cologne—maybe a tad too much, but I don't mind. This is what he always smells like, and over the past year, it's become almost as comforting and familiar to me as the smell of fresh hay.

"Abbs!" he manages to get out through his laughter. At first, he tries to push me away, but when I don't give in, he wraps his arms around me, squeezing me tightly. "You're impossible," he says, still holding me. "I would kiss the top of your head, but I have to draw the line somewhere."

Pulling away from him, I run my hand over the top of my head. The sweat from wearing my helmet earlier has created a cast-like effect. "Yeah, that's rough," I say, looking at my hand afterward.

He walks with me, and I pick up where I left off in the first stall. "I take it you already rode?"

I glance down at myself. "Yeah, I tried to beat the heat, but this is still the result." I look him up and down. "I take it you haven't?" It's always hard to tell considering Spring Oaks has an *air-conditioned* covered arena. It's being renovated this summer too, because apparently, it's not big enough.

Seth shakes his head. "I'm headed there now, but I wanted to see you first."

He pulls up a stool so we can talk while I work. This happens a lot—me working, him sitting. A small part of me always finds it odd he doesn't offer to help. I know it's my work and not his, but I can't help feeling like I'd offer if the roles were reversed. I try to shake the thought from my mind and refocus on what he's saying.

"…but we'll figure it out before tomorrow."

"Wait, what about tomorrow?" I ask in a feeble attempt to get back on track.

Seth stops. "The party? Christina's bonfire?"

"Oh, right." I heave another pile of manure into the wheelbarrow. "Christina."

"You'll be there, right?" The hope in his eyes makes me wish I felt more motivated to go.

Settling on, "I should be able to," I try to shift back to what I'm doing to hide my reluctance.

"Abbs," he says to get me to look at him. When I finally do, he adds, "It will be fun. Come hang out with us. I know Sarah won't be there this time, but we don't bite."

It's not that I don't like his friends. They're just hard for me to relate to sometimes. You wouldn't think that would be an issue since we all love the same sport, but the people at Spring Oaks have money—*more money than they know what to do with* kind of money. While they talk about the latest product releases from leading brands, the only thing I can contribute is the great deal I got on my IRH helmet from a second-hand store three years ago.

Seth and I met competing against each other last year. He went out of his way to introduce himself even though I was the competition. He was charming and courteous, and I couldn't believe it when he told me he rode for Spring Oaks. He seemed so much more down to earth than I imagined their riders. Little did

I know then that he was the anomaly. The rest of them have their noses so far up in the air, I'm surprised they can see where they're walking.

At least when Sarah was here, she and I felt the same way about Seth's friends. It was nice having her there as a buffer. That was the only way I ever had fun with Seth's friends—if Sarah was there, too.

"I know." I offer him my best smile.

He's still watching me, waiting for me to say something. I always tread carefully when it comes to my opinion of his friends, but he knows they're not my favorite people.

His smile widens, reading me too clearly. "Why don't I pick you up at 8?"

"You want to pick me up?" I ask, not bothering to hide my surprise. Sarah always lived closer to me, so she and I usually rode together. Without her here, I figured I'd just drive myself.

He winks, reassuring my unease. "I'll be here at 8." He hops down from his stool. "Well, I better get going. The barn said they'd have Valor ready around 11."

"No problem." I wipe the sweat from my brow with the back of my hand. Stepping around him, I heave the once again full wheelbarrow up and back it out of the stall. He walks with me towards the manure pile, swinging both hands freely as I try and fail to scratch my nose and push the wheelbarrow at the same time.

Seth places a hand on my back, "I'll take a rain check on a

kiss." Taking a few steps away from me, he blows me a kiss in the air instead, making me laugh.

"Have a good ride!" I call after him as he gets into his car. He throws me a wave before slowly backing out and creeping down our long gravel driveway the same way he came in.

Mustering what's left of my strength, I dump the wheelbarrow and head back into the barn.

Ideally, I like to do the barn work first and ride after. Once I'm done mucking stalls and taking care of the horses, riding is the fun part. It's easy to muster up the extra energy to take Sully for a spin when I structure my day that way.

But summers make that impossible. Because of the heat, barn work always comes second, and that means I'm always exhausted from riding by the time I have to get everything done.

"Abbie?" My mother's voice calls from the other end. "How was your ride?"

I pop my head out of the stall so she can see me and give her a smile. "It was good. We were finally able to nail the right lead after the outside line." For whatever reason, Sully hates the two jumps closest to the fence line. Every time we land from the second one, he ends up leading with the wrong leg. If you're going left, the horse should lead with their left leg. If you're going right, they should lead with their right. Sully enjoys mismatching the two, and it's become our biggest challenge lately.

Gently grabbing hold of the metal bars that line the stall,

Mom's lips twist in a smirk. "He finally conquered the dreaded corner?"

I let out a breath of laughter. "Let's hope." If there's one thing I've learned from growing up with horses, it's that they *all* have their quirks. "In my last lesson, Lisa mentioned making sure he lands on the right lead instead of trying to get him to change it after. I know I'll still have to work on the change, but if I can get him to land correctly while we're at the show, I might not have to worry about it."

Mom nods, leaning back as she still holds the bars. "Add outside leg, lift inside rein, and look in the direction you want him to go."

Shoveling my pitchfork into the shavings, my eyes narrow. "Spying, are we?"

She laughs, the skin around her eyes creasing. My mother may not love her laugh lines, but they're one of my favorite things about her. They make her look as genuine as she is. I mean, who wouldn't want to look like they've had a lifetime of laughter? Brushing her blonde bangs away from her face, she says, "I don't spy! I know you're in good hands."

Tossing the pile of manure into the wheelbarrow, I scrutinize her a little longer. "Sure." She's right. Lisa is an incredible trainer, and I'm lucky she comes out here to give me lessons—especially now that Sarah moved. I wasn't sure if she would find it worth the trip now that she's only teaching one person, but she's stuck by me. My mother wouldn't mind teaching me herself, but we've already explored that when I was younger. For the sake of our relationship, it's better if I let Lisa scream at me from the middle of the ring.

"So," Mom says as she grabs the wheelbarrow and starts rolling it toward the manure pile. "I saw Seth came by. How are things with you two?"

I hate that knowing look in her eyes. It's the look that reminds me my boyfriend has big plans of going to Auburn in the fall.

Seven hours away.

In another state.

And I'll still be here, in Geneva, with no best friend *and* no boyfriend.

"We're fine."

Her shoulders lift ever so slightly in a shrug before she hauls the wheelbarrow up and over to dump out its contents. "I just find it strange you two haven't discussed what you'll do once he leaves."

It *is* strange, but I don't want to be the one to bring it up. I'm not the one leaving. Seth hasn't brought up long distance, but I don't think I'd be on board for it. Those relationships never work out—especially when it comes to college. "I'm sure we'll figure it out. I'm not worried about it." It's a lie. And it's a lie she can see straight through, but I stick to it. "Here, I'll take it," I offer as a way of escaping this conversation. "Do you want to bring Jet in now that her stall is clean and turn out George with Sully?"

"Sure thing," she says in the way I knew she would. Ever since my dad left, Mom and I run this place like two halves of a whole. We may only have four stalls, a feed room, and a tack room, but we run a tight ship. My parents' divorce was hard on all of us, but it solidified my mom and me as a team.

Halfway done.

Setting up in front of the third stall, I grab the pitchfork and get to work. Tim McGraw's "Something Like That" plays over- head, and I quietly sing along. There's something relaxing about this type of work. In fact, when it's not 95 degrees outside, I enjoy it. My mind wanders to what Sarah's plans might be tomorrow night. I wish Tampa wasn't two hours away. If she were any closer, I'd probably ask her to drive back so I wouldn't have to brave Christina's bonfire alone.

I'm not sure how much time has passed when the sound of tires kicking up gravel catches my attention. By the time I move to look out the stall window, my brain has already cycled through who it could be. There are no deliveries scheduled, no lesson with Lisa, not a single person is supposed to be here today. Using my hand to shield the glare of the sun, my eyes track a white truck I've never seen, making its way up our gravel drive.

TWO

An old Dodge Ram comes to a stop in the same place Seth's Mustang sat moments ago. Taking note of the silver, rust-peppered bumper, and door dings decorating the passenger side, I watch cautiously for the unexpected visitor. A guy about my age steps out of the truck and opens the tailgate.

My head tilts as I study him. Maybe it's because Seth was here a moment ago looking pristine, but this guy seems the opposite in every way. His dark jeans and shirt are covered in dirt and stains, there's a dirty rag tucked haphazardly in his back pocket, and he has just enough scruff to let you know he didn't have time to shave this morning—or he didn't care to. I barely realize my eyes dragging over his muscled frame until he reaches for something in the truck bed, pulling me from my daze.

"Um," I say loud enough for him to hear, but he doesn't look my way. Leaning my weight on the pitchfork propped up beside me, I ask, "Can I help you?"

Still without looking, he pulls an assortment of tools from the back of his pickup, lifting them with ease. "I'm your farrier."

He looks like a farrier. He has on chaps and seems to have the right equipment to shoe a horse, but he's not *my* farrier. I shift my weight, narrowing my eyes slightly. "No. You're not."

He looks at me then, and I grip the pitchfork a little tighter when his intense eyes land on me.

He's good looking.

Like *really* good looking.

His dark eyebrows pull together. "This the Linley residence?"

Swallowing, I manage to get my bearings. "It is..." I say slowly, determined to hold his stare. Cocking an eyebrow, I add, "But you're still not my farrier."

Our farrier's name is Ed, and Ed is a nice, middle-aged man with a greying beard. Not some dark-haired guy with his hat on backward.

A flicker of amusement crosses his features before he turns away from me again, hauling the rest of his stuff out of the truck bed. "Today I am," he says gruffly. "I'm helping my dad with some of his clients." Equipment in hand, he turns to face me, his eyebrows shooting upward. "Want to tell me where I can set up?"

His brunette eyes pin me in place, waiting for a response. I didn't even know Ed had a son. "Oh, um. The cross ties are over here." I gesture toward the middle of the aisleway, and he follows

14

me into the barn. "So, you're Ed's son?" I ask as he sets down his things and adjusts the toolbelt around his waist.

"Yeah." He nods towards the stalls. "Who's first?"

Still thrown off by him being here, I falter. "Oh. Let me grab Jet." I look toward her stall. She has her head over the stall door, her speckled grey coat still clean after the bath she had yesterday. She bobs her head in anticipation like even *she's* interested in why he's here.

Following my gaze, he asks, "The flea-bitten grey?"

I nod.

"I'll get her." He walks over and grabs the halter hanging outside her stall like he's been here a million times. Slipping it over her head, he leads her out to the cross ties where he clips her in place. He's about to pick up her hoof when he sees I'm still standing here, staring at him.

I blurt, "What's your name? I didn't know Ed had a son."

"Carson," he deadpans. "Anything else? Or can I get to work?"

Seriously? My eyebrows furrow, and I dramatically gesture toward him, offering a, "By all means," before turning away. Once I'm alone in the stall, I roll my eyes at the wall and mimic his voice. "Or can I get to work?"

"Did you say something?" a deep voice says behind me, and somehow, I feel it in my bones.

I spin around faster than I thought humanly possible, a fresh wave of heat washing over me. "What?"

"You said something?" he asks again, stoic and calm.

"No!" I exclaim, and it comes out sounding manic. Pointing to the cobweb-covered speaker overhead, I do my best to give him a smile that doesn't make me look guilty. "Music."

His deep, brown eyes stay on me for a moment too long before he slowly lifts his gaze to find the speaker I referenced. "Right."

"Do *you* need something?" I ask. "Or can I get back to work?" I point my thumb over my shoulder to the stall behind me.

His lips press together like he's trying to figure out if my last question was intended as a dig.

It was.

"I need to know where you keep your broom."

I make sure to keep my response short like his have been. "Tack room is that door," I say, pointing.

He glances over his shoulder before looking back at me, and for a moment, we're both just staring at each other. It feels like a challenge, and I refuse to be the one who looks away first.

"Why have I never met you if you're Ed's son?"

He doesn't break eye contact. I'm not even sure if he blinks. "Because I don't usually live here."

"Why do you live here now?"

"I don't."

I frown, my brow pinching as I try to refrain from giving him

16

too much of an incredulous look. "Then why are you *here?*"

Back to square one.

He holds my gaze for a beat too long before softening slightly and dropping his gaze. Before I have time to celebrate my victory, his eyes are on me again. "Because I'm taking on some of my dad's clients for a little while." He raises his eyebrows like he's asking if his answer is good enough.

I don't know if it's good enough.

Just as he's about to turn away from me, I add, "One more thing!"

He pauses.

"Where is it?" I ask as I study him a little more closely. He's so serious, like if he smiled, he might crack in half. When he continues to stare, I clarify, "The place you'd rather be."

He doesn't try to sugar-coat the fact that I'm right about him not wanting to be here. Instead, he simply says, "Tennessee."

I grimace. "You left the mountains to come *here?*" Shrugging, I add, "Okay, I guess I can't hold this terrible first impression against you."

His lips quirk ever so slightly, and a sense of accomplishment fills me for making him *almost* smile. Seeing it makes my own lips twitch in response. He adjusts his backward hat and says, "Thanks." After another beat, he adds, "I should probably get to work," and nods towards Jet.

His statement feels like a dismissal, and my faint smile fades.

"Probably," I agree, brushing off the feeling.

With that, he walks back toward the front of the barn, and I watch him carefully, curiosity blooming in my chest. I'm not even sure what comes over me when I say, "Hey," before he gets too far. He turns again, staring at me with an unreadable expression. "There's a bonfire tomorrow night. Being here might suck less if you meet people." He looks reluctant to answer, so I add, "There will be pretty rich girls there," and it takes everything in me not to smack myself.

Carson's head tilts.

"I figured maybe you'd have a type," I offer apologetically.

"You figured my type was girls with money?" he asks slowly, his thoughts safely concealed behind his harsh gaze.

I can't help feeling like I've somehow offended him. "Or maybe you don't have a type," I offer with a shrug. "...Maybe you have a girlfriend or something. I don't know."

He seems to consider me before he pulls a metal hoof pick from his belt. "I don't."

"Great," I say, wiping fresh sweat from my brow. "I'll give you the address before you leave." Before he can answer, I duck into the stall and get back to shoveling shit.

He's finished two of the four horses by the time I throw my

last pile of manure into the wheelbarrow. I can usually muck all four stalls more quickly, but it's like him being here has bogged down the gears in my brain. As I head to the manure pile, I can't help glancing at him as he works. He hasn't looked my way since our conversation—even though I've walked past him at least six times.

After dumping the wheelbarrow and putting it away, I stand in the center of the aisle as he works, assuming he'll look at me so I can give him Christina's address. He's bent over with George's hoof held between his knees as he roughly files back and forth.

After an uncomfortably long moment of silence, he says without looking at me, "Are you just going to stand there, or do you plan on saying something?" My words get stuck in my throat until he looks over his shoulder. With an arch of his brow, he adds, "Enjoying the view?"

As soon as our eyes meet, it's like someone slaps some sense into me. "No!" He looks back at the horse's hoof, but I swear I hear faint laughter. "I just figured I'd give you the address for the party before I leave." Without giving him time to answer, I add, "Not enjoying anything. Trust me."

Seth may be good-looking in the boy-next-door, eat-your-heart-out kind of way, but Carson looks like the type of guy who could make a woman's knees weak with a single glance.

I'm assuming.

Definitely not speaking from experience.

He lets George drop his hoof on the floor and stands to face me. For some reason, the way he's standing in front of me with his arms crossed forms a lump in my throat, and I force myself to swallow.

Looking me dead in the eye, Carson asks, "What's your name?" but the way he says it makes me feel like he's asking something far more intimate.

"Abbie," I croak and then clear my throat, not sure why my voice betrayed me.

"Abbie Linley," he says thoughtfully, and the way my name rolls off his tongue should be illegal. "Okay, fine. What's the deal with this party?"

My eyes narrow, and I'm back to feeling more like myself. "The *deal* is that there will be a bonfire, people our age will be there, and you're welcome to show up."

His face remains serious, but I swear the corner of his mouth quirks when he says, "Okay. What's the address?" He takes out his phone from his pocket.

I tell him, and he finishes typing it just as Mom rounds the corner. "Oh, good. You've met Carson," she says with a smile. "He'll be helping out around here for a few weeks."

"What?" I ask with a feeling of panic gripping me even though it shouldn't matter. "Why?"

If Mom senses my reluctance, she doesn't show it. "He's helping with some work that needs to be done. Stuff neither of us wants to do," she adds with a laugh.

My eyes dart back to the guy with his hat on backward. Having him here for one day was off-putting enough. I'm not sure how I feel about him working here. "Don't you have clients that need to be shod?"

He gives me a funny look like he's surprised I care. *I'm* surprised I care. "Only the ones my dad sends my way. I have some time to get work done here."

Awesome.

"Great," I say with my best smile. "Well, I guess I'll see you around."

"And at the bonfire," Carson adds with a twinge of a smirk.

"Right. That too." I nod.

Mom beams at us, oblivious to the tension thickening the air. I wonder if Carson can feel it.

It's probably in my head.

"Oh, that's a great idea, Abbie. I'm glad you're going to introduce him to some of your friends."

If this were any other situation, I'd correct her. They're Seth's friends, not mine. "Right. Well, I better go," I say and awkwardly excuse myself.

And I swear I can feel his eyes on me until I leave the barn.

THREE

Mom has already fed the horses by the time I make it to the barn the next morning. I love starting my days here. The world is quiet, and the not-yet-blaring sun casts soft light across the still-damp grass.

This morning isn't quiet, though. This morning, there's soft, glowing light and *hammering*. Carson, the apparent early riser, has a ladder propped up against the side of the barn as he replaces some of the wooden boards.

His jeans and grey t-shirt are accompanied by work boots and the same backward hat he wore yesterday, and he holds the same stoic, focused façade.

"Morning, Abbie Linley," he says without looking, in a voice that somehow sounds both pleasant and unpleasant.

"You're here early." I've decided I won't be affected by the likes of Carson—whatever his last name is.

Holding a few nails between his teeth, he gives me a sideways glance. "So are you," he points out before taking one and hammering it in place.

I open my mouth to make some sort of retort, but he hops down from the ladder and moves it a few feet away from me. Snapping my mouth shut, I decide to abandon our conversation altogether and head into the barn. I don't think Carson minds.

Sully greets me with a low whinny as I approach his stall. "Hey, handsome," I say as I run a hand down the white blaze that contrasts with his chestnut coat.

What people don't understand about horseback riding is that, at its foundation, it's just like any other relationship. You need mutual respect to nurture the partnership or else it will never work. Sully and I have our partnership down to a science, and we can read each other so well because of it.

Once he's groomed and tacked, I'm about to lead him out to our small arena when my phone vibrates on the tack trunk nearby. Seth's name lights up on the screen with a single message.

Seth: See you for our date at 8!

His message makes me shake my head. I wouldn't exactly call Christina's bonfire a date. I can't even remember the last time Seth and I have gone on an actual date now that I think about it. It was probably when we first started dating.

Deciding not to answer, I lead Sully out to the ring. The larger barns have sand for proper footing, but ours is mostly grass.

The beginning of our ride goes well. Sully engages his hind end underneath him, and we've warmed up over some of the smaller jumps. I know it's time to try the two jumps in the outside line again. When we go to the show, we'll need to be able to pull off changing leads after the jump. My hands grip the reins a little tighter as I gear myself up for practicing Sully's least favorite thing. Picking up a canter to the left, I circle before lining him up for the jump. We pop over the first one with no issues, and I count the strides in my head.

One, two, one, two, one.

On the last *one*, Sully soars into the air and lands on the other side of the jump with a soft thud. A quick glance tells me we're on the wrong lead. If I let him continue this way, it will throw off his balance, so I go ahead and ask for the change.

Nothing.

I ask again, but our window of opportunity closes as we rush towards the fence line. Letting out a frustrated groan, I stop him before we round the bend. Turning around, ready to try the line again, I spot Carson with his elbows propped on the fence a few feet away.

Great.

Gritting my teeth, I try not to let the new audience member get to my nerves as we approach the first jump.

As always, Sully soars over it beautifully.

One, two, one, two, one.

Again, on the final *one*, he soars into the air and over the second jump. As soon as we're back on solid ground, I notice he's on the wrong lead again and ask for the change by lifting my inside rein and adding pressure with my outside leg.

Still no luck.

It happens two more times. Finally, out of frustration, I call out to Carson who's still watching from the sidelines. "Don't you have something better to do?"

Unfazed, he beckons me over with a single wave of his hand.

"This ought to be good," I mutter to Sully as we make our way over. Once I reach the fence, Carson casually extends his hand to Sully, running it down his face and gently scratching his nose with the back of his knuckle. That single touch lets me know a few things.

1. He respects horses.

2. He *cares* about horses.

3. He may like horses more than people... the same way *I* like horses more than people.

"You're too tense," he says, still barely acknowledging I'm here, but that doesn't stop me from glaring at him.

"I'm not. He just hates doing the change in that corner."

He scratches Sully on the nose. "Because you're too tense."

I try to refrain from rolling my eyes. "Would you like to get on and show me how it's done?"

This makes him finally look at me—except now I wish he

would keep scratching Sully on the nose. As soon as his dark eyes meet mine, I have to fight the urge to look away. Something about the way he looks at me leaves me unsettled, like he can see what lies below the surface and he isn't sure how he feels about his discovery.

Thankfully, all he says is a flat, "No," before he steps away from the fence and points toward the jump at the far end. "But do me a favor. Run it again, and this time, stay heavy with your inside leg, and let the change be an afterthought."

The way he keeps his attention fixed on the jump makes me wonder if people don't usually question when he says to do something. With a dubious lift of my brow, I say, "That's your magical solution? Don't think about what I'm trying to do?"

He adjusts his hat before muttering, "We'll never know if you keep standing here."

His response gets under my skin, but I bite the inside of my cheek and force a tight-lipped smile. Leading Sully back to the center of the ring, I pick up a canter and loop around to try again.

Just like before, the jumps are perfect.

As we land from the second jump, I do as Carson suggested, even though everything in me wants to ignore his unsolicited advice. Keeping my inside leg heavy, I ask for the change with my outside leg.

It's not perfect—if anything it's a little choppy.

But he gets the change.

After all the neck pats and making sure to tell Sully what a good boy he is, I look up to find Carson with his back to me as he walks to the barn.

"Hey!" I yell after him, and he stops and turns. Picking up my pace, I bring Sully over to the side of the fence, and Carson takes a few steps toward us. "How did you know that would work? Do you jump?"

A faint smile pulls at the corner of his mouth. "No." He gestures toward me. "I've never worn pants that tight." When I don't say anything right away, he nods and ends the conversation with, "You're welcome."

Ignoring the fact that I didn't thank him in the first place, I say, "Well, you ride. That much is obvious."

His tight smile shifts, but I can't read what's behind that small gesture. "Anyone can see you throwing your weight to the outside. He can't get the change when you're making him cut in."

"So, you don't ride…" I say slowly, urging him to answer my question.

His face hardens. "I used to."

The way he says those three words feels like he just slammed a door in my face. "But not in tight pants," I add with all seriousness.

He softens, his lips twitching as he looks up at me. "Never in tight pants."

"If you say so." I shrug as I ask Sully to walk on. Carson goes to turn back to the barn for a second time, but I call out to him again. "Will I see you at the party tonight?"

Carson uses his hand as a visor against the now-glaring sun. "I'll try to make it. You know, for the rich girls," he says with a smirk. He looks at me for a moment after he says it like he's watching for my reaction.

Shock.

Shock is my reaction.

Did Carson—the guy who looks like he has never smiled— just make a joke?

When I don't say anything back to that, I swear I see him laugh lightly to himself before turning and walking back into the barn.

As much as I hate to admit it, Carson just surprised me, and it makes my lips twist into a smile.

FOUR

"Ed has a son?" Sarah's voice carries over speakerphone as I get ready for Christina's party.

"Apparently." I comb my fingers through my freshly dried hair. Soft pieces frame my face in varying shades of blonde thanks to spending too much time in the sun.

"Weird."

"Yeah."

"What's he like?" The keys of her laptop click in the background.

I'm quiet for a moment, not sure how to answer her.

Reading through my hesitation, she asks, "That hot?"

"Yeah," I answer, and my voice comes out sounding more like a sigh. Clearing my throat, I try to get my bearings.

Her laptop shuts. "Wait, do you really think he's hot? I don't think I've ever heard you talk about another guy like that." She doesn't bother hiding the glee in her voice when she asks, "Do you think he's hotter than Seth?"

I roll my eyes even though she can't see me. "I can objectively say that someone else is attractive… and I'm not comparing him to Seth."

She gasps. "Oh my god, you do. You think he's hotter than Seth."

"Would you stop?" I ask, but I know she can hear the smile in my voice. "There's a lot more to a person than what they look like."

Her voice comes out in a huff when she says, "Yeah. Well…" and I imagine her lying back on her bed. "Seth doesn't exactly have all that much going for him outside of his looks."

We've had this conversation before, and I'm not sure I want to get into it tonight, so I just say, "Seth is my boyfriend. I love him." I let that last statement sink in before adding, "And Carson is… I don't know. He's hard to figure out. All I know about him is that he definitely does not want to be in Florida."

Sarah laughs on the other end of the phone. "Well, that's the case for most people I think."

A smile pulls at my lips. "I wish you could come with me tonight."

"Me too," she says, but I know she doesn't mean it. "I mean, what am I going to do without the latest gossip?"

I let out a laugh. "Don't worry, I'll fill you in."

"Please don't," she says with a scoff. "Unless it involves Brooke and Conner. I really thought they'd break up before I left."

Seth's best friend doesn't ride, but he's dated most of the girls at Spring Oaks through knowing Seth. His latest relationship with Christina's friend, Brooke, has given us constant drama over the past three months, and Sarah ate up every minute of it. "Because it will be better than TV?" I ask, knowing that's what she's thinking. It's what she's been saying about Conner and Brooke ever since they had their first screaming match in front of everyone.

"Better than TV!" she practically cheers through the other end of the phone, and I can't fight my laughter.

A honk comes from the driveway, letting me know Seth is here. The sound usually makes me happy, but tonight, my stomach twists. This is the first bonfire without Sarah, and something in my gut has me nervous for the night ahead.

"Hey, Seth is here. I have to run," I tell her as I grab my house key off the dresser and tuck it into my pocket.

"Try to record anything better than TV."

I shake my head. "I'm not recording their arguments for you."

She sighs. "At least live text it to me then. I want a play-by-play."

"Uh-huh. Bye, Sarah."

"Have fun!"

My shorter brown cowboy boots pair well with cutoff denim

shorts and a plain, light pink tank top. Leaving my hair straight, it falls to the middle of my back. I rarely do much with it other than leave it down when I'm not working in the barn.

Seth honks his horn again, making me shake my head before calling out, "Bye, Mom!" as I bound down the stairs.

She sits in the family room, reading one of her smutty romance novels. If you ask her, they're *love stories*, but I'm old enough to know what that shirtless hunk of a man in a black cowboy hat on the cover means.

"I wish that boy would come to the door," she says with a sigh. I'm pretty sure my mom loves Seth, but when she calls him *that boy*, I know she's fired up about something he's done.

"It's fine, I told him to stay in the car," I lie to take some of the heat off him.

"Abbie, be safe tonight, have fun, and—," She stops. Her speech has always been *be safe tonight, have fun, and be back before midnight,* but ever since I turned eighteen and we worked out my *rental agreement*—me taking over the barn work in exchange for free room and board—the curfew was dropped. Looking up from her sexy cowboy fiction, she says, "Well, damn. I guess just be safe and have fun."

I let out a laugh, and say, "Will do!" before closing the door behind me.

Seth has the passenger window rolled down as he leans over the center console. "Damn, girl! Where are you going, looking like that?"

"You're obnoxious," I say a little breathlessly as I plop into the deep seat.

He grins, taking my hand in his so he can bring it to his lips. "We might need to leave early so we can take a detour on the way back." Wiggling his eyebrows suggestively, he playfully moves to bite my hand.

I snatch it back and shake my head, but his comment still makes my cheeks warm.

Squeezing my thigh, he throws a wink my way as the car rolls down our gravel drive toward the main road. "I'm ready to have some fun tonight."

"Me too." I give him my best smile. "By the way," I add as I reach over my shoulder for the seatbelt. "I invited Ed's son, Carson. He's in town for a while and doesn't know many people."

"Ed has a son?" he asks, giving me a sideways glance.

"Right?" I laugh. "Who knew?"

Seth shrugs. "The more the merrier." He squeezes my leg, and it helps to settle my unnecessary nerves.

It's a bonfire like any other. Christina's family has enough money to keep up with the Kennedys, and her private guest house on an acre of land at the back of the property is big enough for a family of four to live in comfortably.

The outdoor speakers play country music as we sit around her propane-powered fire pit that looks like it's modeled after a bowl you'd find in a museum—filled with fancy rocks. After being with Seth for a year, I've been to my fair share of these parties. I may have been impressed in the beginning. I mean, I had never seen a fire pit shaped like a bowl, but after a while, the parties are all the same. They're more fun for Seth than they are for me.

He used to make sure I was comfortable around his friends, staying by my side for most of the night. It didn't matter who he was talking to, part of him was always touching me.

An arm around my shoulders.

A finger tracing my lower back.

His foot resting against mine as he sat in the chair next to me.

Now he's with his friends, shotgunning beers as Christina and Brooke take a seat on either side of me.

"Abbie!" Christina practically squeals with faked enthusiasm as she gracefully slides into the empty lawn chair. I'm not saying she's *not* happy to see me, but there's no way she's *that* happy to see me.

"Want to take shots with us in the house?" Brooke asks on my other side. Her dark eyeliner is starting to smudge from the humidity and the number of drinks she's had.

Shaking my head, I hold up the still-full beer. "I'm good."

Christina addresses Brooke like I'm not sitting between them.

"She never drinks with us."

"I am drinking," I say as I hold up my beer again, in case they missed it. I'm not drinking. I'm camouflaging. I don't drink, but the first time Seth brought me to one of these parties, he told me to grab a beer for the sake of blending in.

So that's what I do now. I *blend*.

A white pickup pulls up to the automatic gate, and I'm almost ashamed by the sense of relief I feel at the sight of it. Carson may be difficult to talk to, but I can navigate a conversation with him a lot easier than I can with most of the people here.

Carson parks his truck and steps down. He's not dressed much differently than he was earlier today, but he's showered and has swapped out his grey t-shirt for a black one.

He looks like he smells good.

I should *not* be thinking about how he smells.

A backward baseball cap rests on his head, and the predictability of it brings a smile to my lips.

Brooke glances at Carson before asking Christina in a hushed voice, "Who else did you invite?"

Christina looks Carson up and down with hunger in her eyes. "No one, but if he's lost, I'll gladly give him a home."

I'm not surprised she wants to pounce on Carson. She practically oozes confidence with her long, strawberry-blonde hair and toned riding body she's been perfecting since the age of eight. Before Seth and I got together, she used to flaunt herself in front of him all the time.

"Oh, I invited him," I say casually. "He's Ed's son."

Christina and Brooke both frown. "Ed?" they ask in unison.

"The farrier," I offer, but it doesn't seem to jog their memory, so I add, "He's usually at the shows."

"Huh," Christina mutters as she gets to her feet. I don't think she even heard what I said. She's too focused on stalking Carson like the lioness she is.

Christina and Brooke aren't the only ones who have noticed his arrival. The guys walk back toward the fire pit to see what's going on.

Carson looks past Christina to me as I stay seated by the open flames. Throwing him a quick wave, I suddenly feel guilty, like I've dragged him into some sort of trap.

He gives me a nod just as Christina reaches him, ready to sink her teeth in. I can't hear what she says to him, but he *smiles.* Not a small one either. I'm talking white teeth and everything, and it makes him somehow even more devastatingly handsome than I've ever seen him. If anyone could drag it out of him, I guess it makes sense it would be her. They both make their way to the fire pit, and that's when Carson's intense gaze locks on me, his smile fading.

He says, "Hey, Abbie," and I try to ignore the shiver his voice sends down my spine.

"Hey," I answer with a quick nod and tight-lipped smile. If

36

Christina is a lion, I might as well be a mouse.

"Nice to meet you, man." Seth holds out a hand to Carson. "I'm Seth."

Carson takes his hand in a firm shake. "Carson."

Seth nods. "Abbs said you'll be in town for a while." He takes a seat next to me and rests his arm on the back of my chair. "How are you liking it so far?"

If Carson takes note of the gesture, he doesn't show it. "It's taking a little getting used to, but I'll adjust."

Christina hasn't taken her eyes off Carson the entire time. "What made you decide to come to Florida?"

Carson rubs the back of his neck. "It wasn't exactly my decision."

His eyes jump to meet mine, and I tilt my head, my eyebrows furrowing. I want to know more, but Christina speaks first.

"Who do we have to thank then?" This girl is not shy.

He looks at her, but it's brief. Dropping his stare to the crackling flames, he just shakes his head. "Nobody." He glances at me, but I'm still not sure what to make of anything. The more he says, the more questions I have.

Christina's lips twist as she shamelessly looks Carson up and down again. "A closed book, huh? I have something that can help with that." Her voice drips with honey. "Why don't we go inside for a round of shots?"

My eyes dart to Seth because he knows I don't like when he

mixes liquor and beer. He ends up getting obnoxious and argumentative. I stare at him, hoping he'll look my way, but he doesn't even give me a glance before clapping his hands together excitedly. "Let's do it!"

Before I can do so much as give him a pleading stare, he's on his feet and pushing his buddy Liam toward the house.

"Thanks, but I don't drink." Carson's deep voice makes my head snap in his direction. I haven't met many people my age that turn the stuff down. It isn't until he goes on to say, "Work comes early," that I understand where he's coming from.

Because that's the same reason I don't drink.

Well, that and beer tastes disgusting.

Everyone here rides at Spring Oaks except for Seth's friends, Liam and Conner, who don't ride at all. The riders at Spring Oaks don't have to wake up early to feed, muck, and turn out. They can sleep in and go ride in the afternoon, or they can skip going to the barn altogether. The staff are there to take care of the horses around the clock.

At Carson's comment, Christina's upturned smile dips, her shoulders sagging just enough for me to notice. Having already announced her idea to the rest of the party, she says, "Sit and enjoy the fire. We'll be back in a minute."

With the new development, Seth's eyes jump from Carson to me. "Are you sure you don't want to come in?" he asks me, suddenly looking like he may not want to leave me out here now that he knows I'll have company.

"Yup." I nod. "Are you sure you don't want to stay out here?" I ask with a lift of my brow.

Seth shakes off whatever hesitation he had. "Yeah. We'll be back soon." Looking at Carson, he says, "Abbs will keep you company."

I can't help keeping my eyes pinned on Seth as he makes his way into the house with everyone else. It isn't until Carson settles into the seat next to me that I look away from my boyfriend and over at my new farrier.

"No shots for Abbie Linley?" he asks.

I shake my head. "I don't drink." His eyes drop to the beer in my hand, so I lift it and say, "Warm and full."

He cocks an eyebrow. "But you have it because…?"

Peeling at the label, I shrug. "Seth thought it might be better if I hold it since everyone else is drinking."

"And Seth is your boyfriend, I take it?"

"Yeah." I practically sigh out the word as I look back at the house. Large windows give us a clear view of everyone in the kitchen laughing and pouring liquor into tiny glasses.

I can feel his eyes burning into me, but I try my best to ignore it. Changing the subject, I say, "So, why are you in Florida?" He didn't want to talk about it in front of everyone, and I might be pushing my luck, but I have to ask.

Carson fixates on the flames in front of us. "Everyone thought

I could use a change of scenery." He rests his elbows on his knees as he takes in the view around us. When he finishes his scan, he sets his gaze on the flames again. "Everyone but me, anyway."

"What do you think you could use?"

He forces air out through his nose. "Being left alone."

I let out a breath of laughter. "I think I invited you to the wrong place. I've never seen Christina give someone her undivided attention."

A low laugh escapes him as he looks down and shakes his head. "I'm good."

I gape at him. "You're *good?* You did see her, right?"

He nods without looking at me. "I did."

"She's gorgeous," I say, not bothering to hide my shock.

"She is."

"So, what's the problem?"

He looks at me with enough focus to make me falter. I expect him to say something, but he doesn't. He just looks at me, and the sound of the crackling flames gradually gets drowned out by my hammering heart. After what can only be described as the most intense silence of my life, he simply says, "She's not my type."

FIVE

Tossing the beanbag, I grin as Liam lets out a groan. The small bag glides perfectly into the hole and I hop on my toes to celebrate. "That's game!" I say with a laugh. He's the third person I've played at cornhole, and I've won every round.

Probably because I'm not drunk.

But I'm also really good at cornhole.

"Fine," Liam says with a smirk. "I'll let you have this one."

"Yeah, you definitely *let* me destroy you." Tossing one of the bags into the air, I catch it and add, "Thank you for that."

Christina has kept her claws in Carson most of the night, but every time she goes to drink with everyone else, he takes a seat next to me and lets out a breath like he needs a break. I laugh every time, which makes him shoot me a glare. Our little ritual has been the highlight of my night.

Over the past few hours, Seth has gradually gotten sloppier.

He doesn't usually take shots like this. Plenty of times he's had a beer or two and could still drive me home at the end of the night. I don't mind those nights. It's the nights like these—the nights I have to babysit him—that are a lot less fun.

Since they came back outside, Christina has been talking Carson's ear off about her entire life story, and Seth has been busy drinking with Connor. I've stopped keeping track of where he is, but his loud booming laughter tells me he's off to my right somewhere.

Now that my game with Liam is over, I take a seat by the fire with my decoy beer.

Carson's comment about Christina not being his type still baffles me.

You'd have no idea she wasn't his type by looking at him. He seems to be following her every word with rapt attention. Occasionally, I glance at him from across the firepit, but he keeps those dark eyes trained on her.

"Babe!" Seth's voice pierces through the air a second before he's standing in front of me, blocking my view. Bracing his hands on the armrests of my chair, he bends and lands a wet, drunken kiss on my lips. As soon as he steps back, my eyes catch Carson across the flames as I wipe my mouth.

He's staring.

We hold each other's gaze for only a moment because as soon as Seth starts talking again, Carson's eyes drift up toward him. He watches impassively, and I can't help wondering what he thinks of my very intoxicated boyfriend.

Seth puts a heavy hand on my cheek, pulling my attention to him. "Babe," he whispers with heavy-lidded eyes.

"Yeah?" I brace myself for the worst.

He gives a lazy smile at the sound of my voice. "You're so pretty."

I let out a laugh. Okay, maybe this won't be so bad.

"Focus!" Liam yells at him from a few feet away.

Seth laughs. "Oh! Right." He cups my chin with his entire hand, forcing my face up toward him at an uncomfortable angle. "You're probably going to be mad, but I wanted to let you know we're going mailboxing." My face falls, and Seth lets out another drunken chuckle, reading my expression. The appeal of damaging people's mailboxes with a baseball bat will forever be beyond me. "Yeah, you're mad."

"Connor, you and your friends are idiots!" Brooke yells to her boyfriend, nearly spilling her drink as she gestures toward him.

"Don't fucking start with me, Brooke," Conner growls, and I'd probably be interested in watching their argument if I wasn't struggling not to have my own with the guy leaning over me.

As much as I love Seth, he's never had to work for anything and neither have his friends. They see the property damage as *no big deal*, while all I can think about is how I'd feel if someone did it to my mom. It would be one more thing to add to her already long to-do list and one more expense her bank account doesn't need. I have a feeling the neighbors know it's them causing the damage, but no one does anything about it.

Instead of calling him inconsiderate and immature—which is what I'd like to do—I go for the less abrasive approach. I'll save the rest when he's sober. "I have to be home soon. You promised we wouldn't stay late."

"We'll be quick!" he says, already backing away from me.

Getting to my feet, I start after him. "Really, Seth?"

He groans, tossing his head back. "Come on, Abbs. We're just having a little fun." I cross my arms, my frown deepening, and he lets out a sigh. "Stop being lame." He gestures toward me like I'm somehow the one who's disappointed him tonight. "You won't even drink with us. Seriously, I should have just come here without you."

There it is. The liquor clashing with the beer. Biting the inside of my cheek, I throw my arms up in defeat. "Which one of you is driving?"

"Not me!" Seth yells out with a laugh, catching up with his friends, and I only find his answer mildly comforting.

There's a lot more I'd like to say to him, but he's already talking to Liam and Conner as they walk down the driveway, a baseball bat swinging in Conner's hand.

"They're dumb," Christina says with a roll of her eyes. "I hate when they do that."

She doesn't look like she hates it, and she's never tried to stop them. Muttering, "Yeah," I sit back in my chair and dump my warm beer into the grass beside me.

I wish Sarah were here for me to vent to. Because right now, I am heart-pounding mad, but I can't show it. Whatever I say in front of Christina or Brooke will only get back to Seth—probably exaggerated or manipulated.

Keeping my mouth shut, I look down at my phone to check the time again.

11:24 p.m.

As much as I'd love to believe Seth will be done within a few minutes, I know he'll be gone for at least an hour.

I wish my house was within walking distance.

I wish I would have driven myself.

Staring down at the ground, I shove the neck of my beer into the dirt at my feet. Christina's voice picks up again, talking about the renovations Spring Oaks is doing this summer, and I'm assuming she's resumed her one-sided conversation with Carson.

Slowly lifting my gaze to take inventory of the now dwindled party, I catch Carson watching me from the other side of the flames. Christina has her back to me as she goes on about how she wishes she could hire him to take care of her horse's feet, but Spring Oaks has an exclusive farrier on site. If she notices him looking at something other than her, she doesn't show it. Maybe that's the alcohol in her, too.

The way he's watching me makes me feel like he's been waiting for me to look up, and as soon as our eyes lock, he nods towards his truck. "I'll take you home."

"What?" Christina and I say at the same time.

Carson glances between us briefly before clearing his throat. "Abbie, I can take you home."

Christina and Brooke share a look like our exchange is better than TV for them, and it makes me want to roll my eyes.

"Oh, that's okay. You don't have to do that." The words pour out of my mouth like an automated response, and I'm not sure why. I would *love* to go home, and Seth doesn't seem to want me here, anyway.

Another glance at Christina and Brooke's faces solidifies my gut response to turn down the ride. They're both clinging to this interaction the same way dogs stare at bacon. I can only imagine the backlash they'll cause if I go with him.

My eyes float over to Carson again, but his expression is impossible to read. He studies me for a moment longer before he gets to his feet. "If you're sure."

Panic claws at the inside of my chest, but Christina takes the words out of my mouth when she says, "Wait, you're leaving?"

Carson pulls his keys from his pocket. "Like I said, work starts early." He gives me a look that tells me this is my last chance. "I'll pass your house."

Being left here alone with only Christina and Brooke for company is enough to make me reconsider. My eyes dart to each of the remaining partygoers before I say, "I guess if it's no trouble." I can't control how they spin this story for Seth, but I'll worry about that later.

Stammering, Christina gets to her feet. "What about Seth? I don't think he'd like that considering you're supposed to drive his car home." She pops a hand on her hip as she gazes at me, and some of that honey she put out for Carson turns to vinegar.

That was never part of the agreement. Seth offered to pick me up, and in doing so, I assumed he wouldn't pull a stunt like tonight. I'm about to open my mouth to say something, but Carson answers her for me.

"He doesn't seem too concerned about who drives him around," he says in a gruff voice.

A frown pulls at my lips because even though Seth may not care who drives him, I do. If I leave now and something happens, I'd never forgive myself. "Maybe I should stay," I say, not bothering to hide my reluctance.

Carson looks at me like he's trying to figure something out, but I have no idea what he's thinking. Finally, looking between Christina and me, he shrugs. "Can't he crash here if he's too drunk?"

"You want him to stay here?" Christina asks, her eyes darting back and forth between Carson and me before settling on me. "I mean, that would be fine, of course." She lets out a laugh, gesturing to the house behind her. "It's not like I don't have the room."

I nod slowly, but I can't help wondering why the thought doesn't bother me more.

Is it because I trust Seth?

Or is it because I know if he stays here, she'll end up having to babysit him, and I'll be off the hook?

Fortunately, I don't have much time to overanalyze my relationship before Christina blurts out, "I mean that would be fine, of course. I just want to make sure you're okay with it."

Carson lifts his brow, giving me a sideways glance. "Abbie?"

I look down at my phone to check the time again before surveying the dirt road for any sign of headlights. There's no sign of him, though. The only break in the surrounding darkness comes from the fire in front of me.

"Yeah," I say as I take a step toward Carson. "As long as he doesn't drive." Turning to Christina and Brooke, I add, "I'll text him, but will you let him know that I had to go home?"

The girls do a double-take, and it's clear they're still more entertained by this than they should be.

"Definitely," says Christina, and Brooke echoes with an "Of course, we will."

"Thanks," I say with a small smile and Carson tosses them a wave.

As soon as we're a few steps away from them, I can hear the

two girls scheming, but I can't bring myself to look back. Carson doesn't say anything. We climb into his truck, and it's cleaner than I thought it would be. The cloth seats are grey and worn with age, but overall, the truck isn't in bad shape. He puts it in gear and we head down the driveway, turning onto the main road with only the sound of the engine and the country radio station turned low. He drives with his jaw set, his hand tightly gripping the steering wheel, and I can't help feeling like this is a huge inconvenience for him.

"Thanks for driving me home," I finally say.

He doesn't take his eyes off the road as he answers me. "No problem."

Silence falls between us again. I study him, his stern face dimly lit in the soft glow of the dash. His eyebrows are furrowed as he focuses on the road ahead. I want to know what he's thinking, but I force myself to look out the window. Dark trees and the occasional stop sign are all I see. I realize I'm wringing my hands in my lap, and wedge my fingers under my thighs so I'm sitting on them. Talking to him at the party felt easier than this, but being alone with him has shifted the atmosphere, and it's suffocating. When I can't take it anymore, I blurt, "He's not usually like that."

"Not my business."

The lack of emotion in his voice makes him impossible to read. "I just don't want you to think it's always like that. Seth is a great guy."

He nods without looking at me. "I'm sure he is."

I should drop it, but I can't shake the feeling that he's thinking and saying completely different things. "What's that supposed to mean?" I ask, trying and failing to keep the bite out of my voice.

Those intense eyes jump to me before locking back on the road, his fingers uncurling before they wrap around the steering wheel again. "Look, I don't know him. And you're happy, so it's none of my business."

I'm not sure why I'm suddenly feeling so defensive, but when I say, "I am," it comes out like a snap.

He doesn't say anything else, and I stop trying to force a conversation with him. I am happy with Seth—or at least I think I am.

I am.

Six

I overslept.

Rookie mistake not setting my alarm last night. It's already after 9:30 a.m. which might as well be noon for me. I *never* sleep this late, I've usually been up for two hours by now, but last night I couldn't fall asleep. Anxious thoughts kept me tossing and turning until just past two—that's the last time I remember looking at the clock, anyway.

Seth never texted me after I left the party. He was probably having too much fun or ended up passed out somewhere, but I can't fight the worry in my chest.

Is he mad?

Did he get back safely?

Did Christina blow things with Carson out of proportion?

Or all of the above?

My ride home is nothing for Seth to worry about. Carson and

I didn't talk. He dropped me off, I awkwardly said, "Thanks," and he muttered, "Don't mention it."

That's it.

Yet, everything about him, from the way he looks at me to the way he keeps the pieces of himself locked away, seems to make me restless.

I don't have much time to consider those thoughts this morning as I frantically get dressed and head for the door. It isn't that I have to start the barn work at a certain time or anything. Mom wouldn't care if I started late, but if there's any chance of beating the heat, I need to start early.

Our house may not be big, but it would probably feel bigger if Mom didn't cover every inch of wall space with rustic signs. They all have positive affirmations painted on them—most having to do with horses. From where I'm standing, I can see "Ride More, Worry Less" and "All You Need is Love… And a Horse." Not to mention all the signs that label things. Our pantry has a large white sign that says, "PANTRY," the kitchen has a sign on the wall that says, "KITCHEN," and the bathroom even has a sign above the toilet that reads, you guessed it, "TOILET."

Mom stands in the kitchen with a rag as she wipes down the countertops. She lifts her head when I come bounding down the stairs. "I thought about waking you, but you looked like you could use the extra sleep," she says in a voice that sounds too nonchalant for how I'm feeling.

"I'm sorry!" I zoom past her, and my hand reaches for the kitchen door that leads to our backyard where the barn sits. Yanking it open, I add, "Getting started right away!"

She laughs as I shut the door behind me, but as soon as I'm on the back porch, I stop.

It's bright.

And hot.

Too hot.

My heart sinks. Not only did the party cost me a fight with Seth, but it looks like it cost me my morning ride, too.

Pulling on my rubber muck boots with a little too much force, I head to the barn in my riding pants, anyway. Maybe it will feel cooler once I'm there. But by the time I'm halfway to the barn, any hope of riding has been squashed. It doesn't feel cooler. If anything, it feels hotter now that I've been outside for more than fifteen seconds.

Carson stands near one of the paddock fences as I make my way. He gives me a side-long glance. "You look like you've seen better days."

"Yeah. Well, you look…" I give him the once over and stop because he looks good. The sweat and dirt don't take away from his appearance, and it's kind of annoying. Jeans, a t-shirt, and that backward hat seem to be his go-to, but now add gloved hands as he pierces the earth with a post-hole digger. Remembering I need to finish my sentence, I blurt, "too awake," and hope he didn't notice my staring.

He shakes his head as he looks me up and down without shame. "I thought you had to drink to wake up hungover."

"Ha. Ha," I mock. "And I thought you had to know how to laugh to be funny." His mouth quirks before he steps to the side, ready to dig another hole, but that's all I get. "I couldn't sleep," I add, not sure why I feel the need to justify myself.

Holding the hole digger in place, he lifts an eyebrow. "And why's that?"

The look he's giving me is possibly the most interested he's seemed in anything I've ever said. "I don't know," I lie with a shrug. "Must have been too wired from the party… and I was kind of worried about Seth." That part isn't a lie. I *was* worried about Seth last night, but those weren't the thoughts that kept me from sleeping.

I swallow at the thought.

"Yeah," he says in a breath of what might be considered laughter. "How's he feeling this morning?"

I try my best to scan for any underlying condescending tone, but he said the question with no emotion behind it. "I'm not sure. I haven't talked to him since I saw him last night."

He lifts his head to look at me. "Really?"

"Yeah…" I say, my brow slowly furrowing. "Why?"

Looking back at his work, he lifts his shoulder. "Figured he'd make sure you got home okay."

54

The emotion his voice lacks is made up for by how that statement makes me feel. I start in the direction of the barn. "I'm sure I'll hear from him soon."

I kind of wish Seth would have cared enough to check on me, but I'm not having that conversation with Carson.

As I step onto the concrete aisleway, I take a deep breath. I don't like feeling like Seth is a shitty boyfriend. He's *not* a shitty boyfriend, but for whatever reason, recent events have me doubting how much he cares. Shouldn't he have checked on me after abandoning me to get drunk with his friends?

Maybe he would have checked on me if he were sober.

After I give Sully a good morning pat, I grab my wheelbarrow and pitchfork. Rummaging through the box of spare clothes in the tack room, I grab an old pair of running shorts to replace my riding pants. It's too hot to stay in long pants all day. I'm already wearing a sports bra and loose-fit tank, so I keep those on and grab my muck boots.

I've just finished cleaning my first stall when the familiar sound of Seth's Mustang crawling down our gravel drive hits my ears. Setting the pitchfork against the stall door, I head to the front of the barn to find him already parked and stepping out.

"Abbs!" he says with as much enthusiasm as always.

A smile comes to my lips, and I'm relieved to notice it's a real one. *This* is the Seth I fell in love with—the happy-go-lucky life of

the party that, for whatever reason, was interested in *me* of all people.

"I blacked out last night," he says like it's the funniest thing
to happen all week. "Connor and Liam had to carry me at one
point. I think there's a video." My smile dips, and as soon as he's
close enough to read my expression, he groans. "Oh, come on,
Abbs. Don't give me that look."

I hate this feeling—the feeling that I'm an uptight girlfriend
who doesn't let him have any fun. Sometimes it seems like our
ideas of *fun* couldn't be more different.

"I wish you wouldn't have done that." I stare up at him. "Or
at least told me to drive myself."

"Done what?"

My eyes widen, and before I can stop myself, I'm listing on
my fingers. "Destroying people's mailboxes, abandoning me at a
party with your friends, not bothering to see if I got home okay."

"Seriously? It was *one* night." He holds up a finger like I need
the visual to understand, and my jaw tightens. "I don't do stuff like
that all the time. I was just trying to have fun with my friends."

There's that word, *fun*.

"By destroying people's mailboxes?" It's strange how I felt
genuinely excited to see him a moment ago, and now it feels like a
switch has flipped inside me. All the parts of me that wanted him
close now working in the opposite direction, repelling him.

"Really, Abbie?" The words come out of him like a groan.

"Would you get off my back? I'm not giving you a hard time for leaving with another guy."

My eyes widen. "They're hardly the same thing! And the only reason Carson gave me a ride home was because you left."

He rolls his eyes. "For five minutes."

"Five minutes?" I ask, crossing my arms in the process. "Really?"

He scoffs. "I don't know. I didn't time it. I was having *fun.*" *Fun.*

Carson walks into the barn, wiping his hands on a rag, and Seth's eyes track his movement before snapping back to me. "Why the hell is he still here?" he asks with an arm outstretched in Carson's direction. "Did he stay the night or something?"

"What?" I ask, bewildered. "Of course not. He's helping with some stuff around the barn. He works here now."

"He what?" His eyes dart between Carson and me before landing heavily on me. "Why didn't you tell me?"

"Because it didn't seem important?"

Seth grabs my arm to get my attention. "What else haven't you told me?"

Gritting my teeth, I try to pry his hands off me, but it only makes him tighten his grip. "Would you let go of me?"

That's when I catch movement out of the corner of my eye as Carson takes a single step in our direction. His jaw clenches as he watches the scene in front of him unfold. "Hey. She said let go." His voice remains steady, calm even, but there's something in his eyes that I wouldn't want to cross. I can't stop staring at him, but he doesn't take his eyes off Seth.

Dropping my arms, Seth squares his shoulders and faces Carson. "And you," he says, his voice dripping with venom as he points an accusatory finger. "Do me a favor and stay the hell away from Abbie."

"Really, Seth?" I say, but he doesn't even look at me.

Carson looks down at the rag in his hand, running it through his fingers as he lets out a low laugh. I guess the idea of him wanting to be near me is absurd—so absurd it's laughable.

"What the hell is so funny?" Seth takes a step toward Carson.

I expect him to lash out, but Carson just shakes his head, and mutters, "Literally everything about this."

Before I know it, Seth marches up to Carson, seething. "What did you say?"

Carson's eyes jump to me before staring impassively back at my boyfriend. "I said," he says slowly, enunciating each syllable like he needs to speak in such a way for Seth to understand, "literally everything about this is funny."

Seth's hands ball into fists at his sides, and the movement doesn't go unnoticed. Carson lifts an eyebrow, seemingly unimpressed. "What are you going to do? Hit me?"

Seth looks like he's considering it. Before anything can happen, I call out, "Hey!" and rush to get between them. Standing in

58

the middle, my arms outstretched to stop anything from happening, I'm met with a hard shove and thrown off balance. The impact to my chest nearly knocks the wind out of me as my body crashes into Carson, his arms bracing my fall.

Seth realizes he's pushed me and mutters, "Shit," as Carson helps me to my feet. I stare at my boyfriend, wide-eyed. I can still feel the weight of his hands, my shortened breaths making my chest ache even though I know I'm physically fine. When you think you know someone better than anyone else, and then they do something you *never* thought they'd do... there are no words. He didn't even see me. Not because I necessarily came out of nowhere, but because he was blinded by whatever this issue with Carson is.

Carson just stares at Seth, his lips pressed into a hard line. His mouth may not be saying anything, but his eyes are saying plenty.

When Seth speaks, there's panic laced in his voice. "I didn't mean... I'm sorry. But Abbs, look at this guy!" he holds an outstretched hand toward Carson again.

Carson scoffs and shakes his head before giving me his full attention. "Abbie, are you okay?" The concern behind his gaze has me in a trance, and I feel like I can't look away. My mouth opens but no words come out.

I can see him so clearly right now.

He cares.

He's giving me the type of attention I should be getting from

Seth, and the fact that this is all so backward has my head spinning. Seth is the one who pushed me. Seth is my boyfriend. *He* should be asking if I'm okay.

But he's not.

Carson is.

Even without looking, I can feel Seth's stare burning into me. It isn't until he reaches for me that I break out of my daze, recoiling from his touch. His eyes widen and he shakes his head like I've just committed the ultimate betrayal, but instead of saying something, I sneak another glance at Carson.

"Screw this," is all Seth says before storming back to his car.

The urge to chase after him pulls me, but I don't know what to do. Seth and I need to fix this, that much I know for sure. But why does that have to fall on me? Why am I the one chasing after him?

It isn't until I hear the door to the Mustang open that I'm brought back to the present, and my feet move. I know Carson will judge me for this, but I hurry after my fuming boyfriend.

"Seth!" By the time I reach the front of the barn, he's about to get in his car. "Will I see you later?" There are a million other things I should say, but I know we can't fix this while Carson is here. His presence will keep Seth too angry—too distracted to sit down and talk to me.

Space after a fight is my least favorite thing, though. All it does is delay the resolution.

60

He shakes his head, avoiding my gaze. "No. I have plans."

"Plans that will take all day?"

He gets into his car. "Probably." Slamming the door, he backs out and takes off down our driveway faster than I've ever seen.

Seven

What the hell just happened?

Seth and I have had arguments, but never big enough for him to leave.

Never like this.

I make my way back into the barn with a heavy feeling in my chest, only to be met with another troubling sight. "What are you doing?" I ask Carson, my voice raw. He's mucking out my next stall.

"Nothing." He doesn't look at me as he continues to work, shoveling manure with more force than is probably necessary.

I stand there for a moment, taking in the smell of fresh hay and clean shavings, trying to regain my bearings. "You're doing my job," I finally get out.

Tossing the contents of his pitchfork into the wheelbarrow, he says in a gruff voice, "I'm only helping. Get another pitchfork."

I do as he says, but it doesn't stop me from mumbling, "You don't have to do this, you know," as I join him in the stall and start mucking.

His only response is a grunt.

A grunt.

We mostly work in silence. The sound of our pitchforks shuffling shavings and soft whinnies from the two horses in the barn eases some of the tension, but not enough. I'm embarrassed about the way Seth acted and feel guilty for Carson having to deal with him. I wonder what he's thinking. I wonder why he's not saying anything. Eventually, I can't take the quiet anymore. "I'm sorry."

He glances at me as he continues to work. "Don't be." But then he stops what he's doing, his eyes taking their time as they roam over my face. "Are you okay?"

I nod even though I'm not sure it's true. Knowing he witnessed the fight with Seth leaves me feeling exposed, and I wish there was a way for me to hide from the intensity behind his eyes.

Forcing myself to look away, I get to work and thankfully, he does the same. I'm starting to wish I had at least turned on the radio this morning. My heart pounds as we work, and I'm keenly aware of what he's doing at all times, watching him out of the corner of my eye. He never even looks my way. He stays focused on the task at hand with a stern expression, and I can barely think straight with him standing this close to me.

In another attempt to ease the thickening air, I ask, "Why are you doing this?"

Carson finally stops to adjust his hat and wipe some of the sweat from his forehead with the back of his arm. "Because I'm pissed." He sets the pitchfork against the side of the stall wall and steps around me to get the wheelbarrow, now piled high with manure. "I needed to do something, and this was the option that got me in the least amount of trouble."

A frown pulls at the corner of my lips.

"I wouldn't have hit him," he finally says, like I had been worried about it.

I stare at him, not sure what I'm supposed to say to that.

He lets out a sigh. "I'm just letting you know that I wouldn't have. That's not who I am."

"But you wanted to hit him?"

He pauses, staring down at the wheelbarrow in front of him. With a slight shake of his head, he bends down to grab the handles and rolls it backward away from the stall. "Let's talk about something else."

As he starts towards the manure pile, I hurry after him. He was on the brink of opening up, and I feel like the further away he gets, the more that cracked door pulls shut. Scrambling to think of a way to keep the conversation going, I blurt, "So, who do you live with in Tennessee?"

Carson gives me a side-long glance before fixing his gaze

forward again. "My grandpa."

"Does your mom live there, too?"

He doesn't answer me. He doesn't even look at me. Maybe that was too personal?

When it's clear he's not going to answer my question, I ask, "Is your grandpa doing okay without you there?" and it somehow still feels like too personal of a question.

Carson lets out a breath of laughter as he dumps the wheelbarrow. "Trust me, he's fine. He calls me every day to tell me how much he's enjoying having the house to himself."

Talking to him feels like navigating a landmine. He seems so guarded, and it makes me wonder if one wrong step might destroy all the progress I've made. I'm not sure I should consider Carson's willingness to talk to me as *progress,* but that's what it feels like.

I'm pulled from my thoughts, when he says, "Are you sure you're okay?"

I hadn't realized I'd zoned out, and those brown eyes have more warmth behind them than I remember seeing before. I could probably get lost in them if it weren't for the raise of his eyebrows, snapping me from my daze.

"I'm fine," I say too quickly.

The corners of his mouth dip. "Are you worried about what happened with Seth?"

I blink, surprised he would bring it up after saying he didn't want to talk about it.

Shaking my head, I say, "No. I'll call him later. I don't know what got into him."

Carson looks like he wants to say something, but instead, he just picks up the empty wheelbarrow and heads back to the barn. It's obvious he doesn't think highly of my boyfriend, and I can't say I blame him.

"I'm sure he knows what he did isn't okay. I'll clear everything up with him when I call him later," I add to hopefully drive the point home.

"Not my business," is his only response, and I suddenly feel like I'm back at square one with him. His dismissal feels like the end of our conversation, but I don't want it to be over.

Talking about my life doesn't seem like it's moving us in the right direction, so I jump back to asking more questions about him. "Did you have a girlfriend back home? Before you moved here?" I hadn't put much thought into the question before asking it, but now my chest tightens as I wait for his response.

Carson parks the wheelbarrow in front of the next stall and shakes his head. "It wasn't serious."

Curiosity prickles the back of my neck as I imagine Carson in a relationship. He doesn't exactly strike me as the type, so I guess his response fits. "So, what made you decide to move here and get involved with your dad's business?" I ask, hoping to get more than a few words out of him.

Pausing from his work, he stakes the pitchfork into the

ground and stares at me. "You ask a lot of questions."

I can't help the breath of laughter that leaves me as I scoop up a pile of manure. "Yeah. Well, get used to it."

He drops his gaze, going back to shoveling, but not before I catch a faint smile on his lips. It only lasts a moment before his face turns serious again. "My dad is sick. We found out he has cancer."

My jaw drops. "Ed? Are you okay? Is *he* okay?" I feel the blood drain from my face as my throat thickens. Ed might only come here every six weeks, but I never would have known he was sick. I never would have guessed he had cancer. Just the thought of the word, makes me swallow the lump in my throat.

Carson quickly says, "Shit, sorry. I forgot you know him— not the best delivery. The doctors say he'll be fine," and I feel like I can breathe a little easier. "Sorry," he says again. Once he sees me relax, he gets back to work. "Skin cancer," he offers. "They removed it, but they found small amounts in his lymph nodes. They're doing radiation to be safe, and I'll be here to help with his clients."

"They think he'll be okay, though?" I'm not sure what else to say.

"They do," he says with a nod.

I join him in getting back to work. "So, that's why you're here then."

He shrugs.

"I'm glad your dad will be okay."

"Me too." He heaves another pile of manure into the wheelbarrow. "Alright, enough with the questions," he says gruffly. "You're turn. What else is there to know about Abbie Linley?"

For some reason, my cheeks flush at the sound of him saying my name, but I do my best to hide it and let out a scoff. "There isn't much."

He pauses, those dark eyes pinning me in place. "I doubt that."

I may have been able to hide my cheeks turning red before, but I'm definitely failing at it now. "What do you want to know?" I finally ask.

Carson considers my question. "You just graduated, right?"

I nod.

"Are you going away to school in the fall?"

A light laugh leaves me as I hold up a pile of manure. "And leave this life of glory? Never." I dump my heavy pitchfork and start mucking again. "I'll go to a local college, but I don't want to leave home."

"What do you plan on studying?"

His question is refreshing. Seth and his friends only ask me if I'm worried about missing out on parties and that priceless *college experience.* Parties can be fun, but I don't think they'd make me as happy as seeing Sully every morning. "Business." He lifts an eyebrow, and I can't fight my smile. "I know. It will probably be boring and terrible, but it's the road that will get me where I want to go," I say with a shrug.

He's stopped working, and having his full attention might make me sweat more than the Florida heat. "Which is where?"

Bracing myself for his response, I swallow before saying, "I want to have my own barn and teach lessons to kids. I know there's more money in running a show barn, but I'd rather coordinate summer camps and weekly lessons. Kids need to discover a love for horses."

He's quiet, and I squirm, waiting for him to say something. Everyone thinks it's a dumb idea. Well, Seth thinks it's a dumb idea. Mom is just worried it might not pay the bills.

Carson nods before picking up his pitchfork and getting back to work. "I like it."

"You do?"

He glances at me. "Why wouldn't I?"

I don't want to give him another reason not to like Seth, so I just shrug. "You don't strike me as a kid person." It's not the truth I was thinking, but it's certainly not a lie either.

Carson lets out a real laugh, and the sound of it makes me grin. "Kids *love* me."

"Are you sure?" I ask with a crinkle of my nose. "Maybe they just didn't want to hurt your feelings."

He stares at me, not bothering to hide his tight-lipped smile.

"You'll see, Abbie Linley, I'm not as bad as you think I am."

And I have to drop my gaze.

Because I'm afraid he might be right.

EIGHT

Carson goes back to working on the fence, and without him here to distract me, my mind wanders to all the ways my call with Seth might play out later. Even though this isn't my fault, I still feel the full burden of having to fix it. He'll either realize he was acting irrationally, or he'll think he was—and still is—right. The latter sounds exhausting, and the closer I get to speaking with him, the heavier my stomach weighs with dread.

When I finally finish the stalls, I'm almost disappointed I have nothing left to do. My mind keeps replaying Seth and Carson's argument, and the only way to escape those thoughts is by staying busy.

I can't help trying to make sense of where it all went wrong. Seth should have calmed down as soon as he learned Carson didn't sleep here. He should trust me. He should know better than to think I'd have Carson spend the night. I'm not sure what I should be more insulted by, that he basically accused me of cheating, or that he has the audacity to find an issue with who I'm friends with.

I need to talk through this with someone—and it certainly won't be Carson. Taking a seat on one of the wooden trunks in the tack room, I pull out my phone and call Sarah.

"Hey, how was the party last night?" she asks right away. "Anything better than TV happen?"

I put my palm to my forehead and groan. "You mean like me going home with Carson because Seth was too drunk, and then Seth coming here this morning and almost fighting Carson?"

She gasps on the other end of the phone. "Shut up! Are you in the middle of a love triangle?"

"Definitely not," I say with a laugh, and it feels good to laugh about what happened today.

"It sounds like you might be." I can hear her roommate say something about getting food, and Sarah pulling the phone away to answer her.

"Do you need to go?" I ask. It's weird to think she has this other life now. Before she left for college, our lives were like strings so closely entwined they might as well have been part of the same rope. My eyes fall on the bridle hanging in the tack room with her nameplate still stuck to the wall above it, and even though she's only a couple of hours away, it still brings a pang to my chest.

"No," she says casually. "I'm far more interested in the

drama you're stirring up."

I stare up at the ceiling of the tack room. "I'm not stirring up drama." Letting out a laugh, I add, "I know how much you'd enjoy that, though."

"I would," she says without shame. "So, Seth is mad?"

"Yes," I say with a nod, even though she can't see me.

"Because another guy drove you home?"

"That seems to be the reason," I confirm.

"Good!" she practically yells into the phone, making me jump.

"I'm sorry, what?"

"Good," she says again. "Seth takes you for granted. Maybe this will teach him to appreciate what he has."

Getting to my feet, I shake my head. "I don't think that's what's happening." After a pause, I add, "Wait, you think he takes me for granted?"

"Abbie," she sighs my name. "Seth is only ever worried about Seth. You have to have noticed that. His car, his fancy horse, his disregard for anything that isn't his." When I don't answer right away, she says, "So, tell me about Carson."

Grateful for the change of subject, I make my way up to the house, my eyebrows pulling together. "What do you want to know about Carson?"

She lets out an exasperated breath. "Would I be crazy about him if I were there?"

"Yes."

"Damn it," she mutters. "I knew I should have stuck around. Does he make your toes curl when he looks at you too long?"

"Hey," a voice calls out to me, and my head lifts, my spiraling thoughts dissipating. Carson walks toward me with my mom's horse, Cash. I would have walked right into them if he hadn't said something.

"Hey." My cheeks flare, and I hope he didn't hear Sarah's loud voice through the speaker.

"Is that him?" Sarah squeals on the other end.

"It is," I say quietly. "I have to go."

"Call me later!"

I hang up the call without saying goodbye and look from Carson to the horse next to him. "What's going on?"

Carson pats Cash on the neck. "I don't know. He was lying down in the paddock and didn't get up when I went in there to work on the fence. I wanted to make sure he was okay, so I got him up. How did his stall look this morning?"

I try to think back to when I mucked Cash's stall. "I think it was fine. Maybe a little less manure, but nothing concerning."

Carson frowns. "I'm going to see if he'll graze."

"I'll come with you." We diverge from the pathway and head into one of our fields. Carson gives Cash a long lead so he can put his head down and eat.

He doesn't.

He just stands there looking at us. When he does finally lower his head, his knees drop with him like he's trying to lie down.

"Oh, no you don't," Carson mutters as he pulls the horse back to his feet. He immediately starts walking Cash again, keeping him moving. "Probably colic."

"Shit," I say under my breath. Colic can be deadly for horses. "He's had it before, but that was in the winter when the temperature dropped overnight."

Carson, now a good distance away, says, "I'll keep him walking. You might want to get your mom."

I nod and take off in the direction of the house.

For the rest of the afternoon, Carson, Mom, and I take turns walking Cash around the property. When a horse has colic, the best thing to do is keep them moving until they have a bowel movement. If Cash were to roll while lying down, his gut could twist, having deadly consequences. So, even though our feet ache, and we all have red cheeks from being in the hot sun all day, we keep him up, and we keep him walking.

Mom hands Cash to me for the millionth time. "If something doesn't change soon, I may have to call the vet again." She frowns as she looks at her horse, brushing her fingers gently down his face. She looks deep in thought, and I know she's running the numbers of how much that vet visit would cost us. Looking back at me, her shoulders sag. "I'll order pizza for dinner." She looks at Carson. "Are you sure you don't need to head home? You're putting in an awful lot of overtime."

Carson walks toward me with a bucket to see if Cash will eat. He hasn't had much of an appetite for most of the day, but a high-fiber treat can only help. "I'll stay." He gives Cash a pat on the neck as soon as he reaches us. "And it's not overtime. I'm volunteering."

Mom gives him a grateful smile before turning and heading back toward the house.

"How are you holding up?" I ask Carson as he holds the bucket in front of Cash.

"Fine." He nudges the bucket a little closer in Cash's direction. Giving me a sideways glance, he asks, "You?"

I absentmindedly run my fingers through the long hair of the horse's mane. "I'll be better when this guy is feeling better—and when the pizza gets here."

"Me too." Carson grabs a handful of the wet, sloppy bran mash and puts his hand out in front of Cash.

Cash stands there, unimpressed with our efforts. Carson mixes the mash with his hand again before offering his hand to him for a second time.

A wiggling top lip hovers over Carson's open palm, exploring the treat. He snorts out a puff of air like he's ready to snub the food again, but then a pink tongue pokes through, lapping up some of the mash.

Carson and I look at each other, our eyes widening. "That's

76

a good sign!" I say with a grin.

He reaches for another handful, and Cash sniffs and licks his hand again, making a mess as some of it splats on the concrete aisleway. Before reaching for more, Carson holds the bucket out to Cash, but the horse just nudges Carson's hand.

"Fine," Carson says with a faint smile. "You can eat it from my hand as long as you eat."

I look at the state of Carson's arm covered in slop up to his elbow. "You're a mess."

"I don't see you offering to do the dirty work," he says with a smirk as he gives Cash another handful.

I shake my head. "It looks like you've got it covered."

"I don't know," he says as he lets Cash lick his forearm. "It's pretty hard work." As he goes in for more, he snatches my wrist and plummets it into the bucket. "I could use some help."

He lets go right away, but my fingers accidentally graze his as I pull my hand out of the bucket. It's a small touch—a meaningless touch—but every part of my body is aware of it.

Hoping he doesn't think I grazed his hand on purpose, I laugh it off and do my best to shake off some of the slop, but it's no use. Extending my arm out for Cash, I let him lick my hand clean, too.

I shoot him a playful glare. "Thank you for that."

"Any time."

The treat does the trick. By the time my mom comes back

with pizza, Cash has finally passed a pile of manure and seems much happier than we found him this afternoon. Carson and I take turns holding the hose for each other on the side of the barn to wash our hands before we eat.

It's dark when we finally feel like Cash is out of the woods and put him in his stall for the night. Carson says goodnight to Mom and me before getting in his truck, and I watch the red glow of his taillights until he turns onto the main road.

"It's a good thing he saw Cash when he did," Mom says from behind me. When I turn, I see her wiping the back of her hand over her brow. "If it had been much longer… or if Carson hadn't gotten him moving when he did." She shakes her head. "I'm just glad everything is okay."

I give her an understanding smile. "I'm glad, too."

After my shower, I finally look at my phone and cringe when I see three missed calls from Seth. I can't believe he was just here this morning. His fight with Carson feels like it happened weeks ago, and I'm not sure I have anything left to fight with him tonight. Taking a deep breath, I let my thumb tap on his name, my nerves making me pace my room. As I wait for Seth to pick up, my fingers graze over some of the horse figurines I have sitting on my shelf.

The light blue walls have a few horse sketches framed on them, and the knobby oak furniture has been the same since I was ten. Nothing about my room matches the sleek farmhouse décor that's become popular. If anything, it screams, *This person probably owns chickens.*

After five rings, I expect to hear Seth's booming voice tell me I've reached his voicemail and that he'll "try me back later," but instead, I hear, "Hey."

I pull the phone away from my ear to see if I've called the wrong person. Seth has never answered the phone with such a curt greeting. I'm usually met with an "Abbs!" or "Hey, babe!" on the other end.

"Seth?" I ask. "Is everything okay?"

"Sure it is."

Nothing in his voice makes me think he's telling the truth. "What's wrong?"

He sighs, and I get a sinking feeling in my gut. "I called you three times."

"I know. I'm sorry."

"Let me guess," he says, regaining some of his gusto. "You couldn't answer because you were with him."

I shake my head even though he can't see me. "One of the horses—"

"Were you with him?" he asks, with more force.

My mouth is still open mid-sentence when I pause. "What?"

"Were you with him?" Seth asks again, sounding almost robotic.

"Yes, but—"

Cutting me off again, he says, "I don't think I want you hanging around that guy."

"What?" I ask again, my eyebrows pinched.

Seth sighs, and everything about this interaction feels so unlike him. "Carson. I don't want you talking to him."

Heat flares inside of me. Today was stressful and long, and there were more important things to think about than whether my boyfriend would have an issue with me being in the same place as Carson. "Why?"

"Because Abbs," he says with a tinge of annoyance laced in his voice. "I don't like how he looks at you."

A baffled laugh leaves my lips despite my better judgment. "How he *looks* at me?" Was he not there when Carson literally laughed at the idea of wanting to be near me?

"I can just tell. It's a guy thing." His short response makes me feel like I'm talking to a stranger. "Just promise me you won't talk to him anymore, okay?"

After my conversation with Carson today, I can't turn my back on him. I don't want to. He opened up, and after learning the news about Ed and factoring in that he probably helped save Cash's life, I can't shut him out. I won't.

"I work with him," I finally say.

"Seriously?" Seth's voice snaps back with more vigor. "You've known the guy for *two days*."

"I know," I say as I slowly take a seat on my bed, "but that has nothing to do with it." It's not my place to tell Seth about Ed and his diagnosis, so I keep my mouth shut.

"So, what do we do then?" he asks with an edge of anger. "I guess just don't talk to him about anything except work."

His suggestion feels like a slap in the face, and I'm fuming. This conversation isn't like us. We usually spend our time talking about riding, everyday life, and laughing about crazy things our trainers make us do during lessons. But this? This feels like uncharted territory, and I'd give anything to get back on solid ground. Seth's jealousy has never been this bad... or maybe nothing has brought it out until now. Taking a deep breath, I try to stay calm. "Seth, like you said, I've known him for two days. I love you, and I care about our relationship, but you can't tell me who I can and can't talk to—especially when I've done nothing wrong."

I hold my breath as I wait for him to answer. Sarah's comments about Seth only caring about Seth come to mind, but I do my best to push them aside.

It takes him a moment, but eventually, he says, "Come on, Abbs. I'm serious."

"So am I!" I say with a little too much energy into the phone. This whole conversation is ridiculous. "Seth, he's working *at my house*. What do you want me to do? Lock myself in my bedroom while he's here all day? Avoid the barn altogether?" I know I should stop talking, but I can't help adding, "You have friends who are girls. What about Christina? I don't tell you not to talk to her because I trust you."

"Alright. Whatever."

I was expecting more out of him, so it takes me a minute to realize he's not giving me anything to fight against. "Are we okay?" I finally ask, staring at my shelf with the horse figurines and wishing my life was as easy as it was in middle school.

His voice comes out rough as he says, "Yeah," in a way that makes me think he's lying. I want to fix this. I want to get back to feeling more like us, but I can't give him what he wants. I'm about to bring up what happened with Cash again to lead us into safer waters, but he says, "Listen, I have to go, but maybe I'll stop by tomorrow."

"Oh," I mutter, feeling defeated. "Maybe?"

"Yeah."

I pick a stray string on my comforter. "Okay. I guess I'll maybe see you tomorrow then."

"Yeah," he says again, and the phone goes dead.

No "goodbye."

No "I love you."

Nothing.

NINE

I may feel terrible about everything right now, but at least I didn't oversleep this morning. If I had, I would have been late for my lesson with Lisa, and she's already kicking my ass as it is.

"Bend him into the corner!" she hollers from the center of the grassy ring where she stands in her large, floppy hat. It's more of a necessity than a fashion accessory. The hat paired with her jeans and long-sleeve dry-fit shirt make it abundantly clear that it's nothing more than a shield from the sun.

I do as she says, making sure to push Sully further into the corner with my inside leg.

"Good," she calls out once we come out of the bend. "Cut through the middle of the ring to circle him, and we'll start with jumping the cross-rail." She walks over to the jump and lowers the height, forming the two rails into the shape of an X so Sully and I can warm up.

We pop over the fence a few times with ease, and gradually, Lisa raises the height, moving the metal bracket and lifting the wooden posts. Once she's happy with the setup, she combines multiple jumps for us to practice in sequence. We only have four jumps instead of the usual eight, but Lisa and I make it work. Between the two of us, we can usually find a way to double back and do each jump twice in the same run.

I'm in the zone, and Sully takes each jump flawlessly. We go through the course multiple times—each jump echoed with Lisa yelling, "That's it," and "Good. Keep it up!" loud enough for me to hear her over the sound of Sully's hooves and the rush of air moving past my ears.

"Bring him over here," she says eventually.

I'm panting, my voice coming out breathless as I halt Sully next to her. "Everything okay? I thought we did pretty well."

"You're doing great," she says with a nod. Looking past me, she asks, "Who's the spectator?"

A glance over my shoulder tells me the answer to that question. Carson stands outside the fence with his elbows resting on the post. Whipping my head back around, I ask, "How long has he been there?"

Lisa gives me a knowing smile, her blonde ponytail has gradually loosened under the weight of her hat, leaving stray strands to frame her face. "Long enough to make me think he either really likes horses or really likes you."

I force a laugh before swallowing hard. "Trust me, it's the horse," I mutter.

She gives Sully a pat on the neck. "If you say so." Her eyes flicker to me, but when I don't indulge her, she steps back. "Take him around one more time and then cool him out. You both worked hard today."

Picking up a canter, I glance at Carson out of the corner of my eye. He's definitely watching, but I don't think he's watching *me*. His eyes are glued to Sully as we pass him on our way to the first jump.

The course goes smoothly, and I give Sully a big pat on his neck when we finish the final oxer. "Good boy!" I cheer as we slow to a walk.

Wanting to catch his reaction, I look to the side of the ring where Carson stood only moments ago, but he's gone. My eyes scan the property until I find him back at the fence where he was yesterday, replacing some of the rails and posts.

"If you can do that this weekend, you should place!"

My attention snaps back to Lisa, and I grin. "Let's hope," I unclasp my helmet and tuck it under my arm.

"Here, I'll take it," she says with an outstretched hand.

Handing it to her, I wipe the sweat from my brow. "Thanks."

She gives Sully another pat. "I'll meet you at the show-grounds on Friday, and we'll do some schooling to let Sully get used to the grounds. He looks great, though—you both do."

My chest swells with pride thinking about being at the show and competing. I may not be overly competitive, but once I'm in the show ring, I feel the pressure of wanting to take home a ribbon like everyone else.

She seems to read my expression and says, "You'll do great."

"Right. It will be fun." Competing always makes me a little anxious, but I know that I mean it. Shows are fun—or at least they always have been. Being at odds with Seth brings a new wave of apprehension.

She starts to walk back toward the barn. "I'll set this inside for you and then head out." She lifts my helmet and glances at me over her shoulder. "You've made arrangements for Friday night, right?"

"Yeah," I say, but my stomach flips as I think about what those arrangements are. Seth rented a hotel room near the show-grounds, and I'm supposed to stay with him. We were hoping to make a romantic weekend out of it. He's the first guy I've slept with—the only guy—but it can be hard for us to find time alone together, and when we do, something feels off. Lately, whenever we're alone, a small voice in the back of my mind reminds me that I don't know where our relationship stands once he leaves for school. It's a nagging feeling that makes withdrawing feel like the safe choice.

I wonder if he can tell.

And I wonder if he'll still want me to stay with him this weekend after our fight.

"Great!" Lisa calls out, jolting me from my thoughts. "See you then!"

I give her a wave and try to ignore the sinking feeling in my gut.

After hosing off Sully and turning him out, I finish the barn work quicker than usual. Checking my phone, I have another missed call from Sarah. She tried to call me a few times last night, but after my fight with Seth, all I wanted to do was sleep. I love Sarah, but she tells me exactly how she feels, and I already know how she feels about Seth. She won't have sympathy for my strained relationship.

As I make my way back up to the house, I spot Carson further down the fence line, hammering a fresh board into place. He's holding up the railing with one hand, keeping it level, while he hammers away with the other, and before I know what I'm doing, I've stopped walking to help support the board on the other end.

He gives me a sideways glance. "Since when do you fix fences?" he asks, still holding nails between his teeth.

"You helped me yesterday. This makes us even." I shrug even though I know holding a piece of wood in no way balances out the fact that he stayed here for hours yesterday, helping with Cash.

Other than wanting to pay him back, Seth said he *might stop by* today, and if I go into the house, I'll just end up pacing until he *maybe* gets here. Carson steps away from my side of the railing and moves to one end now that he has support. Taking another nail from his lips, he lines it up on the fence. "Looks like you've got a good horse."

I smile, unable to resist a compliment. "He's the best." Looking over my shoulder, I watch as Sully munches away on the grass at the far end of the field.

"Cash looks good today."

My head tilts as I study him, trying to figure out how someone who cares so much about horses has no desire to ride. "Why don't you ride anymore?"

"What?" he asks like my question came out of left field.

"The other day," I prompt, "you said you used to ride. Why did you stop?"

He stares at me for a moment like he's trying to decide something. Then, getting to his feet, he dusts his gloves against his jeans before rummaging through his toolbox. "I stopped after my mom died."

"What?" My heart sinks, and I add in a voice barely above a whisper, "I'm sorry."

Carson still doesn't look at me when he finds a different set of nails and takes a few out of the box. "Thanks," he says absently. "It's been a while now. I was fifteen when it happened."

I can't help thinking about my own mom and how lost I'd be if anything happened to her *now*, let alone when I was fifteen. The thought of having to live with my dad after their divorce was scary enough as a kid, and even in that hypothetical situation, she was still a phone call away.

When I don't say anything, he looks up at me. "Shit. Don't look at me like that," he says with a forced laugh.

"I'm sorry," I mutter again, not sure what else to say.

Carson seems to know how to navigate this conversation better than I do. "It was a car accident," he offers. "Riding was something we did together, and once she was gone, I just stopped."

I frown. Even though what he's saying makes sense, I can't imagine a life without riding. Losing my mom and horses would feel like two parts of me dying. "Did you have horses?"

He nods as he gets back to work. "A few. We sold a couple, but I couldn't part with my mom's horse. She's still up there—her and the pony I rode when I was a kid." He shakes his head. "Mean bastard."

A sad smile pulls at the corners of my lips. "What type of riding did you do?"

He hammers another nail into place before answering. "Mostly trails, but my mom taught me some reining stuff. She even took me to a few rodeos as a kid."

I smile a little wider at that. "You were a cowboy?"

He narrows his eyes. "No."

"Did you wear a cowboy hat?" I ask, my smile shining through my voice.

He pauses a beat too long before simply saying, "No," again.

I have to bite back my smile. "Liar." Carson laughs but refuses to comment on the subject more. After a moment, I blurt, "I'm sorry about your mom."

He takes his time looking at me before answering like he's seeing me for the first time, and it makes me shift my weight. "Thanks," he eventually says again. "Me, too." Clearing his throat, he asks, "Getting ready for the show this weekend?"

His question brings a crease to my brow. "How do you know about that?"

Carson kneels in the dirt and uses the back end of the hammer to pry another old board from the fence. "Dad and I will be there in case any horses lose a shoe." He hesitates before adding, "Well, I'll be there. Dad starts treatment this week, so we'll see how he feels Friday."

Digging my muck boot into the dirt, I ask, "Is he telling people?"

"He's starting to," Carson says, seemingly unaware of my nervousness around the topic.

"I just think my mom would like to know. She'd probably want to reach out or… I don't know, cook him something." My words trail as I catch sight of a red Mustang entering the gate. Seth doesn't bother parking in his usual spot. Instead, he stops the car where we're standing and gets out.

And he's not alone.

Christina gets out of the car too, her long hair reflecting the sunlight as she tosses it over her shoulder. "Abbie!" she cheers.

She goes in for a hug but changes her mind. I'm still gross from doing the barn work and riding. Once she steps away from me, my eyes jump back and forth between the two of them. "Uh, what are you guys doing here?"

Seth leans against the side of his car. "I told you I'd stop by."

I raise my eyebrows to get more out of him, but when he doesn't say anything else, I awkwardly turn to Christina. "So, Christina, what are you doing here?" I don't think I sound rude, but I'm not about to hide the fact that this is weird.

"We were hanging out," Seth answers for her, still standing at his car—apparently desperate to stay as far away from me as possible.

"Yeah, it's been fun," Christina says absently, her eyes locking on the guy with the hammer. "Hey, Carson." She gives him a flash of white teeth and a wiggle of her fingers.

Seth crosses his arms as he leans against his car, looking more casual than I know he's feeling. "Yeah. Hey, man."

Carson gives them a nod but says nothing.

I try to rein in what my face must look like before I say, "Carson is just fixing the fence for Mom." I'm looking at both of them as I say it, but it's meant for Seth.

Seth frowns, his eyebrows pulling together. "I could have done that."

Christina takes the words from my mouth when she says, "You know how to do fences?"

Seth's eyes narrow ever so slightly. His gaze moves to Carson, who gets to his feet, perfectly content with acting like the rest of us aren't here. "It's not like it's hard."

Carson lifts an eyebrow and gives Seth a long look. My breath catches as I wait for what he might say, but eventually, he just shakes his head and gets back to work.

I breathe.

This whole situation feels like peering over the side of a mountain—one false step leading to catastrophe.

Seth stopping by is usually my favorite part of the day, but all I can think about is how badly I want him to leave. I realize why he didn't come alone now. He's trying to make me jealous by hanging around Christina the same way he *thinks* I'm hanging around Carson.

Jealousy isn't what I feel, though.

If anything, it has the opposite effect.

He seems immature and desperate, and it's not a good look on him.

At all.

Not to mention Christina can't take her eyes off Carson, so their whole charade isn't exactly convincing. I can't believe he'd do this. I can't believe he'd go to this extent to try to hurt me. The foundation Seth and I have built our relationship on for the past year has weathered a lot of cracks lately, but this one feels like the biggest hit yet.

Christina skips over to Carson and kneels by the fence to ask him about what he's doing. Her ability to keep a conversation going is truly astounding.

Seth and I just stare at each other, waiting for the other to say something. He's like a statue, his shoulders tense and his gaze sharp. I wait for him to say something—anything. Listening to Carson tell Christina that he's using Oak for the new boards is the only thing keeping me grounded.

"Well," I say, desperately wanting this visit to end. "Don't let me keep you. I'm sure you want to get back to… hanging out." I tried to make my words sound casual, but the look Seth gives me makes it clear I've failed. We both know I don't want him here.

He holds my gaze, and it takes everything in me not to look away. If I look away, I'll look guilty, and I'm not guilty of anything—other than not wanting him here.

Finally, he scoffs. "Yeah. Let's go, Christina."

Christina frowns, her gaze lingering on Carson. "But we just got here."

His eyes dart between Carson and me before he spits, "They're working," and heads back to his car. Yanking the driver's side door open with a little too much force, he says, "Later, Abbie," as he gets in, slamming the door shut.

Ignoring Seth's demand, Christina runs her fingers through

her hair as she starts her doe-eyed farewell to Carson. She lingers like she's waiting for something, but when it doesn't come, she lets out a sigh and says, "See you guys later." Strutting back to the car, her long hair sways from side to side, whipping behind her as she opens the door to get in.

My eyes stay glued to the red Mustang until it's out of sight. Even after they've turned onto the main road, and I'm just staring at the gate, I can't bring myself to look at Carson.

Sweat prickles my brow, and this time, it has nothing to do with the Florida heat.

Daring to bring my eyes back to the guy standing a few feet away, I warn, "Don't say a word."

He fixes his gaze on the fence in front of him, raising his hammer with a trace of a smirk on his lips. "Wasn't planning on it."

TEN

My hands shake as I sit on my bed holding my phone. I showered, ate dinner, and watched Mom's favorite competitive cooking show with her. I've done everything I could to delay this, but even though I've been staring at Seth's contact info for the past five minutes, I can't bring myself to press the green button. I know Seth and I should work things out, but if I'm being honest, he's the last person I want to talk to.

My finger hovers over the *Call* button when Mom knocks on my door frame. "Busy?"

"Not at all," I set my phone face down on my bed, happy for an excuse to postpone the inevitable.

My relief must show because she scrutinizes me in a way that only moms can. "Are you sure? You didn't seem like yourself at dinner."

"I'm sorry." Dinner feels like a blur to me, anyway. I barely remember sitting across from her, pushing my potatoes around with my fork, and trying not to drown in the mundane talk of the annual Summer Fest.

"Abbie," she says softly. Walking over to my bed, she takes a seat next to me. "You don't have to tell me what's bothering you, but I want you to know that you can, okay? I know you're technically an adult now, but…" Her voice trails, and she lets out a light laugh. "But sometimes it still feels like you're the five-year-old who needed me to check for monsters under the bed. Just know I'm here."

I let myself smile a little. Ever since graduation, she's treated me more like an adult, and we've kept things light. There hasn't been a lot of need for serious heart-to-hearts, but with everything going on, I go ahead and reveal the monsters myself. "Seth is being annoying."

Her eyebrows pinch. "How so?"

Staring up at the ceiling, I try to figure out the best way to say what's on my mind. "I think having Carson around is making him insecure, and insecure Seth is a piece of work."

She lets out a laugh before frowning slightly. "Have you or Carson done anything to make Seth feel that way?"

"No—I don't know. I left the bonfire with Carson, but it was only because Seth was having fun with his friends and wanted to stay later." I swallow, pushing down the details of Seth's amateur baseball pastime.

"You guys are probably just a little out of sync right now." She runs a hand over my hair, and I can't help leaning into her.

"I think it might be more than that." My words come out quietly, saying what I've been too afraid to admit to myself.

Mom tucks a strand of hair behind my ear. "You've always been wise beyond your years," she says with a faint smile on her lips. "It sounds like Seth might have some growing up to do."

I force a laugh. "Yeah, you could say that."

Her hazel eyes hold the tiniest bit of sadness. "You'll figure it out. You know what I always say—"

"Communication is key."

"Communication is key," she echoes.

Patting my leg, she gets up and walks out of my room, and I'm left sitting on my bed. Before I can talk myself out of it, I tap on Seth's name.

This time, it doesn't take long for his voice to come through the other end.

"Hey, Abbie."

"Hey," I say in a voice that hopefully hides the fact that I immediately got to my feet and started pacing.

"I was just about to call you."

Those words would normally make me happy, but there's an edge to his voice that creates the opposite effect.

"Okay…?"

"You know that I love you." He pauses, and my room suddenly feels too small to have this conversation.

"I know."

"But things have been different lately."

Those words make me stop in my tracks. "I know they have," I say so quietly I question whether he's heard me.

"I want things to go back to how they were before."

Jumping to agree, I say, "Me, too."

There's a sigh on the other end of the phone. "I mean before you were spending time with Carson. He's bad news, Abbs. I can feel it. I don't trust that guy."

My hands sweat at the mention of Carson. "Why?"

"What?"

"Why don't you trust him?" I ask.

Another sigh. "It's a feeling, but I need you to stop talking to him."

With a furrowed brow, I consider how to respond. "Seth, like I told you last night, he kind of works at my house," I say, frowning. "Did he do something?"

Frustration bubbles in his voice. "No—Listen. If you really love me, you'll do this for me."

A frown pulls at my lips as I hold the phone to my ear. "Seth, if you really loved me, you'd have a little more trust in our relationship instead of acting like this."

"Why do you care about him so much?" he spits, and even

though we're on the phone, I can picture him with narrowed eyes and his complexion turning pink.

"I don't!" My self-control wanes like a dam that's been gradually breaking. "Why do *you?*"

He scoffs. "Because he likes you, and you're not doing anything about it!"

My heart pounds in my chest. We've never fought in a way that makes me want to yell, but I'm on the verge of yelling when I say, "Trust me, Carson does *not* like me." The memory of him laughing at the thought pops into my head again, and I hate that I've held onto it.

"But what if he did?"

"What?" I ask, still analyzing the memory.

"What if he liked you?"

I don't answer right away because I've never let myself consider it. As much as Carson has felt like a breath of fresh air compared to the shitstorm Seth has thrown my way, I've never let myself wonder if things could be different.

"Wow." Seth snaps me from my daze.

I realize I may have been silent for half a second too long. "Can we just get back to how things were?" I finally say, feeling defeated.

"Yeah. I don't think we can." His voice runs thick as it carries through the phone, and it strikes me that I've never seen Seth sad before. He's been a perpetual pick-me-up that's finally turned sour.

"So, what are you saying?" I ask, swallowing the lump in my throat.

He lets out a heavy breath, and the sound of it makes my chest tighten. "I think we need some time apart."

My breath catches, and the ticking of the clock on my wall drowns out the sound of everything else. "Are we breaking up?" I finally ask, trying to keep my voice even despite my eyes burning.

"Fuck," he curses under his breath. "I mean, I'm leaving at the end of summer anyway…" His voice trails until he says with more resolution, "Yeah, I guess we are."

I take a hard seat on my bed with the phone pressed to my ear, the blood pounding in them making it impossible to hear Seth on the other end. I've never been dumped before. Seth was my first boyfriend. He was my first *everything*, and now the ties have been severed. I'm not sure what to make of it all.

"Abbie, are you there?"

"Yeah." I wipe a tear from my cheek. "Wait. I have to ask… were you planning on breaking up with me before you left anyway?" I squeeze the phone tighter.

The other end of the phone is quiet until he slowly says, "No…"

I frown, his voice feeling unfamiliar like he's already a stranger. He's distant—he's *been* distant. He's avoided talking about what really matters for months now.

Then it hits me.

"Were you going to wait until after you moved and *then* break up with me?"

Before he can say anything more, I cut him off. "Never mind. It doesn't matter. I'll talk to you later."

I hang up and collapse in on myself. Hugging my knees to my chest, I let my head fall. Despite how terrible this past week has been, I can't remember any of it. All I can remember are the things I loved about my relationship with Seth—the things I'll never experience again.

I'll never feel his arms wrapped around me in a hug.

I'll never breathe in the comforting smell of him as I lean my head on his shoulder.

I'll never be greeted with an enthusiastic, "Abbs!"

I'll never kiss him again.

I'll never sleep with him again.

I'll never tell him I love him again.

I always saw him as one of my best friends *and* my boyfriend. And now I've lost both.

ELEVEN

I drag myself from bed after tossing and turning all night. Standing in front of my bathroom mirror, I poke the puffy, dark circles now shadowing both eyes. *Thanks a lot, Seth.* I guess taking my virginity wasn't enough—he had to go and take my beauty sleep, too.

I tried calling Sarah last night, but she didn't answer. She sent a text an hour later saying she was out and would call me when she got back, but she never did. I almost didn't call her for fear of undoubtedly hearing, *I told you so.*

Skipping a ride this close to a show isn't something I would normally do, but I know I'm not in the right headspace. The excitement I felt for the show yesterday has been diminished by an overwhelming sense of dread. Christina and Brooke won't be the only two whispering behind my back at the grounds. The horse-show community is small, and it won't take long for everyone to hear the news.

Seth has probably told a lot of them already.

Throwing on my denim shorts and a tank top, I grab my Ariat baseball cap and feed my ponytail through the back. When I head outside, the blue sky and chirping birds seem to mock me with their positivity, but I try to lean into the feeling anyway. Since I woke up, I've been trying to look at this as a fresh start. We'd be going to different colleges in the fall, anyway. Maybe it's better we part ways now.

My positivity fades when I spot Carson checking the arena fence close to the barn. There's no discreet way to avoid him on my way to muck out the stalls, and my stomach tightens at the thought of having him see me like this.

He spots me when I'm only a few feet away and mutters, "Hungover again?"

Lowering my cap over my eyes, I answer, "Something like that," and keep walking.

I think he looks up at me, but I don't stick around long enough to see. Right now, Carson only reminds me of my conversation with Seth last night, and I don't need my breakup on my mind any more than it already is.

I grab the wheelbarrow and pitchfork and get to work. There's no distraction like drowning yourself in physical labor. My mind feels numb as my body sweats and aches, working faster than I ever have. I pass Carson occasionally as I turn out different horses but do my best to avoid eye contact and keep my head down. He hasn't said anything else, which I try to be thankful for.

It isn't even lunchtime when I finish the stalls. Skipping my morning ride put me ahead of schedule, so I look around for something else to do. Sully's head sticks out of his stall as he gives a soft whinny, bringing a smile to my lips. Walking over to him, I run my hand down his white blaze before giving him a pat on the cheek. "Hey, boy."

There's something soulful about a horse's eyes. It makes them look wiser than people realize, and Sully has always had a way of knowing I need him.

Slipping his halter over his head, I lead him into the aisle and hook him to the crossties. I take my time as I curry, brush him, and pick out his feet. I even pull his mane to pass more time and get him ready for the show. Grooming dissolves the storm that's been lingering inside me.

Afterward, I bring him to the side of the arena fence in just his halter and hoist myself up onto his back. I love the show-jumping side of horsemanship, it pushes me both mentally and physically, but there's something about getting on a horse with no saddle and no agenda. It grounds you.

Together, we meander around the front fields, enjoying the frequent patches of shade provided by our large oak trees. Sully occasionally puts his head down to graze, and I don't stop him. Eventually, I lie back and stare at the bright blue sky above, my body jostling now and then when he steps to the side for greener grass.

This morning, I felt alone in a bad way—in an almost hopeless way.

With the world around me out of view, being alone takes on a new light. Because even though I'll miss a lot of things about Seth, there's a lot I won't miss.

Like feeling like he'd have more fun with his friends if I wasn't there.

Or having to listen to the latest drama from Spring Oaks that was never as interesting or important as he thought it was.

And not having to sit idly by as he and his friends destroy other peoples' property for fun.

That last one brings me more comfort than anything else. I never felt less connected to Seth than when he would do that. It made me feel like I didn't know him at all.

"Not practicing for the show?"

Carson's voice sends a jolt through me, and I lift my head to look at him. He's in his usual jeans, t-shirt, and hat combo I've come to expect.

Staring down at him under the brim of my hat, all I offer is a quick, "Nope," before lying my head back down on Sully's hindquarters.

He pats Sully's shoulder. "So, she's finally giving you a break, huh?"

Tilting my head to glare at him, I ask, "Are you talking to my horse?"

Carson ignores me as Sully lifts his head to look at him. Holding Sully's face gently with one hand, he says, "Probably for the best. She seems like she's in a mood." Leaning forward like he's about to tell Sully a secret, he whispers, "I think you dodged a bullet."

"Stop talking to my horse," I say flatly, still glaring at him.

But then Carson brings his eyes to me, and I realize I should have let him stay focused on Sully. "What's with you today?"

Looking back at the sky, I mutter, "Nothing," and hope he'll go away.

"I'm not buying it."

Still not looking at him, I say, "You don't have to."

Even though I'm staring at the sky above, I can feel Carson's gaze burning into me as he tries to figure me out, but I don't want him to figure me out. "So, you just woke up this pleasant?" There's an accusatory tone in his voice that I don't have patience for.

Pushing myself upright, I grab hold of the lead draped over Sully's neck. "Yup."

Carson opens his mouth to say more, but by the time he gets the first word out, Sully and I are already halfway across the property and gaining speed.

TWELVE

Popping a grape into my mouth, I sit at the kitchen table to eat a quick breakfast before heading to the barn. As soon as I sit in the rustic wood chair, my phone vibrates against the wood tabletop, creating a loud buzz that seems to reverberate through the quiet house.

Turning my phone over, I see Sarah's name on the screen and answer immediately. "Hey, is everything okay?" She's never called me this early. Even when she lived here, I'd have to call her to wake her up on the days we were supposed to ride together.

"Of course!" Her voice is accompanied by the sound of cars passing in the background.

"Where are you headed?" I ask, taking a sip of my water.

"Zumba, but I'm late." She huffs. "I should have known better than to register for a class this early. This campus is so spread out. That's what they don't tell you. They tell you there's a gym, but do they tell you that the walk to the gym is a workout on its own? No. No, they don't."

I can't help scrunching my face. "Wait. Since when do you do Zumba?"

"Since the instructor is a hot guy named Jared. It's fun, though. Next time I'm home, we should find a class." Before I have the chance to turn her down, she says, "Hey, I'm sorry I didn't call you back the other night. We ended up staying out way too late. Nancy said I tried to sleep in the wrong bed when we got back. She had to escort me across the room. I was exhausted."

I'm going to go ahead and assume she was a little drunk, too. "Nancy's your roommate, right?"

Her breathing gets a little steadier, and I imagine her standing at a crosswalk, waiting for her turn to cross the street. "Yeah! I think you'd like her."

If Sarah thinks I'll like her roommate, I probably will. Even if I'm a little jealous of her at the moment. "She sounds great. I'm glad you're having fun. Enjoy the break while you can, your horse is getting fat."

She lets out an open-mouthed laugh that I can picture perfectly. "Georgie's putting on the pounds? Doesn't he make a cute chubby pony, though?"

"Fat and lazy."

"Fat and *happy*," she corrects, and I can hear the smile in her voice. "Hey, why were you calling the other night, anyway? It was late."

"Oh, right." I eat another grape. "Seth and I broke up."

"What?" Somehow, even though I can't see her, I know that sentence stopped her in her tracks. She's probably standing in the middle of a sidewalk as people work their way around her. "Really?"

"Really," I answer with a nod.

"Shit," she mutters. "Are you okay?"

"Yeah." I am okay. "It would have never worked out."

"Tell me everything."

"What about Zumba?"

She's on the move again. "Forget Zumba. Tell me everything."

My heart swells, and I have to bite the inside of my cheek to keep my emotions in check. "Where are you going now?"

It sounds like she's yanking a door open. "I have no idea, but this building has chairs in it." She drops her voice to a whisper. "I just can't start yelling about how much I wish that asshole would fall off his horse. They might kick me out."

"Probably," I say with a laugh. And just like that, it doesn't feel like we're so far apart at all. It feels like she's sitting with me in my kitchen as I tell her everything.

Mom sweeps fallen hay in the feed room as I organize my plastic bin of polos I used to wrap around Sully's legs for extra support. Lifting a pair of pink cloud print ones from when I was younger, I laugh at the thought of putting them on him now.

It's been three days since my breakup with Seth. It feels like the chapter has ended, and now that a little time has passed, it doesn't consume my every thought like it did that first day. I'm starting to feel more like myself.

After I told my mom about the breakup, she did everything a mom is supposed to do. We watched a few 90's romantic comedies, ate pizza out of the box, and it was the perfect remedy. She's only brought him up once since that night to ask if I'd heard from him.

 I haven't.

He hasn't called—not that I was expecting him to. He's probably busy training for the show this weekend.

At least, he could be.

I don't know, and surprisingly, I don't care what Seth is doing in his spare time. I thought I would. I thought I'd wonder how he's coping, but the part of me that was tied to him has shut down. It turns out that life without Seth isn't much different than life with Seth. He was my boyfriend, but he didn't contribute to making my life better. If anything, not having to worry about him these past few days has felt like a break I didn't know I needed.

More than thinking about my breakup, I've been thinking

about the show. As much as I don't regret Seth calling things off, I can't deny that the thought of seeing him makes me mildly nauseous.

Which is why I'm not going.

Shows and competing are supposed to be fun, and if I'm stuck dodging Seth the whole time, that's the last thing this show will be. I'd rather sit this one out, but I know Mom won't understand.

"How was your ride this morning?" Mom asks as she continues to sweep. Her usually casual question holds some hesitation like she thinks she needs to be careful with what she says around me.

"It was good," I say with a shrug. It was. Sully has made a lot of progress with getting the change in the corner ever since Carson gave his advice. But the fact that he's been doing so well during our rides doesn't make me as happy as it normally would, given I'm skipping the show. Now it feels like a wasted effort.

"You both make the course look seamless out there," she says with a smile, pausing to rest her hands on the top of the broomstick. "I wish I could see you compete this weekend."

My cheeks flush. Does she already know? How? I haven't even told Lisa yet. "Uh, yeah," I mutter.

She tilts her head, giving me a funny look. "Alright," she says, setting the broom aside and taking a seat on one of the containers of feed. "Out with it."

"What?" I ask over my shoulder as I continue organizing polo wraps like my heart isn't pounding in my chest loud enough for us both to hear.

"Abbie, look at me," she says, and her tone isn't as gentle as it usually is.

I turn, letting my hands grip the edge of the bin behind me. "Yeah?"

She frowns. "What's up with you? You say you're fine with the breakup, but you haven't seemed like yourself since."

There are two approaches to doing things you aren't comfortable doing: easing into it, one sliver of discomfort at a time, or getting it over with—like when you rip off a band-aid in a single pull.

I go with the band-aid approach.

"I'm not going to the show this weekend." I bite my lip, waiting for her reaction.

She draws her head back slightly, blinking a few times to allow what I've just said to sink in. "Okay... let's talk this out."

I nod.

"Why aren't you going to the show?"

"Because I don't want to see him."

To this, the corners of her lips fall. "But you and Sully have both worked so hard. Hell, Lisa has worked so hard. Don't you owe it to both of them to go?"

Everything she's said, I've already thought about. I feel guilty about my decision, but I can't shake the feeling that going to the

112

show would be a terrible idea. "I really don't want to go."

"We aren't quitters, Abbie."

"Mom." I give her a heavy-lidded stare.

Putting her hands up, she says, "Fine. I don't agree with it, but if it's what you want to do, I can't force you." I can hear just enough snippy judgment in her voice to let me know I'm disappointing her.

Carson rounds the corner, and I hope he didn't overhear us. He doesn't seem concerned with our conversation as he grabs a flake of hay from one of the bales, gripping it with both hands. "I'm going to toss this to Jet. She's pacing at the gate." When he registers we're both staring at him, he says, "Did I miss something?"

I say, "No," at the same time Mom says, "Abbie's dropping out of the show this weekend."

I widen my eyes at her, but she just mirrors my reaction like she's silently saying, *Well, you are!*

"What? Why?" Carson looks at me. "You guys have been practicing nonstop."

Mom gestures a hand to Carson, clearly agreeing with him, before walking out of the feed room, leaving me alone with the guy that indirectly caused my breakup and the reason I've been harboring guilt for the past three days.

He's still staring at me, his dark eyes pinning me in place, so I just shrug and say, "I don't want to deal with the drama."

"What drama?"

I may have been ready to tell Mom about my breakup, but I'm definitely not ready to have this conversation with Carson. "There's always drama between barns. I just want to stay out of it."

He stares at me with his eyes slightly narrowed like he can see straight through my excuse, and I'm starting to sweat under the pressure of his glare. Eventually, he says, "Abbie, go to the show."

The corners of my mouth dip. "I don't want to."

"Bullshit."

"It's not bullshit!" Everything I've been feeling recently seems to come out in those three words. Taking a deep breath, I try to make my voice more even as I add, "I'm telling you I don't want to go."

He rolls his eyes as he says, "And I am telling you it is bullshit."

I scoff, turning to the shelf of supplements. I rotate the containers, so the labels face out and try to ignore the feeling of his eyes burning into my back.

"Listen," he says. "I don't know what your problem is or why you've been avoiding me lately, but you've worked too hard to let whatever's bothering you keep you from that show. It's the last show before they break for summer, so deal with your shit then."

I glare at the supplements, rearranging them in no particular order. Carson has worked here for less than two weeks. He doesn't know me. I can't believe my mom threw me under the bus in front of him, and I can't believe he thinks he knows what's best for me.

He doesn't.

And I'm about to tell him just that, but when I turn around, he's gone. The feed room is empty, and the fact that he's not wrong only grates me more.

THIRTEEN

"Is that all of it?" Mom asks as she slams the trailer door shut. We've just finished loading everything Sully and I will need for the show, and I'm about to start the hour and a half drive to the showgrounds in Ocala.

"I think so." I stare at the trailer, my mixed feelings only growing.

Even though I'm not looking at her, I can feel her eyes locked on me. "It's good that you're going. You and Sully have both worked for this." She walks over and puts a hand on my shoulder. "You'll have fun once you get there."

She might be right, but I'm not convinced. When Carson called me out, I couldn't unsee the points he made. Everything he said was right, but that doesn't mean I'm convinced this is a good idea.

"And when seeing Seth is weird?" I ask, finally looking at her.

She smiles that infectious smile of hers. "Well, then all the more reason to focus on your horse."

She's right. I know she's right. But that somehow doesn't make this feel any easier.

"I know you love staying at the grounds," Mom says, bringing my attention back to her, "but try not to stay too late. I don't want you driving home in the dark."

No Seth means no hotel room to stay at the grounds overnight. Driving an hour and a half back won't be terrible, but I have a long day ahead of me, and I'll need to be at the grounds again early tomorrow morning. "Trust me," I tell her. "The last thing I want is to stick around longer than I have to. I'll be careful."

"I know you will," she says as she runs her hand over my ponytail sticking out the back of my hat. "I'll grab Sully for you."

"Thanks." I get my water bottle for the road. My eyes fall on the new fence Carson installed near the riding ring; the fresh wood not yet stained. Today is the first day he isn't here since he's going to the show too, and even though this is how the barn has always been, the absence of his relentless hammering leaves a void I wasn't expecting.

He knows I'm going to the show this weekend, but other than that, our interactions have been nothing more than the sum of a few awkward glances.

I see the irony. Seth broke up with me because I wouldn't cut Carson out of my life, but now I seem to have cut him out of it anyway. I can't help it. Every time I look at him, I'm met with a mixture of guilt and negative feelings connected to my breakup. It feels easier to keep my distance right now, and considering he hasn't gone out of his way to talk to me either, I don't think he minds.

"Here he is, the man of the hour!" Mom says brightly as she walks down the aisle with Sully in hand. "Sullivan's Secret!" she announces in her best commentator voice.

Clad in his leather halter with a gold nameplate displaying his show name, Sully dutifully walks with Mom. Once they're close enough, I hand my water to her and take Sully so I can load him onto the trailer.

He follows me on without an issue. Pushing him aside and clicking the divider into place, I step down and latch the door shut behind him.

"That horse loads like a dream," Mom comments fondly as she hands back my water.

"He always has."

The showgrounds are packed. It's the last show before a break in the season, and it seems like nobody wants to miss it. Even though June is just as hot as July and August, they still manage to squeeze in one more show before the two-month hiatus.

I park my trailer near the row of stalls Lisa rented for her students and hop down from my mom's navy-blue F-150.

"Abbie!" Lisa calls out as she waves and jogs over to me. "Perfect timing," she says, catching her breath as I walk around the back of the trailer and unlatch the door. "Take Sully for a walk around the grounds to get him acclimated, then put him in stall number 19. There's hay in there for him already. I'm headed to the schooling ring, but meet me over there when you're done?"

"Yeah, of course." I step up into the trailer and back Sully out. I'll gladly stay with Lisa for the rest of the afternoon if she needs me to—anything is better than running into Seth.

By the time we're both on solid ground, Lisa is already a good distance away, standing next to a small girl in braided pigtails on a grey pony. The little girl looks sharp in her show jacket, and it reminds me of when I came to shows at her age. A man I'm assuming is her father stands next to her, holding the reins of her small pony to guide him in the right direction.

My dad used to act as my caddy too, following close behind with anything I may need. For a while, he never missed a show. It's strange to think about, considering he doesn't even know I'm here now.

"See you in a bit!" Lisa calls out with another wave, snapping me from my thoughts.

Sully and I make our way around the grounds. He's been to this location a few times, so it doesn't take long for his excited jig to relax into his usual gait by my side.

A familiar, booming laugh rings in my ears, and I look over my shoulder to see Seth with Christina and Brooke. Christina has her hand over her mouth as she watches Seth, still with his head thrown back in a howl of laughter. She's looking at him like whatever made them laugh in the first place isn't as amusing as his reaction to it. I've had my fair share of those looks over the past year.

The already humid air feels thicker as I watch him. He's animated as he talks about something I can't make out. My stomach turns over. I wasn't expecting him to mope around the showgrounds all weekend, but he shouldn't be this happy either. Before they see me, I sneak back to Sully's stall unnoticed and put him away.

As I make my way to the schooling ring to find Lisa, I can't get rid of the sinking feeling in my stomach that I shouldn't have come here. Just *seeing* Seth got to me. I don't think I'm ready to face him. Maybe I can avoid him—at least for today. Tomorrow we'll be competing against each other, so there's no controlling that, but with a little luck, I might be able to get through today unscathed.

I'm still stuck on seeing Seth when I walk to the schooling ring to find Lisa. Horses of all different sizes and colors are being worked by their riders in preparation for tomorrow. I wait for a black Thoroughbred to pass before ducking under the white fence and meeting Lisa in the middle of the ring.

"How was the drive?" she asks, not taking her eyes off her student.

"A little longer than usual, but it was fine."

"Good." She's distracted, so she doesn't notice I'm distracted, too.

"Are the rest of your students here?"

She nods toward the girl on the grey pony I saw earlier. "That's Chelsea and Shadow." She gives me a sideways glance, the corner of her mouth quirked. "Show name is 'Up in Smoke.'"

"Cute," I say with a light laugh.

"That's good, Chelsea, but check your diagonal!" Lisa calls out to the young girl. Turning to me, she says, "I have you in my last slot of the day at 5:30. That okay? A lot of these parents have other commitments, and you're staying close to the grounds, so I figured it would work."

"Yeah. Of course, that's fine." I'm not about to make Lisa restructure her schedule on my account—even if it means I'll definitely be driving home in the dark.

"Great." She gives me a pat on the back. "I think Seth is over there if you're looking for him." She jogs back to the middle of the ring, saying, "Chelsea, keep him straight!"

The scene of Lisa running up to the pony and helping the girl by grabbing the reins would normally make me laugh, but her mention of Seth has me squirming. Daring to look, I catch Seth staring at me. For a split second, I wonder if I can pretend I don't see him, but I know it's too late. Taking in a deep breath, I grit my teeth and throw him a casual wave.

He doesn't wave back.

Instead, I get a tight-lipped smile that could easily be mistaken for a grimace. Then with a slight shake of his head, he brushes Christina's arm with his hand, waving her over to follow him to the bottom bleacher outside the ring.

It isn't until he pulls her onto his lap that he looks my way again. Christina's cackle feels like nails on a chalkboard, and as much as I want to stop watching, I can't seem to tear my eyes away. You'd think Seth and Christina would look like two halves of a whole together, but something about seeing her on his lap feels… off. It's like those kid's activity books where you have to circle the thing that doesn't belong. It's them—they're the thing.

Oblivious to me watching them, she drapes her arms around his neck.

"What the hell?" I mutter to no one in particular. Seth still looks at me as he whispers something in her ear, and she playfully bats his arm.

"Isn't that your boyfriend?" An unmistakable voice sounds behind me, making the hairs on the back of my neck stand up.

I spin around to find Carson standing a few feet away, watching Seth and Christina with his lips pressed into a thin line.

Hot embarrassment flushes my cheeks. "Uh, ex-boyfriend."

He gives me a sideways glance and an unconcerned lift of his brow. "Since when?"

"A few days ago."

He nods like something finally makes sense to him. "I'm sorry." Carson's gaze drifts back to Seth, his body tensing. I follow his line of sight back to my ex and the girl he swore was just his friend, instantly regretting it.

Seth has his arms wrapped around Christina as he kisses her. She stills, clearly taken off guard, but there's only a moment of hesitation before she melts into him. Seth's hands are in her hair, and his tongue is in her mouth like she just ate his last M&M and he wants it back.

The sound of the showgrounds turns into muffled, far-away noise. Heat flares through me as my heart races and pounds, my pulse jolting through my body.

I'm not angry because of their kiss, or because of the breakup. I'm angry because he's doing this on purpose. He doesn't care about hurting me—he *wants* to hurt me, and that realization steals the air from my lungs.

Desperate to do something, I turn back to Carson. "Hey—" but he's already walked away.

FOURTEEN

My eyes scan the bustle of people and horses for the guy in the backward hat.

I spot him near a horse trailer a few feet away. His farrier equipment and tools are set neatly in front of him in case any of the horses throw a shoe.

By the time I reach him, he's taking off his chaps and setting them on a nearby chair. "Hey," I say again once I'm closer. "I need your help."

He looks over his shoulder at me but continues what he's doing. "What kind of help?"

When I don't say anything, he turns, his eyes burning into me as he waits for an explanation.

I hate that I can't read him.

"Will you help me?"

He leans his back against the trailer, crossing his arms. "Depends on what you need me to do."

I take a step toward him. "I know you find me repulsive, but I need you to act like you don't—I need you to act like you're into me."

Carson cocks an eyebrow. "I'm not doing that."

Leaning into him, I put a hand on his chest and give him my best award-winning smile. "Please?"

He stares at me with a hardened expression, his eyes searching mine. I've never been this close to him. If I wasn't already using him for support, I think my knees might buckle. My eyes are glued to my hand as it slowly slides from his chest to his abs, feeling every groove under the material of his t-shirt.

I look up to find him watching me, and heat flares in my cheeks. Those dark eyes dip to my hand before meeting my gaze again. "Three things," he says, his voice rough. With a single step, he flips us around, so he's the one who has me pinned to the side of his trailer. His hips press into mine, making it impossible to move, and my breath catches at the contact, his body hot and solid against mine.

There's no Seth.

No Christina.

No horse show.

There's just Carson in front of me, igniting my core, like the sun, burning from the inside out.

His face is inches from mine when he says, "One: This is stupid." His hand gently adjusts the brim of my hat so he can look me in the eyes. Leaning closer, he says in a low voice, "Two: You're better than this." He has his hand on either side of me, locking me in. "And three." He lowers his lips to my ear, and in a voice too smooth for my own good says, "I don't find you repulsive."

Pushing off the trailer, he steps back and stares at me for a moment, waiting for me to acknowledge that I understand.

I don't understand.

If anything, I think I may have blacked out. I'm dazed by whatever magic he just pulled, unable to move, or think, or speak.

He turns and stops. "Oh, and Abbie?"

It seems like words have abandoned me altogether. I don't even think my mouth has fully closed from the shock of what he just did—and the effect it had on me.

"Next time you touch me, make sure it's because you want to—not to make that asshole jealous." He points over his shoulder with his thumb to where Seth might be.

Rubbing the back of his neck, he turns and walks away.

My eyes scan the area around me. Everyone is still doing what they were doing ten minutes ago—what they've been doing all day. People get their horses ready, kids play as they wait for their time to ride—nothing is different.

But at the same time, nothing is the same.

126

Forcing a deep breath into my lungs, I adjust my hat and start walking to Sully's stall with my head down.

Or at least that's where I'm trying to go when I crash into someone. Staggering back a step, I look up to find Seth towering over me, his porcelain complexion pinker than I've ever seen.

"What the hell was that?" he spits.

"What?" I ask, looking over my shoulder to the space he's referring to, but Carson is long gone.

"Don't play dumb with me. I knew there was something going on between the two of you." His neck has turned splotchy and red now, his voice struggling to stay within normal speaking range.

I laugh, despite everything. "You're joking, right?"

He blinks.

"You and Christina?" I nudge to remind him of the girl whose mouth he was just inspecting with his tongue.

He groans, doing a poor job of hiding his frustration. "That was nothing."

"Right." I'm losing my patience. With a breath of laughter, I add, "You know, I wasn't sure about our breakup at first, but I think it was the right choice." Before giving him a chance to say anything else, I step around him and start toward Sully's stall. I don't care if it's not 5:30, I'd rather wait by the stables than stay here.

Seth's hand wraps around my wrist, pulling me back with enough force to throw me off balance. "I'm not done talking to you."

"I don't care." I rip his fingers from my wrist with my other hand. "*I'm* done talking to *you*." I turn and head towards the stables. This time, with more determination.

Behind me, Seth says, "Come on, Abbs," and for a moment, he sounds like Seth—*my* Seth. I hate that part of me wants to turn back at the sound of my name. He still sounds like home even though he shouldn't.

I shake off the feeling.

As familiar as he once was, he's a stranger to me now. The Seth I loved isn't the guy standing a few feet away, determined to hurt me. And I won't let him get close enough to try.

Seth doesn't follow me back to the stalls. Hot tears burn behind my eyes, and I tug the brim of my hat down. I can barely see Sully swing his head over the stall door to greet me, his chestnut face a blur as the tears start to spill over. I don't realize how fast I'm walking and nearly crash into the wooden door. Fumbling with the latch, I slip inside.

The metal bars of the stall don't give much privacy, and I can still hear the chatter of people around the stables, but I let a heavy tear fall. It glides down my cheek as I scratch the soft part of Sully's nose. He nudges me, looking for carrots, and I let out a breath of laughter as I wipe my eyes. "Sorry, buddy. I didn't come prepared."

He whinnies softly like he's letting out a sigh and turns back to his hay. The snub only makes me smile. No matter how much he loves me, he'll always love food just a little bit more.

FIFTEEN

"Let's try it again!" Lisa calls out to me from the center of the schooling ring.

I grit my teeth and ask Sully for the canter and circle him for a good approach to the first jump. The heat has broken as the sun starts to set, and I've lost count of how many times we've done this run.

"Steady! Steady!" Lisa's voice rings out. I can't see where she is now, my eyes are locked on the jump as Sully and I quickly approach it. "Sit back, Abbie!"

I lean back, but throwing my weight only makes Sully chip in, his hooves stopping short just before the jump until he lurches himself over the rail at the last minute.

"Damn it!"

"Pick him up! Recover!" Lisa says with an edge of annoyance in her voice. "One, Two, One, Two, ONE!" She counts our strides, and we soar over the second jump on the last *one*. Sully lands heavily on the other side, cantering around the corner on the wrong lead and giving me a small buck as a result.

"Whoa," I ease as I pull on the reins, bringing him back to a walk.

"Alright. Bring him in." Lisa waves us over.

I know it was bad. Our entire ride has been bad, and I know it's my fault—it's always the rider's fault. Horses are never the ones to blame.

Lisa pets Sully as she grabs the reins to stop him. "He's puffing," she says as she takes in his hard breathing. "We're going to have to cool out on that." After giving Sully a smile, she looks up at me, and her smile fades. "What's going on? Earlier this week you killed this."

"I know," I say, angry with myself. "I'm distracted, and I shouldn't be. I'm sorry."

She raises her eyebrows. "Don't apologize to me. It's your horse who deserves the apology. Get your stuff worked out by tomorrow for his sake."

"I will." I pat Sully's neck, still unable to shake the way Carson made me feel earlier.

The way his dark eyes burned into me when I put my hands on him.

The shock of electricity that went through me when his body pressed against mine.

And the embarrassment I feel for acting the way I did. His words still ring in the back of my mind.

This is stupid.

You're better than this.

He was right, of course. I don't want to stoop to Seth's level, but in the heat of the moment, all I could think about was getting even.

"Abbie?" Lisa's voice snaps me back to the present.

Shaking my head, I say, "Sorry," and she presses her lips together.

"Get a good night's sleep. Tomorrow will be a better day." She pats my leg before leaving me to cool out Sully.

It's already getting dark, so there's no point rushing home. My ride went longer than expected, so I take my time walking Sully out. Walking with him around the grounds allows a sense of calm to wash over me. When I eventually make it back to the stables to untack him and hose him off, most of the other riders have left for the day. The sound of horses eating their dinner after a long day of training fills my ears. People in the distance from other barns are happy and loud as they wrap up their day, but all of Lisa's other students have since left.

Once Sully is clean and put away in his stall, and I've showered at the facility, I load my saddle and the rest of my tack into my trailer. I'm hanging up my bridle when a voice behind me says, "You're here late."

Looking over my shoulder, I spot Carson standing a few feet away, wearing the same shirt I had under my fingertips earlier. "Yeah." I step down from the trailer and swallow my pride. "Listen, I'm sorry about earlier."

His eyebrows pull together. "Don't be," he says, but I can't help hearing something in his voice that sounds like I should.

I head over to Sully's stall to check on him one more time. "It was stupid."

He joins me by Sully's stall. "Yeah, it was."

I can't help glaring at him. "I know. Trust me, it won't happen again. I don't even know why I did it."

Carson scoffs before patting Sully. "I'm guessing it's because you want him back."

My eyes narrow. "That's not true. I don't." I don't want to talk about this—especially with him.

"Clearly."

Grabbing my keys, I mutter, "Whatever," and head toward the truck. "I don't have time for this. I have to get home."

Looking over his shoulder, he asks, "Home?"

"Yeah." I'm done indulging him.

He frowns, taking a step towards the truck. "You're driving back tonight?"

Fighting a yawn, I say, "That's the plan."

He seems conflicted, but something behind his harsh eyes softens. He finally points to his trailer a few feet away. "There's a bed in there," he says, almost in defeat.

Glancing to where he pointed, I ask, "In the horse trailer?"

He looks over at the trailer, and I wonder if he's avoiding my gaze. "Dad doesn't put the horses in this one. It's clean, and there's a mattress in it. He was never one to splurge on hotels when he had to come out here."

"That's smart." I look over at the parked trailer. Turning back to Carson, I ask, "But why are you telling me?"

His jaw tenses before he settles his eyes back on me. "You can sleep there."

I frown. A few minutes ago, I could have sworn he was annoyed with me. Looking between him and the trailer, I ask, "Why are you offering it to me?"

He adjusts his hat. "Why wouldn't I?"

Sixteen

I can think of a few reasons why he wouldn't want me sleeping in his trailer.

And I can think of a few reasons why I wouldn't want to take him up on it—starting with the fact that I humiliated myself in front of him today. "Um… because you don't like me right now?"

"First, I find you repulsive, and now I don't like you?" He shakes his head with a low laugh. "Shit."

"Well, I just mean—" But I stop there because I'm not sure what I mean.

"You just mean that after not talking to me all week, you thought I'd be happier about you throwing yourself at me to make your boyfriend jealous?"

With crossed arms, I glare at him. "Ex-boyfriend, and I did *not* throw myself at you."

"No?" He lifts his eyebrow. "Looked like it from where I was standing."

"I wanted your *help*."

He nods. "Right. To make Seth jealous." The look he gives me might as well be a neon sign telling me how dumb I am.

"Forget it," I say, rolling my eyes. "I'm leaving."

Rubbing a hand over his face, he groans. "Damn it, Abbie. Would you just sleep here?"

"With you?" The question hangs between us, and I hope he isn't putting the wrong connotation with it. *Want me to sleep with you, Carson?* I shouldn't be allowed to speak for the rest of the night.

He falters slightly. "No. I'll sleep in the truck." He heads toward the trailer.

My feet hurry to catch up with him. "*I'll* sleep in the truck. You keep your bed." I'm not sure why I'm even considering staying given his attitude, but I'm exhausted and have to be back by 7:00 a.m.

With his hand on the latch, Carson looks over at me. "You're not sleeping in the truck."

"Why not?"

He unlatches the trailer to reveal a mattress with clean, light-blue fitted sheets and a thick, woven blanket folded neatly on the bed. "I wouldn't be able to sleep."

"Because you think I'll drive you somewhere?"

"Yeah," Carson tosses a pillow at me. "That must be it."

He starts toward his truck, but I call out after him. "I won't be able to sleep with you in the truck either, you know!"

He turns, holding an outstretched arm. "Because you think I'll drive the trailer somewhere?"

"No." I throw the pillow back onto the mattress where it belongs. "Because I'd feel bad about stealing your bed." Sleeping in a truck is bound to be uncomfortable for anyone, but Carson is bigger than me—it'll be worse for him.

"It's not stealing if I'm giving it to you."

I bite the inside of my cheek. I'm competing tomorrow, and I can only imagine what my body will feel like if I sleep in the cab all night. Letting out a sigh of defeat, I look back at the bed. There's only one pillow and only one throw blanket, but there's plenty of room. "Why don't we just share it?"

"The bed?"

"Platonically," I add, my heart racing.

"Share the bed platonically," he echoes.

I swallow the lump in my throat. "Or not," I backpedal. "I don't mind driving home."

"No," he says with enough force to make me jolt. "It'll be fine."

Nothing about the way he's acting seems *fine*. Tilting my head, I ask, "You're sure?"

"Yup," he says with a curt nod. He walks toward me and takes off his boots, setting them neatly inside the trailer. Lowering himself onto the bed, he rests his back against the trailer wall. "Are *you* sure?"

His words fall on my ears like a challenge, and I do my best not to give him the satisfaction of achieving whatever he's trying to achieve. I copy his, "Yup," and sit cross-legged on the opposite end of the bed facing him.

His lips quirk at my response. "I saw you training today."

There's no point in trying to hide my grimace at the thought of him watching one of my less than finer moments. "Yikes... I'm sorry you had to see that."

He lets out a laugh. "You're just stuck in your head."

"Oh, are we a psychologist now?"

"Just an observation," he says with a subtle lift of his shoulder.

My eyes narrow. "Do you observe everyone as much as you observe me?" As soon as the words leave my mouth, I wish I could take them back.

The corner of his mouth lifts as he takes his hat off and sets it neatly next to him. "No."

I clear my throat. I've never seen him without a hat on.

Usually, when someone wears a hat during every waking hour, it's because they look significantly better with it—or they're balding. But as I stare at Carson, I come to the infuriating realization that he looks great with the hat *and* without. His dark brown, crew-cut hair matches the color of his eyes, which only seem more intense now that there's no hat to steal my attention.

"No?" My voice comes out sounding more like a croak.

"Not particularly," he deadpans.

Part of me wants to ask what he means, but I'm too scared to know. "So, um… No Ed today?"

Carson shakes his head. "He wasn't feeling up to it."

"Is he okay?" I ask, a frown pulling at the corners of my lips. That's probably not a great question to ask about anyone undergoing radiation, but I want to know—I need to.

"He will be," he says with a definitive nod, and I wonder if he's trying to convince himself that those words are true.

An uneasy silence falls between us, and I wring my hands in my lap. I should have driven home. This is too awkward. Stealing a glance at Carson, he doesn't seem nearly as phased by the quiet as I am. Add it to the list of things about him that leaves me restless.

Reaching for my phone, I tap on my text thread with my mom, I send her a quick message letting her know that I found a place to stay overnight and not to wait up.

Once the message sends, I find Carson watching me intently. My hand reaches for the pillow, and I hug it to my chest. I'm wearing leggings and an oversized t-shirt, but the way he looks at me makes me feel exposed.

"Why didn't you tell me you and Seth broke up?"

My mouth goes dry, but I do my best to hide it. More than anything, his question confuses me. He doesn't strike me as someone who would care. I search for a quick-witted comment, but the truth tumbles from my lips instead. "I was embarrassed."

Carson leans forward, matching my cross-legged position. "Bullshit."

I force out a laugh. "Excuse me?"

His mouth quirks. "Bullshit." When I continue to stare at him, he adds, "You don't embarrass that easy."

"Oh yeah?" I challenge. "And what makes you think that?"

"It's not you," he says in a matter-of-fact tone.

"Who am I then?" He's right. I usually don't get embarrassed easily—only when it comes to him apparently.

"I'm still trying to figure that out, but it would be a lot easier if you'd stop lying."

I let out a huff and roll my eyes. "Right." I flop back onto the mattress. The back of the trailer over the hatch door is open, giving me a clear view of the sky. The stars are out tonight, and I let my eyes wander as I figure out what to say. "I think Seth might be a little immature."

He lets out a breath of laughter. "I've noticed."

Turning my head to look at him, I add, "I didn't tell you because none of that became clear to me until you got here. And the fact that I never saw it before then is…" I look back at the stars with a shrug, "embarrassing." I expect him to say something, but he doesn't. "It's weird," I say softly. "It's like you being here—" I shake my head, not wanting to finish that thought. "I don't know."

"You don't know?" Carson lifts a brow, and for once, I can

see what he's thinking so clearly. I know he can see straight through me.

"Alright—fine. Bullshit!"

I expect him to laugh or make fun of me, but instead, he just scratches the side of his head and says, "Hey, you don't owe me anything."

I know I don't, but for whatever reason, I find myself blurting, "He felt threatened by you." I avoid his gaze as soon as the words leave my lips. "He wanted me to stop talking to you, and when I wouldn't, he felt like I was choosing you over him." I sneak a glance at him before looking back at the stars. "I wasn't, but I wasn't going to give in to an ultimatum like that either."

"Are you okay?"

I sit up and turn to face him, crossing my legs. It's the same way we were sitting before, but this time, our knees are almost touching. I try not to notice. Smoothing my hair back with both hands, I nod. "Yeah. I know it was for the best, but I wish it didn't end the way it did, you know? I tried telling him you didn't see me that way, but he wouldn't listen."

Carson leans back slightly, his eyebrows furrowed. "What makes you think that?"

"Think what?"

"That I find you repulsive."

"Oh." I will my cheeks to stay their natural color. "You laughed."

"I laughed?" he asks with a tilt of his head. Those molten eyes waiting for me to make a fool of myself by admitting I even took notice of such a thing.

"It's not a big deal. People look for different things in a partner—or a person. But when Seth told you to stay away from me, you laughed. Because you don't see me that way."

"That's not why I laughed."

My face falls as I think back to that day. "Then why did you?"

Carson looks thoughtful before answering. Finally, after a long pause, he says, "I laughed because if I were trying to take you away from him, I wouldn't have tried to hide it."

"Well, if you ask him, you were definitely up to no good," I mutter, my sarcasm being the only defense against how this conversation is shifting.

"Seth was just worried because he knew he didn't set the bar very high." He shrugs. "I'm not saying you would have gone for it. He should give you more credit, too. What if you find me repulsive?"

I nod solemnly. "I do."

Carson gives me a real smile, and I think my heart spasms at the sight.

He doesn't find me repulsive.

It shouldn't, but that small detail makes it feel like the air has shifted around us, making it harder to breathe.

"See," he jokes in a tone I'm not used to hearing, "It's a good thing I didn't go for it."

"Definitely." I nod and pick at the material of my leggings, suddenly feeling like I'm treading dangerous waters. "That would have been embarrassing for you."

"It's a good thing I'm not that guy."

"What do you mean?"

"I'm not the guy who goes after someone he knows is in a relationship," he says simply. "That's not who I am."

Bringing my eyes to meet his, I can't help asking, "Who are you then?"

Carson doesn't answer right away. One of the horses in the distance lets out a soft whinny, and the steady drum of my heart quickens as I wait for him to answer. He stares down at our knees, and with one subtle movement, his fingers lightly graze my bare ankle. "You want to know?"

I stare down at his hand touching me, unable to tear my eyes away from it. "Yes." I'm frozen, afraid that the tiniest movement might make him pull away.

"I'm the guy," he says, the sound of his voice pulling my attention back to him, "who shouldn't kiss you."

My heart pounds in my chest, and I feel myself being pulled to him until he starts speaking again.

"I'm the guy," he says again, and I look back at his eyes, "who can't show you how you should be treated." His hands slowly glide from my ankles up to the backs of my knees, hooking behind my legs and pulling me toward him. "And I'm the guy," he says in a voice barely above a whisper, his gaze dropping to my mouth, "who wants to do it all anyway."

He's so close when he pauses, his gaze lifting as if to check for my reaction. Despite being frozen in place, I somehow manage a faint nod, my entire body buzzing.

His calloused hand finds my cheek, and I've completely stopped breathing. Skimming his nose against mine, Carson pulls my mouth to his. The kiss is gentle, his lips tenderly parting over mine. It's a kiss with intent.

When he pulls away, I'm breathless. I can't speak. I can't breathe. All I can think about is how I want more—another kiss, another touch, another minute of feeling wanted by him.

Carson cups the back of my neck, his thumb grazing just below my ear. He touches me like I'm his to touch, and everything inside me responds to it. His gaze only flicks upward to meet mine for a second before his fingers are in my hair and his mouth is on mine again, this time with a hunger. His tongue grazes over my bottom lip, and I let him kiss me deeper, my hands resting on his knees as I lean toward him, desperate to get closer.

Pushing me back onto the bed, he moves on top of me, firmly gripping my waist. Our clothes are the only barrier between us, and yet I still want to be closer to him—I need to be. My hands explore his body, feeling every muscle in his back, and when his hips press against mine again, a sound leaves the back of my throat, making him bury his face in my neck, his lips burning against my skin.

Carson claims my every curve as he kisses my neck. By the time he trails lower, my hips have started to roll. Carson grips tighter, a groan dragging out of him, and the fact that I affected him in such a way only makes me want to do it again.

Before I have time to think about it, my hand reaches for the bulge in his jeans. I feel every part of him over the denim, and he kisses me harder. I've never been kissed like this—like our lives depend on it. We're both panting and desperate, and when Carson pulls away and breathlessly says, "We can't do this," I freeze.

"Oh." I scramble to get out from under him.

Hugging my knees to my chest, I guess I do a poor job of hiding the rejection I feel because he adds, "It's not because I don't want to." He runs a hand over his hair. "I want to."

"Right, but you can't, and you shouldn't, and all that," I offer, avoiding his gaze.

A nod is his only response. He's never been a big talker, but for once I know what he's *not* saying.

That he regrets the kiss.

Because if he were feeling a fraction of what I'm feeling right now, no reason would be strong enough to make him want to stop kissing me.

"Okay," I say, as I try to hide what I'm feeling.

"Abbie, look at me."

I do, but only because it would be childish not to. I instantly regret it, though. Being this close to him after he made me feel like I wanted to toss caution to the wind is too difficult. My eyes betray me, dipping to his mouth again, and all I can think about is how much I want to taste him again. My gaze jumps to meet his, and I hope he can't tell what I'm thinking. "It's fine," I say, my voice coming out a little too cheery. Doing my best to tame it, I add, "I understand. We should get some sleep, anyway. Tomorrow's another early start."

"It's just that…" his voice trails off and he rubs the back of his neck, trying to find the right words.

"Carson, it's fine."

He doesn't seem satisfied with my answer, but eventually, he nods, those dangerous lips pressing into a hard line again.

"Well, goodnight." I lie down and turn to face the wall of the trailer, wishing I could disappear.

It takes a moment, but eventually, I feel the shift of Carson's weight as he lies down next to me. In a voice that doesn't reveal an ounce of what he's feeling, he says quietly, "Goodnight, Abbie Linley."

SEVENTEEN

My eyes flutter open to the soft, early morning light, and it takes me a moment to remember where I am. Staring at the metal of the trailer wall, I brace myself before rolling over. I'm not ready to face Carson after what happened.

Last night, I stayed awake for what felt like forever, but I didn't want him to know. Staying as still as possible, I willed myself to sleep. All I could think about was him stopping the kiss. I thought it was a good kiss—a *great* kiss. Could it really have been that different for him? Wouldn't I have been able to tell if he wasn't enjoying it, too?

What it felt like when he touched me, his mouth burning sweetly against my skin, played on a torturous loop. I only have one relationship to compare it to, but nothing has ever taken my body by storm the way he did. I was completely at his mercy, and I know I would have let it go a lot further if he hadn't stopped things.

Which isn't like me.

Maybe it's for the best. Because if I had slept with him, and he regretted *that*, I'd feel a million times worse. It's better that he realized it after the kiss.

But that doesn't mean I have to like it.

And that certainly doesn't mean I want to see him as soon as I wake up after lying next to him all night.

The only saving grace is that after my brain had exhausted all thoughts of Carson, I was able to drift off to sleep. The bed was comfortable, and I didn't have to set my alarm since I'm already at the showgrounds.

But now I need to get my day started, and I'm afraid to face him. I'm dreading the awkward *good morning* and afraid of how I'll feel once I look him in the eyes again.

Taking a deep breath, I roll over as slowly as I can in hopes of not waking him.

But the bed beside me is empty.

What the hell?

Scrambling to my feet, I slide on my muck boots and step down from the trailer.

I do a quick scan, but there's no Carson in sight. It isn't until I notice Sully's stall door open with a wheelbarrow parked in front that I realize where he is. My eyebrows pull together as I make my way to the stall. Sully pops his head through the opening to greet me, happily munching away on his morning hay. Past him, I spot Carson with a pitchfork.

"What are you doing?"

He's wearing his backward hat again, and as much as I liked how he looked without it, I'm a fan of the hat.

He stops, adjusting the brim behind his head like he can read my thoughts. "Mucking."

My eyebrows pinch. "Yes, I can see that. Why?"

He goes back to doing the work at hand. "Horses shit a lot."

"But why are you shoveling *my* horse's shit?"

Carson's lips quirk into a faint smile. "You don't know how to take help, do you?"

"I don't need your pity." I squeeze past the wheelbarrow and into the stall. Standing with my arms crossed in front of him, I gesture with an outstretched hand. "I can take it from here."

He stops working but still grips the pitchfork as he leans against the back stall wall. "You could just say, 'thank you,' you know."

"Thank you. I can take it from here," I repeat, gesturing for him to hand it over again.

Casually spinning the handle, he asks, "You think I pity you?"

"No," I snap.

He tilts his head. "Why would I pity you?"

My cheeks flush. He probably pities me because he rejected

me last night, and now he's trying to make up for it. I'd rather not bring up last night, though. So instead, I say, "Forget it. Would you just give me the damn pitchfork?"

"This pitchfork?" he asks with faked innocence. My eyes narrow, but this seems to only make his amusement grow. "Sure, Abbie." He takes a step toward me. "I'll give you the pitchfork. But first, tell me why you think I pity you."

Being this close to him again has me feeling more alert than three cups of coffee. My lips part as I stare at him. "Because," I say to buy myself time. "I had to listen to you snore all night."

Carson releases a deep laugh, and I hate how happy it makes me to know I'm the one who caused it. He leans in closer, our noses almost touching. "If that's the case, you should be the one pitying me."

I gape at him. "I do *not* snore!"

"Try telling the horses that," he gestures to the line of stalls on the opposite side of the trailer.

Laughter bubbles in my throat, but I do my best to keep it down. "You're dumb," I finally say.

"You like it," he answers. "Here." He hands me what I've been asking for. "Have your precious pitchfork. Most of the stall is done anyway."

"Where are you going?" I ask as I take it from him.

He walks out of the stall. "Now that there's no cute girl passed out in my trailer, I've got work to do."

150

He said those words so casually—like they don't have the power to make my heart stutter.

☼   ☼   ☼

Sully and I stand outside the show ring as I wait for the announcer to call our number. We finished a flat class—the one with no jumping—this morning, but *this* is the class that matters most.

This is the class where all our hard work pays off.

Staring at the eight jumps in the ring, I go over the course pattern in my head for the millionth time. The showgrounds are packed now that it's late morning. Everyone is dressed their best in britches, dress shirts, and show jackets. I didn't plan on making the drive dressed in all that, so luckily my show clothes were already in the trailer ready to go.

Trainers call out pointers from the side of multiple rings as riders of all ages wait for their classes to start. I'd probably find it all more exciting if my ex-boyfriend didn't just have a perfect run and wasn't glaring at me from across the ring. There's a reason Seth has already been accepted by the equestrian team at Auburn. He stands with Valor, ready to watch the other competitors— ready to watch *me*. I'm back to feeling small. Even when I try to focus on the other riders, his burning gaze sears into me. My heart rate rises, my palms sweat, and I can't stop anxiously petting Sully's neck as I stand next to him.

"Don't let him get to you," Carson says, startling me.

I scoff, glancing over my shoulder at him. "Did you see him just now?"

Carson places a hand at the small of my back like it's the most natural thing he could do, and my nerves seem to settle at the contact. Leaning in, he says, "I don't need to see him ride." He turns me to face him and tips the brim of my helmet up so he can look me in the eyes. "You're better than him."

The announcer's voice booms through the loudspeaker. "Next, we have rider 426: Abbie Linley riding Sullivan's Secret!"

"I guess we're about to find out." When I lift my gaze, I'm met with Seth's cold glare again.

But this time, I don't shy away from it.

This time, I glare right back at him until Carson offers to give me a leg-up on Sully. "Ready?"

I nod.

He cradles both hands together, and I set my foot in the middle of his palms, and he hoists me up. Swinging my leg over, I grip my reins and scratch the side of Sully's neck with my pinky.

Once I'm given the okay, I lead us to the ring entrance where Lisa stands waiting for me. She gives Sully a pat as we pass. "You guys will do great."

I force a smile and head down the center line, pausing before picking up a canter.

I let the steady sound of Sully's hooves drown out everything else. We approach the first jump at a steady pace, and he soars over it beautifully.

Keeping him straight, we head down the line to the second jump.

Another seamless takeoff.

He lands on the correct lead, so we round the corner and head to the next line of jumps.

And the next.

Only one line left. My heart drums in my chest as we head into the first of the two jumps. Some of my adrenaline seems to rub off on Sully. He picks up his pace, and I end up having to steady him before the jump. He holds back and ends up going over the jump perfectly.

Then there's only one.

The last jump quickly approaches and as soon as his feet are off the ground, I know we've nailed it.

I drop the reins to let him relax. "Good boy!" I whisper to him excitedly as I give him all the reassuring pats of a job well done.

Lisa beams at us as we meet her at the ring exit. "I don't know where that came from, but I'll take it!"

"Me too," I say with a laugh.

"Take him for a walk around the grounds, and I'll find you when they're ready to announce who placed."

"Okay." I give Sully another pat and keep him on a loose rein

153

as we start our walk toward the outside of the show ring where Carson stands.

"Observing?" I ask in a teasing tone.

He smiles, and a sense of pride fills me. "That was a great run."

"Thanks." The word comes out sounding happy, and I realize I *am* happy. Seth disappeared after my ride, Lisa's pleased with us, and even Carson seems to be in a good mood. And even if none of those things were true, Sully and I kicked ass out there. I wish my mom could be here, but I'll tell her how it went once I'm home—and with any luck, I'll have a ribbon in hand as I do.

"Mind if I walk back with you?" Carson asks as he takes hold of Sully's reins.

"Everything okay?"

He nods, but his face slips back into that serious façade and it makes my stomach tighten.

Hopping down from Sully in one swift movement, I fall into step with Carson. "Spit it out."

He does a quick adjustment of his hat, and I frown as I wait to see what he has to say. "I wanted to apologize for last night."

My riddled nerves dim my happiness. "There's nothing to apologize for."

"There is," he says sternly, his free hand reaching for the back of his neck. "Listen, I know how it must have looked when I stopped things last night. I didn't want to stop, but I don't plan on staying here after my dad finishes his treatments—I can't. I need to go home, and I don't want to complicate things."

Complicate things.

I'm a *complication.*

"I understand," I answer more brightly than I feel. "You want a clean break from the state of Florida and everyone in it."

He nods, but his gaze stays locked on the ground ahead of him. "Something like that."

"And it's not a girl." I know he said he wasn't dating anyone, but I can't help wondering what or *who* waits for him in Tennessee.

Carson lets out a breath of laughter that fails to soften his expression. "Not a girl."

"It's okay," I give in. "Really. It was only a kiss. It never happened." I try to sound light, but my stomach sinks lower with every word.

Watching out of the corner of his eye, he asks, "You're sure?"

I can't look at him and lie, so I fix my gaze forward, and the sight in front of me makes me mutter, "Shit."

Seth sits in a lawn chair with his narrowed eyes locked on us before he pushes himself up with too much force and marches over.

"So, what do we have here?" he asks, trying and failing to keep his voice casual.

Carson brings Sully to a halt but never takes his eyes off Seth.

"Well?" Seth asks again, zeroing in on me. "Having fun?"

Not bothering to hide the roll of my eyes, I say, "Trying to." I move to step around him, but he cuts me off. "Can we not do this right now?" I ask, even though I have a feeling he won't go peacefully.

"Oh, you don't want me to embarrass you in front of your new boyfriend. Is that it?" He gestures toward Carson like he's not standing two feet away and listening to every word.

"We have nothing to talk about." My gaze flickers to Carson. He eyes Seth warily but doesn't say anything.

"Did you tell him, Abbs? Did you tell him how desperate and pathetic you are? That you'd throw away a relationship you had for a *year* just for a chance with him?"

"Oh, my god," I say, and Carson takes a single step toward Seth.

Seth looks at Carson and scoffs before turning back to me. "It's true, isn't it?"

Something inside me snaps, and before I've fully thought about what I'm doing, I've poked a finger at Seth's chest. "You know what's true? You're insecure, Seth. You're too immature to handle a relationship, and I'm better off without you." I'm breathing hard by the time the last word leaves my lips, and Seth is staring back at me, apparently at a loss for words.

It isn't until I turn to walk away, my temper flared, that he mutters behind me, "Desperate and pathe——" Before he can finish the word, Carson steps toward him again, this time grabbing a fistful of his button-down shirt.

He's still holding Sully's reins with one hand, careful not to yank on the bit as he holds Seth in place with the other. Carson's jaw ticks as he pulls Seth toward him. In a dangerously low voice, he says, "Do not talk to her like that."

Seth laughs, but it's unnatural sounding—higher than his regular laugh.

My mouth hangs open as I frantically look back and forth between the two of them. The last thing I need is for a fight to break out between them in the middle of the show. Gently putting a hand on Carson's shoulder, I gave him a pleading stare.

He looks at me, but nothing changes. He still holds Seth in place. It isn't until I give a slight shake of my head, that Carson's shoulders drop and he lets go. He turns to lead Sully back to the barn, and I hurry to catch up with him, leaving Seth alone.

"I bet she's already thrown herself at you, hasn't she?" Seth barks at us. "Fucking slut."

Carson stops dead in his tracks.

"It's fine. Let's get out of here."

Carson's intense gaze stares straight ahead until he turns to me, taking my hand in his. "I'm going to need you to hold him for a minute," he says as he sets Sully's reins in my open palm.

Before I can protest, he's already let go of the reins and walking toward Seth who suddenly looks a lot less confident.

In one easy movement, Carson shoves Seth with both hands.

I wince at the sight and when my eyes open again, Seth is in the dirt—looking a little less pristine for the first time.

"What the hell, man!" Seth exclaims, trying to brush off the dirt before he's even stood.

Crouching down in front of him, Carson uses both hands to pull Seth toward him like a ragdoll.

People start to take notice, but no one approaches them.

"Okay!" Seth finally yells. "I said, okay!"

Carson stares at him before roughly letting go and walking back to where I still stand with Sully. As soon as he approaches, he takes the reins from my hand. "Yeah. Let's get out of here."

My feet somehow know they need to move, but all I can do is stare at him with wide eyes.

"What?" he asks with a furrowed brow. "I told you I wouldn't hit him."

"Yeah, but…" My voice trails. Pointing a thumb over my shoulder, I say, "But you—"

"I didn't hit him."

He waits for me to acknowledge what he's said, so I nod even though my brain is slow to process the scene that just happened. "I can take Sully," I finally offer, realizing he's still holding my horse.

"No, I'll untack him and put him away." He doesn't even look at me as he speaks.

"Why?"

158

"Because I need to stay busy." He stops to look at me, his expression still sharp. "All I want to do is punch that asshole in the mouth so hard that his teeth fall out or…"

"Or…?" I wait impatiently for him to finish his sentence.

Carson shakes his head and keeps walking. "Nothing."

"What is it?" I ask, reaching for his free arm to stop him.

He glances down at my hand on him. It only lasts a second, but when his eyes meet mine again, they're a shade darker than I'm used to seeing. "Or," he says, "distract myself in ways I shouldn't." His gaze falls to my lips, lingering just long enough to make my mouth go dry. My tongue instinctively wets my bottom lip, and his eyes shoot back up to meet mine. "Both are bad ideas."

EIGHTEEN

The far end of the tack room houses the same bulletin board Mom has been hanging ribbons on since I was six. She stands on her tiptoes as she tries to find a place to hang my ribbon from the show. "We'll find a spot. I think there's still some room over here." There's no organization to how they hang. The only method of dating is the dust that's settled over the years.

"Second place," she muses as she stares down at the bright red ribbon in hand. "That's wonderful, Abbie. How many were in your class again?"

"23," I say with a tired smile. I already told her this when I got home from the show yesterday and again when we ate dinner last night, but I think she likes hearing it. Or maybe she likes *me* hearing it.

"Wow," she says again as her gaze drifts back to the crowded board, scanning for an open spot to stick my latest achievement.

"And Lisa said you were competing against some talented riders. You should be proud."

Seth took home the first-place ribbon. Considering Mom hasn't asked, I have a feeling she already knows.

"Aha! Here we go." She reaches for the top right corner of the board, managing to tack the new ribbon in place.

"We should really throw some of these away." I gently pull on a faded and dirty yellow Walk-Trot ribbon from when I was younger.

Her eyes widen. "I would never."

I shake my head, but there's a smile tugging at my lips. "Well, I need to get back to work. I still have to turn out the horses and clean the last two stalls." Sully always gets the day off after a show, and Mom fed the horses this morning, so I bumped my barn work out a little later than usual. At this rate, I won't be done until dinner.

"Okay," Mom says casually over her shoulder. "Carson's coming by. George lost a shoe. I found it in the paddock, so he just needs to tack it back on."

"What? Why?" I try to hide the panic from my voice. The last thing I need is for Mom to sense something going on between Carson and me.

After he put Sully away at the show, it was time for me to meet Lisa to see who placed. By the time I had my ribbon in hand, Carson had put Sully in his stall and was nowhere to be found.

Seth's insult still echoes in the back of my mind.

Desperate and pathetic.

Deep down, I know I'm not either of those things, but right now, I feel like I'm both.

Because Seth was right, I *did* throw myself at Carson. It may have been for the sake of making Seth angry, but I still did it.

And when Carson kissed me, I wouldn't have stopped it from going further. I would have done a whole lot more than that if he hadn't put an end to it.

Fucking slut.

Mom's staring at me with a furrowed brow. "He's coming to put George's shoe back on... like I said." She tilts her head. "Are you okay?"

"What?" I shake my head. "Sorry, I'm fine. That's fine." Adjusting some of the bridles in the tack room, I try to make myself look busy.

"Uh-huh."

"Well, I better get back to work," I say and make a conscious effort to slow my pace, so I don't look like I'm trying to run from this conversation.

And hide from our new farrier.

Our extremely attractive new farrier that I haven't been able to stop thinking about since he kissed me in the back of a horse trailer.

The one who instantly regretted that kiss because he's leaving and doesn't want to complicate things.

The one who probably thinks I'm desperate and pathetic now.

I go to leave the tack room too quickly and crash into a broad muscular chest that feels more familiar than it should.

Carson reaches out to steady me, his hands holding my arms on either side. "In a hurry?"

My fleeing thoughts leave me with nothing, and I'm stuck staring up at him with an open mouth and no words. He's not moving me out of his way. He's just standing there, holding me in place, and the warmth of his hands pulls all my body heat to the surface.

"Is that Carson?"

It isn't until Mom's voice sounds behind us that Carson drops me, and I yell, "George!"

Carson raises his eyebrows at my outburst.

As my mom approaches, I manage to get out, "George threw a shoe."

"Right…" Carson says. "That's why I'm here."

Mom watches us with a trace of amusement that makes me want to melt into the concrete. For once, I'd like to be able to hide something from her, but I swear the woman is omniscient.

"Right," I say, stealing Carson's words because I can't come up with any of my own. "I'll go get him."

"You do that." Mom laughs, and I want to curl up in a corner and die.

I take my time walking to George's paddock, muttering variations of, "Way to go, Abbie. Now he thinks you're pathetic, desperate, *and* a lunatic," the whole way there. By the time I reach the large, dark bay Warmblood and slip the halter over his head, it's turned into a mantra of "a pathetic, desperate crazy person."

"What's that?" Carson's unmistakable voice says behind me, making me jump.

Spinning around, I snap, "What are you doing?" not bothering to hide the accusation in my tone.

"Figured you might need some help," he says with a shrug.

I give him a dubious look. "Bringing a horse in from the paddock?"

He ignores my question. "Weren't you saying something?"

"No," I mutter, turning back to George and petting his face.

"For the record," Carson's low voice is right behind me now, sending goosebumps down my spine. "You're not pathetic or desperate." He takes the lead from my clenched hand and walks George out of the paddock. Then looking over his shoulder, he adds, "But verdict's still out for 'crazy person.'"

"Do you think you're funny?" I call after him. "Because you're not funny."

Carson's shoulders shake with laughter as he keeps walking. "I have my moments," he calls back, and my lips twist into a smile.

☼   ☼   ☼

Carson seems completely comfortable with moving on from what happened between us, but it's all I can think about. As I work on cleaning my two remaining stalls, I'm overly aware of where he is and what he's doing at all times.

Tacking a shoe on should take minutes, but Carson takes his sweet time. He hasn't even looked at me, and it's making me want to bang my shovel against one of the metal feed bins just to get his attention.

The longer he stays, the more I walk by him, and every time I walk by him, it's harder to breathe.

Peeking my head out of the stall, I check to see that he's still working before ducking back inside and texting Sarah.

Me: I have to tell you something.

The three dots appear right away.

Sarah: Is it better than TV?

I bite my lip as I think about Carson kissing me. It was *definitely* better than TV.

Sarah: You're taking too long to answer. That means yes.

Sarah: Is it a juicy something or a serious something?

My lips twitch as I type my response.

Me: Juicy.

Sarah: Can I guess?

Me: No.

Sarah: Did you kiss Ed's son?

My cheeks burn from the text alone, and I steal a glance to make sure Carson's still at the other end of the barn.

Sarah: Because if you kissed Ed's son, I might scream.

Me: Don't scream.

Sarah: Did you kiss him???

Me: No.

I start typing again, a smile pulling at my lips.

Me: He kissed me.

Sarah: SCREAMING!

Sarah: Tell me everything.

Me: Sarah, it was so good.

Me: Like dangerously good.

Sarah: Did your toes curl?

Sarah: When are you doing it again?

I choke back a laugh, but the thought alone makes my smile fade.

Me: Never. He's leaving in a few weeks, and we're pretending it never happened.

The three dots don't appear again. I stare at the screen for a few more seconds but no answer comes. Biting my bottom lip, I hope for a new text so I can get her take on things—so she can tell me what to do. I hold out a little longer before deflating and slipping my phone back into my pocket. I know she's not brushing me off. She's probably in class, or maybe her roommate needs her for something. I know she'll get back to me when she can, but I was hoping she'd have some advice for what to do when you're developing feelings for a guy who's leaving the state.

After dumping my final wheelbarrow, I pause at the crossties where Carson stands with George's hoof between his legs. I watch him swap different tools from his toolbelt, mesmerized by his practiced fluency.

"Abbie," he says as he continues to work.

I jolt, not realizing I had zoned out. "Yeah?"

"I'm going to need you to stop checking me out," he playfully shoots me a look over his shoulder before hammering the shoe onto George's foot with ease.

I open my mouth, determined to tell him that's *not* what I was doing, but there's no point trying to talk over the noise. Once the hammering stops and he sets George's foot down, I say, "Shouldn't you be done by now?"

Carson turns to face me, wiping his hands with a rag from his back pocket. "Well, the shoe your mom found was bent. I tried to straighten it but ended up having to put a new one on him." He points to the hoof he just set down. "That was the part you saw."

"Yes, thank you," I say flatly. "So, are you leaving now?"

"Are you trying to get rid of me?"

I cross my arms. "Maybe."

He gives me a long look before saying, "Okay, Abbie."

I'm not sure why I'm pushing him to leave. I don't want him to go, but I don't love how it feels having him here either. He makes me agitated and unsettled, distracted by things I want but can't have.

"How long do you think you'll be here, anyway?" I ask as he uses a large magnet to pick up any fallen nails.

"If you're that desperate to get rid of me, tell your mom to find someone else to do the work around here." He stands up straight, and I notice the sharp lines of his face. My eyes betray me, skating from his jaw to his lips, reminding me of what it felt like to have him kiss me.

And how he'll never do it again.

I roll my eyes. "How many weeks?"

"Four more weeks, and you'll have to find someone else to actively avoid."

My cheeks flush with anger or embarrassment, or maybe a mixture of both. "And what about you?" I ask, determined to hide how much he affects me.

"What about me?" His eyes drop to the rag in his hands.

"In four weeks you'll have to find someone else to seduce in the back of a horse trailer."

His eyes jump to meet mine, and he breaks into a grin. "No." Stepping toward me, he hooks his finger under my chin. "That was only for you." Too soon, his smile fades and he releases me. The corner of his mouth quirks like he's trying to recover the playful mood, but I wonder what caused his mouth to turn down only moments ago.

Crossing my arms, I cock an eyebrow. "Only for me?"

Straightening, he runs both hands over his head, adjusting his hat. "What do you think?"

In the heat of his gaze, I bite my lip, but I'm not sure how to answer him.

One side of his mouth turns up. Grabbing his equipment, he says, "See you tomorrow, Abbie Linley," as he walks out of the barn.

I stare after him with a newfound ache at the bottom of my belly. "Bastard."

Nineteen

It sounds like he's hammering right outside my window. I groan and peek one eye open to check the time. 7:12 a.m. Rolling onto my back, I stare up at the ceiling with a new reason to curse Carson.

Tossing back the covers, I step out of bed and make my way to my bedroom window. Sure enough, Carson's replacing some of the slats in our back porch railing below. He's dressed in work gloves, jeans, a charcoal-grey t-shirt, and that damn hat.

Catching me out of the corner of his eye, he stops hammering and holds his hand up as a visor to block the sun.

I open my window and lean out. "You do know it's barely 7 a.m., right?"

"It's 7:15," he says, matter-of-factly. "Is that what you sleep in?" he asks, gesturing toward me with his hammer.

Looking down at myself, I curse under my breath. I'm wearing cotton shorts and a tank top that barely covers all things that should be covered. "You know," I say as I cross my arms to try to hide. "You wouldn't need to block the sun if you turned that stupid hat around."

Carson lets out a low laugh I can feel in my bones. "Yes, ma'am." He gets back to work, but not before he swiftly turns his hat around. With his hat facing forward, I catch him peeking up at me from under the brim, his tight-lipped smile mirroring my own.

"Don't you have a horse to ride?" I spin around to find Mom casually leaning against my door frame with that same amusing smile from yesterday.

"Are you trying to kill me?" I ask with a hand on my chest. "You can't just go lurking around corners like a psycho."

"Oh, I can lurk all I want," she says with a grin. "It's my house. You are my daughter." She points to my bedroom window. "And that is a young man who seems to have knocked you right off your feet."

I huff. "Hardly."

She cocks an eyebrow. "No? So, you didn't spend the night with him at the show, and he didn't get in a fight with Seth the next day?"

I gape at her. "How do you even…"

"It's a small town," she whispers playfully like she's letting me in on her big secret.

"No." I shake my head. "Geneva may be a small town, but the show was in Ocala, and Ocala is not a small town."

"I have my ways."

"Well, your ways creep me out." I go into my closet for a pair of riding pants and an athletic tank.

I expect her to be gone when I walk out of my closet, but she's still standing there, looking like she has more to say.

"Yes?" I ask expectantly.

"I like him," she finally says.

"Who?"

She gives a nod toward my bedroom window. "Carson. He's a hard worker, down to earth, and focused. If I were you, I wouldn't write him off."

I'm not sure where this is coming from. She's never pushed me like this when it comes to my personal life. She's never told me *not* to date someone, but she's never encouraged anything like this either.

"He's leaving," is all I can bring myself to say. I'm careful to keep my focus on the clothes in my hand, knowing she'll be able to see everything I'm feeling if I look at her.

"That's a shame," she says softly. "Ed mentioned he was helping out during his treatments, but I didn't realize he wasn't staying."

"Wait. You know about Ed? How was he feeling when you

spoke to him?"

"Yeah, he mentioned it." Mom weighs her head from side to side. "He says he's doing fine, but I think it's taking a lot out of him. You can hear it in his voice."

"And he wasn't at the show."

"Exactly," she says with a nod. "I may see if he's up for a visitor. I know Carson is helping with his clients and the work that needs to be done, but I doubt he's cleaning and cooking over there, too."

"That would be impressive," I say with a laugh. "I think that's a good idea, though. If Ed's up for a visit, you'll have to tell him I say hi."

"Will do," she says with a smile. As she leaves, she gently hits the side of the door frame twice. "Have a good ride out there, okay?"

"Thanks, Mom." Closing the door behind her, I get dressed.

Still a little worn out from the busy show weekend, I decide to only do flat work with Sully—no jumping. As we approach the far end of the ring at a trot, I spot Carson walking by with his toolbox in hand. Setting it down, he stops to watch us, scrutinizing both of our movements and making me feel more susceptible to judgment than I did at the actual horse show.

As we pass, he says, "You guys look good together."

I try to ignore the fact that those words, coming from him, make me happier than placing at the show. "Are you checking out my horse?" I ask as I circle to stay close enough to continue the conversation.

"I might be." When I circle again, he's not staring at Sully anymore, his eyes are locked on me. Heat flushes to the surface of my skin, and I pull Sully to a halt. "You can take him for a spin if you want," I somehow manage to say in a light tone.

This pulls Carson out of whatever thoughts were circling his mind. "I told you. I don't ride."

"But you miss it." It's not a question. I can see that he does.

Carson looks at his work boot as he gently bumps his foot against one of the new posts he put in last week. Glancing up at me from under the brim of his hat, he says, "Sometimes I think I do, but not always."

"How many years has it been since you rode?"

"Five."

And since his mom passed away.

"What would she think?" I ask, hoping I'm not overstepping.

"About what?"

I run my thumb over the leather reins. "About you giving up riding."

At first, he doesn't say anything, but when I look at him, I'm relieved to find a faint smile pulling at the corner of his mouth. "She always put horses first, so she'd probably make some smart-ass comment about how I don't deserve to ride with that attitude, anyway."

174

I smile. "She'd have a point." Signaling Sully to walk on, I add, "Well, if you ever change your mind, you're welcome to ride Sully."

Carson lifts a brow. "And sit in that tiny saddle?" he says with a smirk.

"I thought real cowboys could ride in anything."

He shakes his head as a light laugh leaves him. "That's your first mistake," he says as he turns his hat back around, adjusting it to its usual backward position. "I'm nothing like a real cowboy."

Something in the way he's looking at me makes my stomach flip. Circling Sully while keeping him in sight, I say, "The verdict's still out for that one."

The side of his mouth quirks, but it doesn't last. His face turns serious as he taps his thumb against the railing, deep in thought. "A trail ride might be fun." The words make me whip my head around so fast I could have given myself whiplash.

"A trail ride?"

Carson looks unsure, but says, "Yeah... I've been thinking about it for a few days now."

I stop Sully in his tracks and study Carson. If I'm understanding correctly, this is a big deal—like a really big deal. And the fact that he wants me to be a part of something like this makes my heart swell in my chest. "Let's do it," I say, not wanting to give him a chance to back out. "When?"

He still looks at me like he's not sure he should have said anything, but he answers, "Friday? I don't think I have any clients that day."

I nod, and perhaps too quickly, say, "Yes."

He laughs, amused by my over-eager reaction. "Okay," he says. "Friday."

He turns and walks back toward the house to get back to work, and I let the smile linger on my lips. Carson is going to ride again, and knowing I played a small role in that choice makes my whole body feel lighter.

He's going to get back on a horse.

And I get to spend time with him.

I just have to pretend I don't want to kiss him.

TWENTY

Steam from my shower fogs my reflection in the bathroom mirror, and I stand with a towel wrapped around me. Reaching for my hairbrush, I comb out the wet tangles. Mom left to go grocery shopping before I got in the shower, so the house is quiet, my mind wandering as I brush my hair longer than needed.

Knowing Carson's leaving and doesn't want to complicate things should make me second-guess spending time with him. I know time alone with him probably isn't a good idea, but it's too tempting. The selfish part of me wants to soak up as much of him as I can, even if there's a chance it might cause more harm than good. Carson and I should be friends, nothing more. We can have a fun, four-week friendship, and then we can go our separate ways.

Because if we don't, I could get attached.

Things could get messy.

I could end up hurt.

But I've already been hurt. A few weeks ago, I thought I'd be heartbroken when things ended between Seth and me, and I was at first, but now I'm not. I'm okay, and maybe I'll be okay when Carson leaves, too.

My stomach tightens, not believing the thought.

Once my hair is free of knots, I open the bathroom door. I only make it one step into the upstairs hallway before jumping back, my hand gripping the towel around me like my life depends on it. "Son of a bitch, Carson! What are you doing here?"

The warmth of the shower steam is quickly replaced with cold, air-conditioned air, only adding to my awareness of how incredibly naked I am right now.

He immediately steps down from the step stool and shakes his head. "Sorry, I was just uh…" he points up at the smoke detector.

Swallowing the lump in my throat, I nod as I hold the towel around me tighter. "Replacing the battery?"

"Yeah," he says, his eyes never leaving mine. "I didn't mean to…" He gestures toward me. "I figured I'd be done before you…"

"It's okay." I try to get my bearings again. "I just need to get to my room." I gesture just past him to the door on his opposite side.

He steps aside.

"I didn't realize you were working inside the house." I head toward my room, trying not to dwell on the fact that this towel is shorter than I'd like it to be.

Carson nods, avoiding my gaze. "Your mom has a list of things for me to do in here. I figured I'd get some of them done today since I'll be helping my dad with his clients all day tomorrow."

I turn my body to sidestep past him. "So I'll just see you for our date on Friday then." I freeze. My eyes jump up to meet his. We're almost pressed against each other in the narrow hallway, and it makes it impossible for me to think straight. "I didn't mean—it's not a date. I just meant—" I let out a huff. "I meant I'll see you Friday then."

He opens his mouth to say something but seems to change his mind. With a subtle crease of his brow, he asks, "Do you want it to be a date?"

My eyes widen. Why did I say that? This isn't supposed to be about me or my feelings for him. This is supposed to be about Carson finally getting on a horse again. "No," I answer, surprised by how convincing I sound.

His gaze burns into me. "No," he echoes.

"No," I say again with a shake of my head and try to ignore how thick the air has suddenly become. "A date would complicate things."

He lets out a breath of laughter, his eyes falling to my mouth for half a second before he clears his throat. "Abbie, you standing here in a towel complicates things."

"That was unintentional." Blood flushes to the surface of my skin and coils at the bottom of my belly. I press my thighs together under the towel, and my tongue instinctively wets my bottom lip. His eyes dip to my mouth again.

He swallows hard. "So, not a date."

"Not a date," I confirm, even though disappointment fills me.

He nods, but neither of us makes a move to leave. My feet feel like they've sunken into the floor. I can't help looking at his mouth, remembering what it felt like to have his lips on mine. All it would take is half a step and a tilt of my head for me to make it happen again. It sounds so easy when I put it that way, but it's not easy. Nothing about this is easy.

"Abbie," Carson says, his body rigid.

"Hm?" I ask, but my eyes stay trained on his mouth.

"I'm going to need you to go put some clothes on."

My eyes jump back up to meet his. "Right, sorry." I give an embarrassed smile as I sidestep past him and reach for my bedroom door. Pausing, I catch him standing with his back up against the wall before his head falls with a slight shake. I slip into my bedroom and quickly close the door, afraid of what one more glance might do to me.

Pressing my back against my bedroom door, my chest rises and falls as I try to come down from whatever just happened.

I am so screwed.

Twenty-One

It's probably a good thing Carson wasn't at my house yesterday because it feels like it's taken me this long to recover from him seeing me in a towel. Even as I drive the winding, country roads to get to his house, anxiety meshes with my excitement. Ed has a couple of horses Carson said we could use on the trails that back up to their property. Even if Mom and I had access to trails from our house, Sully is a complete nuisance in the woods and thinks everything is trying to attack him.

My racing heart doesn't match the events that will take place today. Carson and I will go for a trail ride. He'll rediscover his love for riding, and that will be it.

End of story.

But as much as I *know* Carson and I need to be only friends, there's a flutter of anticipation in my chest that won't quit.

I lock away the feeling and toss the key. *He's leaving—as in, going to another state with no intentions of coming back.*

My face falls at the thought, but I don't have time to dwell on it because I've reached the property gate where Carson stands, waiting for me.

He holds the gate open so I can drive through and then closes it behind me. Once he slides the chain around the post to secure it, he jogs over to my passenger door and hops in.

He's not wearing anything I haven't seen him in before. His dark grey shirt has a Dodge Ram logo over the front pocket, and his jeans are faded and worn. Large work boots make him look like he's ready for any task that might be thrown his way, and his faded backward hat might as well be the cherry on top.

Even though he looks exactly as I expected him to look, I still notice the way the sleeves of his t-shirt stretch over his arms, and the sharp angles of his jawline. You'd think it would stop coming as such a shock at this point.

Carson looks good—always.

"Hey."

"Hey." I smile and try my best to hide my thoughts.

The gravel drive splits in two directions, and he points to the left. "The barn is over there."

We pull up to the barn right around the corner, and Ed stands at the fence, throwing hay to the horses. A West Highland Terrier mix dances at his feet, and a sigh of relief leaves my lips.

Ed will break the tension—and there's a dog—it's almost impossible to feel awkward while petting a dog.

"You have a dog?" I ask as I put the truck in park.

Carson stares at me. "You've never met Phil?"

I laugh. "I'm sorry. Did you say, *Phil?*"

Carson opens the truck door and hops down. "Yeah." Then with two fingers in his mouth a loud whistle rings out.

I get out and walk around the front end, and a small white dog with pointed ears happily bounds up to Carson. He rolls onto his back, and Carson crouches down, rubbing the dog's belly. It seems like the pup can't sit still because, within seconds, he's back on all four legs, circling and wagging his tail.

"Hey, Phil, this is Abbie." He glances up at me. "Abbie, meet Phil."

I can't fight my smile as I kneel to pet the furry ball of energy. "Hi, Phil," I shy away from his sloppy kisses, laughing when he catches me on the cheek.

Carson grabs the dog by the collar. "Alright, I know she's pretty," he casually says, like those words don't have the power to knock me off my axis.

"Well, look who it is!" Ed's familiar voice calls out, and I turn to look at him. I don't know what I was expecting, but I thought he would *look* sick.

He doesn't.

"Hey, yourself," I say with a smile as I get to my feet. Ed has always had a tall wiry frame, and now that I think about it, I don't think I've ever seen him without a baseball cap. My eyes jump to Carson's backward hat staple, and my lips pull up at the connection.

"I hear you're finally getting this one back in the saddle." He claps a hand on Carson's shoulder. "I've only been trying for years."

"Yeah, well…" Carson stands, his voice trailing off as he dusts his hands on his jeans.

As casually as Ed brings it up, I have a feeling he doesn't know the reason behind Carson's decision to walk away from horses.

"So, I'm assuming you have access to some nice trails out here?" I ask.

"Oh, yeah," Ed replies and Carson's shoulders seem to relax at the change of subject. "If you go out the back gate, you'll find a path that takes you around a three-mile loop."

"Sounds great." I grin. My eyes wander to the barn a few feet away where two horses—one buckskin and one a paint—stick their heads out over the stall doors. "Will we be riding them?"

"Yeah." Carson points to the buckskin. "That's Hank." He then points to the paint next. "And that's Williams."

My eyes flicker between the two men next to me. "Hank and Williams? As in Hank Williams?"

Ed's smile grows wider. "Oh, I knew I liked you."

Carson shakes his head. "Dad's a big fan." His stoic façade

184

can't hide his amusement as he stares at his father.

"Well, I'd better get inside," Ed says as he dusts his hands on his jeans. "This stuff takes all the energy out of me. Come on, Phil."

Phil obediently trots behind Ed as he turns to make his way toward the house.

"He looks good," I finally say once he's out of earshot.

Carson watches his dad. "Some days the treatment knocks him on his ass, but I think he's getting stir crazy sitting in that house all day."

"So, who's helping with the horses while he goes through his treatment?" I ask as we head toward the barn.

Carson gives me a sideways glance. "I am."

I stop. "What? How? *When?*" Gaping at him, I add, "Earlier this week you were at my house by 7 a.m."

He shrugs and keeps walking. "Someone has to do it." He stops, waiting for me. "Are you just going to stand there, or are we going for a ride?"

My feet scramble to catch up with him. "What time did you wake up this morning?"

"I don't know," he says as he tries to remember. "Five, I guess?"

"*Five?*" I stare at him, wide-eyed. "Is that why you're always in such a great mood?"

Carson gives me a heavy-lidded stare before gathering the

tack and dipping into the first stall. He balances a western saddle over his shoulder and holds a saddle pad in his other hand. Then he effortlessly tosses the pad and saddle on before tightening the cinch underneath.

"Are you sure you haven't done this in a while?"

He slips out of the current stall and moves to the next. "I haven't ridden, but I've tacked up a lot of horses. I worked as a groom at a big stable back home before I started shoeing."

"Ah, that explains it." I'm reminded of the stable hands at Spring Oaks and hope Carson tacked up horses for people who carry their noses a little lower.

Once both horses are saddled, he hands me a bridle. "You take Williams. Both of these guys are pros on the trails, but he's a little sweeter than Hank."

Taking the bridle from him, I let out a laugh. "Who knew you were so chivalrous?"

Carson gives me a smirk as he tosses the reins over Hank's neck. "I have my moments."

Birds chirp in the trees overhead as we bring the horses over to the fence so we can mount up. Even in the late-morning heat, the many trees on Ed's property provide enough shade to keep us cool.

The fact that I have a great view doesn't hurt, either.

"It's beautiful out here," I say to Carson in front of me.

He looks up at the trees like the thought never occurred to

him. "Yeah, I guess it is."

Wedging my foot between the fence railing, I put my other foot in the stirrup and hop on Williams. We walk in a circle near the barn while I wait for Carson to get on Hank.

He doesn't use the fence like I did. He stands with a firm hand on Hank's neck, giving him a few pets as he stares at the saddle.

I don't rush him.

He could change his mind, right now, and he wouldn't hear a peep out of me.

He doesn't, though. After that moment of hesitation, Carson hoists himself up like he's done it a million times. Seated comfortably on Hank's back, he looks like he never stopped riding. The western saddle may feel bulky to me with its horn and large stirrups, but Carson seems right at home.

Comfortably holding Hank's reins in one hand, he points to an opening in the trees. "The trail is through there."

I smile. "After you."

He lets out a low laugh as he steers Hank in that direction, and I follow in step behind him. Carson looks up at the trees overhead as he leads the way.

"It probably can't compete with the trails in Tennessee," I offer, assuming that's what he was thinking.

Glancing over his shoulder, he smiles. "Not even close," he says, and when he turns back around, he adds, "I wish I could show you."

My heart flutters, but I do my best to brush it off. "Yeah." Looking up, I take in the sunlit trees.

"But Florida has its beauty, too."

I look at him. He has one hand resting on the back of the saddle as he looks back at me. Trying to fight my smile, I say, "You should probably watch where you're going considering you barely know how to ride."

His eyebrows shoot upward, but he does a poor job of hiding his grin. Facing forward again, he laughs and shakes his head, and I let my own smile blossom across my face.

This is not good.

Even after Seth and I started dating, I never felt this. He never made my heart stop with a single look. With Seth, I was mostly surprised he had taken an interest in me. He was the cutest guy to ever like me, he was popular, and he was one of the best riders at the shows while I was just a girl with her horse. He made me laugh, and I adored him, but he never ignited a spark in me with a single touch. I never daydreamed about kissing him to the point where I walked my horse right into his.

"Shit. Sorry." I pull Williams back a couple of steps.

Hank had jigged forward when Williams bumped into him, and now Carson looks at me like he's waiting for an explanation. "Where'd you go?"

I blink. "Nowhere."

"Right," he says, but his eyebrows furrow. Pointing ahead,

he says, "I was stopping to say there's an open field just through there." He looks back at me with a glint in his eyes. "Want to race?"

"You haven't been on a horse in five years."

"So?"

"So... don't you think you should take things slow?"

His response is a slow, easy grin. "Where's the fun in that?"

Before I have time to answer, he takes off on Hank at a lope, and the two disappear out of sight. I barely have to ask Williams to do the same. He's already on their tail, not wanting to be left behind.

Around the corner, the trees clear, and we pick up our speed to a gallop side by side. There's something liberating about riding this way. The wind in my hair and the power of the horse underneath brings a smile to my lips.

Carson looks over at me, not bothering to hide his grin. "I forgot to tell you something!" he yells over the sound of us cutting through the air.

"What?" I ask, raising my voice to be heard.

A wicked smile crosses his lips. "Hank is faster!" With that, he kicks Hank into high gear, still looking like he hasn't missed a day of riding since the age of six.

I throw the reins forward on Williams' neck, urging him to open up. He does, but Hank still has us beat.

When we reach Carson and Hank, they've stopped at the far

edge of the field. My heart races from the adrenaline of going that fast, and I'm panting. "That wasn't fair."

He lets out a breathless laugh. "Maybe not." He gives Hank a pat on the neck. "But you're right. I've missed this."

It's impossible to wipe the grin off my face. "We should do this again before you leave." I give him a sideways glance. "But, next time, I'm taking Hank."

Carson tells Hank to walk on. "We'll see about that."

Falling into step beside him, I glare at him. "I never had you pegged as someone who cheats."

He lets out a laugh that warms my entire body just from the sound of it.

The field we meander through is beautiful. Tall grass with wildflowers of all different colors brushes against the horses' legs as we walk, the stalks swaying like an ocean of petals every time the breeze picks up. I've never had a reason to visit Ed's property, but it's certainly something to look at.

"Your dad really lucked out with this."

Carson follows my gaze, but he just shrugs. "I guess he did. My mom used to love it here. She was always outside."

"She sounds great."

He nods, as he looks out at the field. "She was."

An easy silence falls between us. There's nothing but the soft sounds of birds and horses to fill my ears, and I don't mind. I'm used to riding in tight riding pants and a helmet that traps the heat, but out here in my jeans with my hair down, I feel free. I turn my face toward the puffy white clouds overhead and close my eyes with my mouth turned up, loving the way I feel in this moment.

Because I *am* free.

I'm free of Seth, Christina, and the rest of his friends. I'm free to be here with Carson and not feel guilty about it. It feels like I can do anything.

Opening my eyes, I look over at Carson. "What made you change your mind?"

"About what?"

Leaning back, I give Williams a pat on his hindquarters. "Riding."

Carson doesn't look at me as he considers my question. His eyes are fixed on something in the distance as he brushes his hand along Hank's neck. "I stopped riding because it wasn't fun anymore, but I thought if I went with you, it might be fun again."

My lips turn upward even though there's a pang in my chest from his answer. "You never told your dad why you stopped?"

Dropping his stare to the reins in his hand, he rubs his thumb over the thick leather. When he does speak, it's slow and careful. "My dad and I haven't always had the best relationship."

I mull over his response. Ed is one of the kindest people I know, and Carson is... Carson.

"He used to drink." My lips part as I search for something to say, but Carson adds, "That's why my mom left and took me to

191

Tennessee."

"I had no idea," I finally say. "That must have been hard."

Carson nods. "It was, but I was young. I barely remember their divorce." He hesitates and stares down at Hank. "I blamed him after the accident." He glances at me, those brunette eyes capturing mine. "I was young, and I figured if he never ruined their marriage, my mom would still be in Florida. She never would have been on that mountain road in the rain." Carson shrugs. "It's a backward way of thinking about it, but at the time, I was looking for someone to blame. He was the easiest target."

I can't imagine losing a parent and blaming the other. Doing that would feel like losing two people instead of one, but I can see where he was coming from—even if he shouldn't have thought the way he did.

"I think it's normal to feel that way," I say, and it's my turn to look down at the horse in front of me. Weaving my fingers through Williams' mane, I add, "My mom has had to do a lot on her own over the years. I wasn't always old enough to be helpful with the barn, and she's had to work twice as hard because my dad left." I hesitate before looking up at him. "I know it's not the same, but I blamed him, too."

Carson gives me a sad smile. "When I stopped riding, I wasn't talking to my dad. The only person who knew the reason behind it was my grandpa." He brings his eyes to meet mine. "Well, I guess you know now, too."

192

My eyes widen. "Why did you tell me? I'm nobody."

"Abbie." He shakes his head, and I love the way he says my name. "If there's anything I know, it's that you're somebody."

I let a small smile come to my lips because, over these past few weeks, he's become somebody to me, too. I may not know what the end of summer holds, but I know he's become my favorite person to talk to. I know that when he isn't around, I wish he were.

And I know that I'll miss him when he leaves.

Carson looks at the sky above, the crease between his brow deepening. "Looks like a storm is headed this way. We may have to turn back early."

I look up at the overcast skies, disappointment flooding me.

Carson points in the distance. "Rain has already started over there, and it's coming this way."

My heart sinks as a gust of wind picks up. I'm not ready for our time together to end, but when he steers Hank back the way we came, I let Williams follow close behind.

TWENTY-TWO

Thunder bellows in the distance by the time we reach the property. We ended up having a second race to get back here before the storm. As we jump down from the horses, light rain starts. It cools my sun-kissed skin, leaving goosebumps down my arms. The metal roof plays the beat of the rain as we put the horses away and untack them in their stalls.

I follow Carson into the small tack room and hang my bridle on the wall hook. "I guess I should get going."

"Or you could stay." Carson's voice sounds behind me, his arm reaching over my shoulder as he hangs his bridle next to mine. I wonder if he meant to say those words all warm and melty, or if I'm just hearing them that way. Turning to look at him, I expect him to take a step back, but he doesn't. His shirt, damp with rain, clings to his muscular stomach, and I can feel the warmth radiating from him on my cool, damp skin.

My eyes search his, trying to understand what he's thinking. Carson tucks a strand of hair behind my ear, and my eyes flutter shut at his touch. I don't want this to end.

He presses his lips to my forehead, letting them linger there as he strokes my hair again. He shouldn't be allowed to look the way he does—make me *feel* the way he does—and then leave. It's not fair.

"Why do you have to go back?" I whisper. My cheeks flush when I realize I've said the words out loud.

Stepping back, he frowns.

"I mean, I know why you have to leave. It's your home, and you don't want to be here. That's a good enough reason."

I hope my last question didn't come across like I'm asking him to stay. My dad stayed in Florida for my mom, and look how well that turned out. Sometimes as much as you want something to work, it just doesn't. Trying to force it will only delay the inevitable. Carson will go back to Tennessee the same way my dad went back to Chicago. I won't waste my time trying to convince myself otherwise.

I expect him to brush me off, but he looks deep in thought. "It's not just that."

"It's okay. You don't owe me an explanation." I go to walk around him, but he puts an arm up against the tack room wall, blocking my exit.

Stopping, my eyes trace the lines that run from his forearm

195

to his bicep before they disappear under the tight sleeve of his t-shirt. He looks from me to his hand on the wall and quickly drops it.

Sinking my hope along with it.

I shouldn't be hoping for anything. From the beginning, he's been painfully clear, and I promised we could put the kiss behind us.

I can do that.

I can pretend it didn't happen.

But when he's standing this close to me, I can't deny I want to kiss him again.

My palms sweat as I wait for him to say something.

He grips the back of his neck and shakes his head. "No, I want to tell you why I'm here."

"Because your dad is sick?"

Carson nods. "That's part of the reason."

"What's the other part?"

Taking a step away from me, he avoids my gaze. "I may have gotten into some trouble back home."

I want to step after him, but my feet stay frozen in place. "What kind of trouble?"

He looks at me, his eyes jumping back and forth between mine as he debates what to say.

"Whatever it is, just tell me."

Carson takes a seat on a wooden tack box across from me.

Slipping off his hat, he runs a hand through his hair. "You'll see me differently."

"Try me."

He finally looks at me then, holding my gaze for a beat longer. Sliding his fingers over the brim of the hat in his hands, he says, "I was arrested before I came here."

Whatever I thought he might say, it certainly wasn't that. I blink. "What? Why?"

He's back to keeping his eyes trained on the hat. "I got in a fight."

"You were in a fight?"

His foot lightly bounces against the concrete floor. I've never seen him like this. I've never seen him nervous about anything, and it's only making my own nerves stand on edge. "I was at a bar in town with a few friends. We all had fake IDs, but our friend bartends there, so it's not like we needed them." He pauses. "This guy started harassing her that night. She doesn't take shit from anyone, but we all knew it was getting to her. " He shakes his head. "She was starting to get freaked out, but he wouldn't stop. I couldn't listen to it anymore." His eyes jump up to meet mine. "I was pissed, Abbie, and I was drunk."

My heart sinks. "What did you do?"

"I hit him. Hard." He holds my stare. "My friends did too, but I started it. I threw the first punch."

I'm almost afraid to ask my next question. "Is he okay?"

Carson nods. "He's fine, but whoever he was with called the cops." He rests his elbows on his knees and holds my stare. "I know what I did was wrong, and I'm lucky he didn't press charges, but everything in Tennessee is messed up because of this."

I walk toward him, taking a seat next to him on the wooden box. "How?"

He looks over at me and his jaw ticks. "Most of the people back home know my dad had a drinking problem." He shrugs. "After the arrest, they all started to look at me like I did, too—like the apple didn't fall far."

"And do you… have a drinking problem?" It's a question I have to ask.

Carson shakes his head adamantly. "I don't."

"But that's why you don't drink."

Putting his hat back on, he shrugs. "I don't want to give people a reason to think that I do. I'm not a loose cannon. I can control myself, and I need to go back home so people can see that. I need to fix what I did."

"You mean, you need to prove them wrong."

He nods and gets to his feet.

I stare down at the concrete floor and try to wrap my head around everything. I can't picture Carson at a bar, drinking. I can't picture him getting in trouble with the police. It all seems far-fetched, but when I bring my eyes to meet his again, I know he's telling the truth. I know he's just shared the darkest part of himself, and now I have to decide what I want to do with it.

When I don't say anything right away, he adds, "I'm here because my grandpa thought the change of scenery would keep me out of trouble, and my dad needed the help."

"Why are you telling me all this?"

He crouches in front of me, his hands gripping the box on either side of me. "I'm glad I'm here for my dad. I would have been regardless." His thumb gently grazes the outside of my jeans, and the touch sends a jolt through me. "I'm glad I met you."

I give him a faint smile, knowing there's about to be a *but* added to that statement.

Carson stares at me, and for the first time, there's vulnerability behind his eyes. "My life back home is a mess, Abbie. I'm the one who messed it up, and I'm the one who needs to fix it."

"I get that." With a slow smile, I tease, "You're kind of distracting. It will be good for you to go anyway."

Carson's mouth quirks. "*I'm* distracting?"

"Yes," I say as I give a sharp nod. "You and that stupid hat of yours are distracting."

Carson looks up before taking off his hat and holding it up. "This hat?"

"That's the one."

He looks between me and the cap. "Distracts you."

My tongue wets my bottom lip before I can stop it. "Annoyingly so."

199

Those molten eyes snag on my lips before he shrugs it off. "I can fix that." He reaches up and hooks the hat around my head, facing it backward. He helps me to my feet and takes a step back to get a good look at me. "Problem solved."

My mouth twists as I fight my smile, but my stomach twists, too.

Because wearing something of his has only made the problem worse.

He looks relieved that I'm willing to joke with him after his confession. I'm relieved, too. He made a mistake, one he's determined to right. I can't hold a single mistake against him, especially when I wasn't there to witness what happened.

His lips pull into a faint smile. "I'll walk you to your truck," he says like he's assuming I don't want to stay after what he told me.

But I still want to be here. I still want to spend as much time with him as I can. My heart rate rises as I say, "Or I could stay."

TWENTY-THREE

Carson stops. "You want to stay?"

I nod, and my nerves make me bite my bottom lip.

For a moment, he looks torn, like he's debating whether or not he should let me. Finally, he says, "I have some dry clothes you can change into."

I'm grateful he turns away because the thought of wearing his clothes sends a wave of heat over me. "Yeah, that would be great, but shouldn't we wait out the storm?" I ask as I hurry to catch up with him.

In the aisleway, Carson points to a tucked-away wooden staircase at the other end of the barn. "I stay in the loft when I'm here."

"You live in the barn?" I give him a perplexed look.

He doesn't bother hiding the trace of amusement that crosses his face. "Yeah. I guess I do."

"Well, that certainly explains some things," I mutter as I walk past him and make my way up the stairs. I hear a low chuckle behind me, followed by his heavy footfalls echoing mine.

The stairs lead to a surprisingly large bedroom with wood-paneled walls. A large window AC unit sits in the smaller window, and on the far wall, a huge window takes up most of the space. Even with the rain, natural light pours into the room. It feels open and comfortable.

"Hey." I look back at Carson standing a few steps below. "This is *nice*." I didn't mean to come across as sounding surprised, but my disbelief carries every word.

He breathes out through his nose, giving me an *almost* laugh. "Thanks."

"Like this doesn't even look like it's in a barn."

Scratching the side of his head, he clears his throat as he eyes his bed behind me.

It's only when he closes the door that it dawns on me that I'm in Carson's bedroom. I scan the four walls for details about his life, but it's bare. He didn't grow up here. There are no pieces of his past and no signs of a future. No pictures, no sports trophies from when he was younger, and no posters of his favorite musicians. It's just a room—a room where he sleeps.

My eyes wander to the large bed with its dark grey bedding, and I feel like I might as well be reading his journal.

"Here, you can change into these."

He stands with an outstretched hand, holding the clothes I'm supposed to wear.

His clothes.

"Oh, um… thanks." I take them and hug them to my chest, trying to resist the urge to inhale the intoxicating scent of him. Even from here, the faint notes of cedar and spice have my thoughts reeling. "Was the house not big enough for you?"

Carson smiles, but there's a sadness behind it that makes me regret asking. He leans against the dresser, crossing his ankles. "My dad and I learned a few years ago that being under the same roof wasn't good for either of us."

I look down, pretending to be interested in the material of the dry t-shirt in my arms. "But you two are okay now?"

"Yeah," he answers simply. I'm not sure what to say, so I continue to smooth the cotton fibers between my fingers.

Then a low rumble of laughter pours from him, and my eyes dart upward. He has his arms crossed as he stares at me with amusement in his eyes. "You're right. The hat is distracting."

The corners of my mouth pull into an easy smile as I take off the hat, holding it up for him to see. "This hat?"

Pushing off from the dresser, he walks toward me. "That's the one." He takes it from my hand and slips it back on my head, running his hands over the top as if to smooth it down. "It looks good on you," he says quietly, and I wonder if he meant to say that last part out loud.

As I look up at him, my breathing shallows. He drops his hands, his fingers brushing the sides of my neck ever so slightly, and his touch leaves a trail of fire behind it.

Carson glances over his shoulder. "The bathroom is right through there."

When I don't move toward the door, his eyes return to mine. My pounding heart pulses in my ears loud enough to drown out everything around us. Every thought, every sound, even the pelting rain doesn't reach me. If I wanted to kiss him, I wouldn't even need to take a step.

My eyes flicker up to meet his before settling on his lips. With a steadying breath, I push up ever so slightly, and when my mouth is centimeters away from his, I pause, waiting—*hoping*—for some sign that this is okay. I've never made the first move, and even though Carson technically kissed me first, this still feels like I'm out on the edge of a cliff, waiting for him to either pull me back onto solid ground or let me fall.

Carson's eyes somehow seem darker than the shadows of the storm outside as he stares back at me, his jaw set in a hard line. "I thought we agreed this is a bad idea," he finally says, his voice rough.

"Yeah." From here, in the cast of the soft light, I can make out flecks of honey in his eyes. "But we could pretend it never happened."

His jaw ticks as he takes a lock of my damp hair between his fingers. "I don't think I'd be able to do that."

"Me either," I admit.

We're both frozen in place, teetering on the edge of head and heart.

"This isn't going to end well."

I'm about to take a step back when his fingertips graze the back of my arm. That's all it takes for me to close the gap between us.

Carson's lips find mine, and it's like every part of me comes alive. I grip the material of his shirt, pulling him to me as my lips move over his. Hesitantly brushing my tongue across his bottom lip seems to wake something inside of him. His hands move to my hair as he backs me into the wall. His hat nearly falls off my head when the brim meets the wall first, but he slips it off me and tosses it behind him, letting it land somewhere with a soft thud.

His hands cradle my face as he kisses me deeper, his tongue sliding over mine. "You're perfect, you know that?" he murmurs against my lips.

I can't help letting a light laugh escape me. "We just went for a trail ride and got caught in the rain." I turn slightly to kiss his neck. "I'm pretty sure I'm bordering on disgusting right now."

His lips pull into a smile against my skin. "That makes two of us." Finding my mouth again, his kiss tells me that he couldn't care less about the sweat and dirt.

It isn't until he moves to kiss my neck that my eyes flicker to the bathroom door and an idea takes over. "We could take a shower."

I can't believe those words just left my lips.

Carson pulls back and searches for something behind my eyes before he rests his forehead against mine. His hands pin me against the wall, and his thumb drums against the wood paneling as he thinks about what I've said. "You want to take a shower," he echoes.

I nod slowly, my eyes never leaving his. I want this—I want him. Pushing up on my toes, I gently kiss his lips. "Go ahead. Make your move."

He lets out a groan. "Damn it, Abbie." Then hooking his hands under my thighs, he picks me up and carries me to the bathroom. "You're going to be the death of me."

TWENTY-FOUR

I squeal as Carson picks me up and carries me toward the bathroom. He pushes open the cracked door with his foot, kissing me as soon as he sets me on the counter. He claims my mouth with his, holding my face between his hands. Without his lips leaving mine, he reaches to turn on the shower in the tiny bathroom. Fumbling with the handle, he curses under his breath when he has to pull away to turn on the water. I laugh as the running water merges with the sound of the rain, and it's like we're the only two people in the world.

He grips my waist, pulling me closer to the edge of the counter—closer to him. My legs fall to either side of him, and I tighten my arms around his neck, pressing my body flush against his. As every part of me is touched by him, I feel alive.

When he breaks the kiss, the shower has left a layer of steam over the bathroom mirror. "We should probably get in," he says against my lips.

"Hm?" I can't seem to pull away. Gently sucking on his tongue drags a sound from his throat that I will never forget, and when we both come up for air, he says, "You're too good at that," as he pulls my shirt over my head. I love seeing him lose control. I'm about to press my lips against his again, but his hands are on my body, and I can't move, or think, or breathe—I can't do anything.

He reaches to unclasp my bra, his fingers grazing my skin as he slides the straps down. Gently setting it aside, he moves to cradle my face in his hands, his nose skimming mine before he softly brushes my lips with his. The fact that he's not tearing my clothes off with his teeth is a new kind of torture.

The *best* kind of torture.

His hands trail from my cheeks, to my neck, to my breasts and the ache between my legs intensifies. He presses warm kisses on my neck, and my back arches as I suck in a breath.

Carson pauses. He's studying me, how I react to his touch, and knowing he's watching me pulls new heat to the surface of my skin. His lips press against the sensitive spot just below my ear and my mind is a blank slate again. A soft sigh leaves my lips when the sensation of that kiss reaches my toes.

He pulls back and tucks a strand of hair behind my ear. As his hand slowly falls, his gaze follows. He shamelessly locks onto each part of me as his eyes work their way down.

208

Carson kneels on the bathroom floor, gently pulling my jeans down my legs, and seeing him look up at me this way makes it harder for me to breathe. Then my jeans are on the floor, his hands sliding up my bare legs until he's standing in front of me again, his thumbs hooking under the cotton at my hips.

I kiss him without hesitation. I kiss him with enough intensity to let him know he doesn't need to treat me like I'm fragile. His grip tightens in response, and then my underwear are on the floor.

With the final layer at my feet, my nerves spike. I'm completely naked while he's still fully clothed, and it's not fair.

Heat flutters in my lower belly, and I reach for the hem of his t-shirt. Carson pulls it off the rest of the way, and I let my fingers explore his stomach, unable to tear my eyes away.

His body stills at my touch.

My fingers find their way lower and meet the waistband of his jeans. I unbutton them and let my hand slip inside. His eyes flutter shut at my touch. The feel of him sends another wave of heavy heat between my legs. I need more. I slip my hand under the thin layer of his black briefs, my breath catching as I palm him, and Carson lets out a groan.

"You. Shower. Now." His voice is rough. I hop down from the counter, and by the time his pants and briefs hit the tile, I've pulled him into the shower with me.

As the door closes, he presses his body against mine, pinning me against the shower wall. The cool tile sending a chill down my spine, offsetting the heat of everything else.

The water.

The steam.

Him.

My hands run down the muscles that shape his body, every part of him more beautiful than the last. Pulling away, he looks at me, his eyes devouring every part of me before brushing my wet hair away from my shoulder, exposing me completely. "You," he says as he hooks his finger under my chin, "are beautiful."

I smile, but when he releases me and grabs the bar of soap I ask, "What are you doing?"

Carson's mouth quirks as he works up a lather. "We're taking a shower." His hands run over my neck and shoulders, and he kisses my forehead. He's almost methodical as he takes his time massaging my skin, leaving a trail of soap suds in his wake. I watch him move from my shoulders to my breasts. He runs the soap over himself as he does, but somehow, he always has at least one hand on me. Lowering himself, he pulls one of my taut nipples into his mouth, and a wave of pleasure I've never known washes over me.

I try to stifle the noise that comes from my throat, but he's already caught on. He looks up at me with a devilish glint, his mouth teasing until I have to brace my hands on his shoulders. "I want you."

Carson smiles against my skin but shakes his head. "Not yet." I watch him lower himself more, his lips marking a trail of kisses

210

to the base of my stomach until he's kneeling in front of me. He lathers the soap in his hands again as he glances up at me with a smirk. "You still smell like a barn."

I shoot him a glare, but it only seems to make his amusement grow. Turning his attention back to my body, his fingers massage and work their way down the length of my legs.

My chest rises and falls as his hands run from my calves to my thighs. He's getting dangerously close to where I want him to touch me most—where I *need* him to touch me. He looks up at me, and the satisfaction in his eyes makes my knees buckle. He knows exactly what this is doing to me.

His lips press into the top of my thigh, and another involuntary sound leaves my throat. "Carson," I pant.

His mouth moves between my legs where he murmurs, "What, Abbie?" against my center.

"Fuck." My head falls back against the shower wall, the ache between my legs too much. "I need you inside me."

"Soon," is all he says before he runs his tongue over me, making me gasp. My legs are already shaking after the first few strokes of his tongue, and he groans, digging his fingertips into my thighs as he grips me harder.

He stands and turns off the water, shocking me.

"What are you doing?" I wrap my arms around myself as a shield from the sudden cold.

He reaches for a towel. "You deserve a bed."

MAKE YOUR MOVE

TWENTY-FIVE

Carson drapes a towel around me, and I walk back into the grey-lit room. The sound of pelting rain still hitting the tin roof creates a peaceful tranquility. After the heat of the shower, the fresh smell of rain makes this feel more real. The day casts light on what's happening between us, and how much this will change things.

Good.

I want things to change. I want a future that looks like this, even if it's temporary.

I barely have time to ring the water from my hair before Carson comes up behind me, gently taking the towel and tossing it on the floor. I feel him hard against my lower back and move my hips, pushing into him. He lets out a low, guttural sound against my ear. "I'm going to need you to get on the bed," he says, and shivers run down my spine.

I do, and he walks to the bedside table to get a condom from the drawer. Tearing it open with his teeth, he rolls it on. Carson carefully holds himself over me. He plants a kiss on my lips, one on my neck, and another on my collarbone. "You're going to wreck me."

Hitching my leg over his, I pull him closer.

His eyes meet mine.

There's no going back after this—there's no way to uncomplicate things. But I don't want simple.

I want him.

My breath catches when I feel him position himself against me. Holding my gaze, he slowly pushes into me, cursing under his breath as he does. My nails dig into his shoulders as he fills me completely, my head falling back.

He pauses, letting me adjust to him. The first roll of his hips is slow and torturous like he's savoring this—savoring *me,* and it pulls a soft moan from my lips.

"You feel so good." My voice comes out dream-like. Sex has never been like this. It has always been rushed, and I could never get out of my head enough to enjoy it. Carson groans, burying his face in my neck as he pushes into me deeper.

My hips roll, meeting him.

"Fuck," he mutters, catching my bottom lip between his teeth. "Do that again."

I kiss him, letting my hips roll more freely to meet his thrusts, and he swears into my mouth, gripping me tighter. We move until

214

we're both panting as he brings me further away from myself and closer to my breaking point. My legs start to shake, my body tightening around him. The sensation is completely foreign to me. It's a little scary... the loss of control, but at the same time, I chase it—I want more of it. "Like I said," he says through heated breaths, "you're fucking perfect."

And that's all it takes to send me over the edge. My lungs lock, and pleasure tears through me. I dig my nails into his back as he picks up his pace. It's like watching me come undone is enough to send him over the edge, too. Carson swallows my moans before adding his own, his body tensing as he finds his release. Seeing him fall apart at the seams thrills me, and I'm surprised by how much I want to make him do it again.

I'm happy when he doesn't pull out of me right away. I'm not ready for this closeness to end. Lowering his head, he kisses the spot just below my ear. "That was..."

I gently trace my fingers over the muscles in his back and love the way he seems to relax even more at my touch. Letting out a breath of laughter, I ask, "Is that what sex is supposed to be like?"

Carson brushes a strand of hair away from my face, his expression thoughtful. "Only if you're lucky."

Tilting my head, I can't help asking, "Is that what sex is always like for you?"

His eyes settle on mine. "No." He slowly pulls out of me, and I press my head back against the pillow as the feeling sends another trickle of pleasure through me. Carson rolls onto his back and stares at the ceiling before looking over at me, a lazy grin pulling at the corner of his mouth. "No, that was something else."

I barely have time to smile back at him before his mouth is on mine again. I reach for his face, feeling the dark stubble against his jaw as I kiss him deeper.

"Abbie," Carson says against my lips. "I'm going to need you to go put some clothes on."

I laugh. "You're no fun."

He smiles sweetly against my skin. "Go."

Letting out a huff, I throw open the covers. I walk back to his dresser where the clothes he picked for me still lie folded. He's watching me walk around his room with nothing on. I can feel him tracking my every moment. Pulling his t-shirt overhead, I snatch the towel from the floor and toss it to him. "Isn't there something you should be doing?"

Carson lets out a deep laugh as he catches the towel. He gets up from the bed. "Yes, ma'am."

To say his clothes are big on me would be an understatement, but this doesn't stop him from pausing to take in the sight of me as he walks out of the bathroom after hanging our towels.

"What?"

He shakes his head as he walks over and plops down on the bed next to me. He runs those intense eyes over my body, his gaze lingering on my thigh where the hem of his t-shirt rests. "I am so fucked," he says with a laugh as he rubs a hand over his face.

I can't help having the same thought as I take in his bare chest, each muscle clearly defined from his pecs all the way to the chiseled lines that disappear under the hem of his shorts.

"Want me to leave?" I ask, jumping to my knees on the soft mattress. "Because I can go…" I look over my shoulder at the door, trying and failing to fight my smile with my threat.

Carson snatches my wrist, pulling me back to him in one swift movement. "Don't you dare."

Laughter bubbles in my throat as I collapse on top of him. When my eyes drift to meet his, he runs his knuckles against my cheek, and I can't resist smiling. Stopping it would be like trying to stop the sun from rising. There's too much warmth and light inside of me right now, and it can't be hidden.

How can this person I didn't even know *existed* a few weeks ago suddenly feel like my tether to solid ground? How is it he has known me such a short amount of time, and yet he seems to know me—seems to really *get* me—better than anyone else?

How is it possible to feel this lucky and unlucky?

Because in just a few weeks he'll be gone. He'll be back in Tennessee, picking up his life where he left off, and I'll be here alone, trying to make something of the pieces he'll leave behind.

Part of me wants to believe I'll be okay, but another part can't help wondering if I'll ever come back from how intense my feelings are for him. Seth may have bent me, but Carson could break me.

Right now, with him lying here within reach, I already miss him.

"What's wrong?" He smooths his thumb over my furrowed brow. "You look like you're trying to work something out."

Instead of giving him an honest answer, all I can think to say is, "It's irritating how good-looking you are. Do you know that?" I playfully glare at him. "You have to know that."

A deep laugh rumbles in his chest.

"And what about you? You've been chipping away at me since we met." His hand travels from my thigh to my hip, pushing the shirt up as he goes, then his thumb traces circles on the bare skin just above my cotton underwear. "And knowing you had a boyfriend killed me."

"It did?"

"More than I'm proud to admit," he says. "Ever since the night I drove you home from the bonfire, I couldn't get you out of my head. All I could think about was how badly I wanted to pull over and kiss you, right there in my truck."

I frown as I remember that night. "But you didn't even talk to me on the ride home."

"I couldn't. What would I have said?" His eyes find mine, and he adds, "That you deserved better?" He shakes his head, dropping his gaze to where his fingers brush my skin. "It wasn't my place."

I open my mouth to say something, but he cuts me off.

218

"Plus, I knew I was leaving, and that I couldn't offer you anything more."

"Turns out you did have something to offer." I turn my face up to softly kiss his neck.

His calloused hand runs up my bare thigh. "I don't know about that."

"I do." Crawling onto his lap, I straddle him. "I'm glad I met you." I lean down and kiss him.

Holding the back of my neck, he kisses me deeper. "Me too, Abbie, me too."

TWENTY-SIX

The sound of excited paws bound up the stairs, quickly followed by Phil scratching at the door. Carson gets up to let him in.

"Hey, boy." I crawl toward the edge of the bed. Phil pops up on his hindquarters, his mouth open and panting as his tongue lulls to the side while I pet his head.

"Time for dinner?" Carson asks the pup as he gets to his feet and pulls a clean t-shirt over his head.

"Dinner?" I reach to tap my phone on the bed a few feet away. It's only 4:00 p.m. "Now?"

"We still have to cook it. Phil's just coming to get us."

A laugh passes through my lips. "Your dad sent Phil to get us?"

Carson bends down to pet the dog's white, wiry fur. "Dad is always sending Phil to do his dirty work." His eyes drift up to me, still lying on my stomach, draped over his bed, and I love how easy his smile is. "Want to stay?"

"And watch you cook?" I ask almost gleefully.

He raises an eyebrow. "That excites you?"

I prop myself up on my elbows, resting my chin in my hands and crossing my ankles up in the air like the pining girl I am. "More than you could imagine." Lifting my head, I feign a gasp. "Will you wear an apron?"

"For you," he says as he steps forward, cupping my chin in one hand, "I'd wear anything." He gives me a chaste kiss that still manages to daze me.

"Or nothing?" I ask with a playful raise of my eyebrows.

I don't even realize I'm looking him up and down until he says, "Abbie, I'm going to need you to stop picturing me naked."

My cheeks flush, but I try to brush it off by getting to my feet. "Hmm..." I reach for my jeans and pull them on. "No promises."

He shakes his head, and I catch a glimpse of the smile that comes to his lips. Then he grabs his hat off the bed and hooks it over his head in his usual way. "You're a mess."

I throw my hair up in a messy bun. "Don't act like you don't do the same."

When I walk past him, he catches my wrist and pulls me close. "Trust me, I've already imagined all the ways I can have you before I leave, and I'm still coming up with new ideas."

I swallow. "Okay."

His lips twitch before he lets go of me and heads down the

stairs. "Come on, Phil."

I stand there for a moment, willing my beating heart to settle. My body buzzes with anticipation, but his words, *before I leave*, cast a far-off shadow. Shaking my head to clear my thoughts, I head down the stairs after him, determined to keep the darkness at bay.

☼   ☼   ☼

"Got this in the mail today." Ed tosses something that looks like an invitation down on the table. "Abbie, I'm sure you've got one at home just like it."

"What is it?" Carson asks over his shoulder as he seasons a few steaks. Unfortunately, there was no apron to be found, but I still enjoy watching him while I poorly peel a pile of potatoes in my distracted state.

"The Summer Fest." Ed pulls out a chair at the kitchen table and takes a seat. "I walked to the mailbox today. That was my big adventure."

I smile and hope my worry doesn't shine through.

"Let's see." I wipe my hands on a rag before abandoning my post to sit with Ed. Then reaching for the invitation, I take a closer look, and my stomach drops.

"Lisa is hosting this year's Summer Fest," I say quietly.

Carson turns to get a better look at us. "Isn't that the annual award ceremony they do?"

"No, that's in December," I say, my eyes still glued to the invitation in my hands. "The Summer Fest is like a big, outdoor banquet for the local show barns. It's more... social." I frown. "It's usually held at Spring Oaks, but I guess they want Lisa to host since they're still undergoing renovations."

Carson shakes his head as he puts three raw steaks on a plate to bring out to the grill.

If this invitation were from Spring Oaks, I'd probably have the same reaction. The last thing I want to do is go to a big, fancy party with Seth and his friends.

But it's not from Spring Oaks.

It's from Lisa, and I owe her so much. I know I'll have to go.

"It will be fun," I try to reassure myself.

Carson looks over at me, a dubious eyebrow raised. "You think?"

"Maybe." I get up from the table and head back over to my pile of potatoes. "You probably won't have to worry about it. It's a couple of weeks away. You might not be here."

"I'll be here."

"But you don't even know the date—"

"I said I'll be here," he says, locking his eyes on me.

"Great!" Ed claps his hands together. "I sure as hell don't want to go, but you guys can bring me back some of Lisa's cherry pie. I always say she makes the best pie in all of Florida."

Looking over at him, my lips turn up. "You've got it, Ed."

Carson goes back to prepping our dinner, but his shoulders hold more tension than they did a moment ago. I can't help watching him out of the corner of my eye, hoping to catch a glance, but he hasn't looked at me.

Ed's phone rings and he gets to his feet. "Call from a client. I've got to take this." Looking back at Carson, he adds, "Which day did you say was light next week?"

"Wednesday should be good."

"Right, Wednesday." Ed leaves the room, answering the call as he does.

I turn to face Carson, my back leaning against the countertop. "Do you want to tell me what's bothering you?"

He looks up as he washes his hands, surprise written in his eyes. "Nothing's bothering me."

"I wouldn't blame you if you didn't want to go to the Summer Fest. The only reason I plan on going is for Lisa."

"And I plan on going for you," he says before I have time to add anything else. I watch him dry his hands on a dish towel, and he adds, "Listen, I'm not bothered by the Summer Fest. I'm sorry if it came across that way."

There's a rigidity to him. I scan over his features, trying to catch a glimpse of what he might be thinking, but all I see are sharp angles and harsh lines.

"But…?" My feeble attempt to pull the truth from him.

He sighs and runs a hand over his face. "It bothers me how

224

much I hated the idea of you going alone."

"Oh."

"Yeah."

An uneasy silence falls between us.

"I'm sorry about earlier," I blurt. He had made it clear that he didn't want to complicate things, and what did I do? I asked him to take a *shower* with me. My insides tighten, and I suddenly feel like I've ruined everything. "I don't know what I was thinking." I shake my head and turn back to the potatoes.

Carson comes up behind me and turns me to face him. "What? Why?"

"You didn't want this. I shouldn't have… we shouldn't have—"

He looks in the direction of the other room where Ed can still be heard. "Abbie, stop," he says so adamantly that I'm forced to meet his gaze. He pulls me to him, and I can feel his body relax against me.

I whisper against his chest, "I complicated things."

He shakes his head. "Things have been complicated for a while. Today…" He lets out a short laugh. "Today was the best day I've had in a long time."

I bite the inside of my cheek.

He smooths a strand of hair away from my face, a slight frown settling at the corners of his mouth as he studies me. "I don't want to hurt you."

"You won't." We both know I'm lying through my teeth. "And if you do, it's okay." I let my head lean back against him. "Plus, you'll miss me. If anything, I should be the one worried about you. I'm known to leave quite the impression."

Wrapping his arms around me, he kisses me on the cheek, and it warms my entire body. "That we can agree on."

TWENTY-SEVEN

Since the day Carson and I went trail riding, I've been waking up with a perpetual smile on my face. I open my eyes, and my heart flutters knowing I'll see him again. Even if we only spend one minute together, it's the best part of my day.

This morning he's unloading hay from the back of my mom's truck, stacking bales in the feed room. Thick work gloves cover his hands, and the rising sun gives his tanned skin a golden glow. I lean against the door frame as he hoists one bale on top of another, wishing every morning could start like this.

He catches me out of the corner of his eye, and his face softens. I love the way he goes from stoic Carson to this lighter, easier-to-smile Carson—*my* Carson. "What are you doing?" he huffs as he straightens the bale.

My mouth pulls into a faint smile. "Enjoying the view."

He gives me a sideways glance. "Is that so?"

"Mhm," is my only response and my lips twist.

He shakes his head, but his mouth quirks in the way it always does when he's amused. He walks towards me and turns sideways to squeeze past me in the doorway. "Don't you have a horse to ride?" He checks for my mom before giving me a quick peck on the lips.

Grabbing his t-shirt, I pull him back for more.

Carson groans and presses his weight into me, pushing me up against the door frame. I loop my two pointer fingers through his front belt loops, smiling against his lips. When we pull apart, he points a finger at me. "You," he says, "are bad for business."

I watch as he walks toward the truck stacked with hay. The way his t-shirt stretches over the muscles in his back as he unloads another bale makes my teeth sink into my bottom lip. And when he turns, my eyes drop to the muscles in his arms, straining against the weight of the hay.

"Abbie."

My gaze darts upward to meet his. "Yeah?"

"Two things," he says, and he suddenly has my full attention. He stops in front of me. "One, move."

I laugh and step out of his way.

"Two," he says as he stacks it neatly next to the other bales. "If you keep looking at me like that, there's a good chance I'll do something that'll get me fired."

I roll my eyes. "You're not getting fired."

He cocks an eyebrow. "No?" He walks up to me and leans in close. "I think you're underestimating the things I'd like to do to you in this barn." He kisses me on the cheek before stepping away. Then pointing to the door, he says, "Now, get out of here."

I let out a laugh and head toward the door, my mind still reeling over the possibilities.

My ride on Sully goes smoothly. Now that there's a break in the show season, our rides have become more relaxed. Most days we don't even jump. This morning, after we did our basic flat work, I took him for a walk around the property before spending a little extra time grooming him.

I put Sully away and finish up the barn work. As I head toward the house, ready to take a shower, my phone rings. Sarah's name pops up on the screen, and I answer right away.

"Hey, I was wondering when I'd hear from you."

She sounds breathless. This girl is always on the go. "I know, I'm sorry! Things have been crazy around here. The school doesn't have much going on since it's still technically summer, but we've made up for it with parties. Hey! When you come to visit, I'm taking you to one. They're nothing like Christina's bonfires—they're fun."

"Yeah… sure." Before she can call out my sarcasm, I add, "Where are you headed now? Zumba?"

"Not Zumba. I just got home, and the only exercise I'm doing today is clicking, 'Next Episode.'"

I flop onto my own bed. "It was that good of a party, huh?"

"It was *such* a good party!" she practically groans. "Definitely worth me feeling like death today. So, are you and the sexy cowboy still pretending nothing happened?"

"He's not a sexy cowboy," I say with a laugh. "He's…" my voice trails off as I try to think of the best way to describe Carson.

"A sexy cowboy," she says flatly. "That's who he is in my head. Let me keep him that way."

"If it will make you happy." I can't fight the smile that comes to my lips.

"It will," she says. "Why is he leaving?"

I trail my fingers over the material of my comforter. Telling her about Carson's past doesn't feel right. It feels like something I want to keep to myself. "He's only visiting. He has to get back to Tennessee."

"Are you okay?"

"I'm okay." It's not a lie. After our day together on Friday, I'm more than okay.

"Do you like him or is this just a fun distraction?" I can hear the low volume of whatever show she decided to watch in the background.

I know I like him. I like him more than I should, but I can't bring myself to admit it out loud. I don't want everyone to know about Carson and me. It will only put me under a microscope when everything ends. They'll all be waiting for me to fall apart.

"Is that the Salvatore brothers I hear?"

"Yes," she says matter-of-factly. "I will rewatch this series until I die."

The Vampire Diaries has been Sarah's comfort show ever since I made her binge it with me in ninth grade.

"Seriously," she goes on to say. "Ian Somerhalder could ruin my life, and I would do nothing but *thank* him. But you never answered my question about Carson. Are these real feelings or what?"

My mouth opens, but my words are caught between not wanting to lie and not wanting to tell the truth.

The downstairs door opens and closes, and I hear Carson's voice. "Abbie?"

"Upstairs!" I call back, covering the bottom of the phone.

Sarah perks up, and I imagine her suddenly sitting upright. "Is that him?"

"Yeah, I have to go. I'll talk to you later?"

My heart races with the sound of each step he takes up our wooden staircase.

How have I never felt this before?

How is it possible to date someone for a year—to truly believe that you're in love with them but never feel your heart flutter as they make their way up to your bedroom?

"Stop wasting time pretending it didn't happen. Do dirty

things to him so you can tell me about it. I wish I had a sexy cow-boy."

Carson rounds the corner, his hand on my door frame. "Hey."

A few stray pieces of hay cling to his shirt and jeans, and his arms show evidence of dirt and sweat, and I smirk because Sarah is half right. It kind of makes him look like a sexy cowboy.

"I have to go. I'll call you later."

"HI, SE—"

I hang up before she can finish. "Hey." I shove my phone under my pillow like I'm worried Sarah might be able to hear us still.

He cocks an eyebrow as he kicks off his boots by my door. "Were you busy?"

"No." I shake my head. "It was just my friend Sarah. She's at school in Tampa."

"Sorry to cut the call short, but I wanted to ask you some-thing." He takes a few steps toward my bed and glances down at himself before looking back at me. "Is it okay if I sit?"

A light laugh escapes me as I move to make room for him. "Of course."

He rubs the back of his neck as he takes a seat. Carson is cute when he's nervous. But I haven't seen him nervous since he told me about his arrest, and it's making my own anxiety prickle.

"Are you okay?" I ask.

He nods but seems distracted as he looks down at his hands. "Yeah."

I frown, studying him. "If this is about—,"

He looks over at me. "Can I take you out on Friday?"

My brain processes his question with a delay. "What?"

Carson turns, sitting with one leg folded on my bed, while the other foot stays on the floor. "Sorry," he mutters. Then, seeming to get his bearings, he says, "I want to take you out on Friday." This time, all nerves seem to have disappeared.

"Oh." I blink. Tilting my head, I ask, "Like a date?" We may have complicated his leaving already, but doesn't going on a date complicate it even more?

He nods. "Like a date."

I frown. "Do you think that's a good idea?"

He shrugs. "I mean, we already hang out all the time. We'd just be doing it somewhere else."

"Going on a date is a little different than hanging out." I give him a dubious look, and his lips turn upward.

"A little," he admits.

Hugging my knees to my chest, I weigh the consequences of getting in deeper than we already have.

"Abbie, it's one date."

Hesitating, I say, "Can I know where we're going?" I don't know why I'm trying to buy time. I'd love to go on a date with him, but part of me is scared—scared that a date with Carson will ruin me for all future dates without him.

"No."

I playfully glare at him. "Why?"

He shrugs. "Why do you need to know?" When my mouth opens but no words come out, he cuts me off. "I'll pick you up at seven."

"Fine," I give in. He leans forward and presses his lips to mine. I expect it to be a light kiss, but he gently pushes me back onto my bed, and my entire body reacts to the feeling of him pressed against me.

My breath catches as his warm lips trail my jaw. He nips at my bottom lip, and I slip his hat off so I can run my fingers through his hair. "I thought you were worried about getting fired," I tease.

His eyes get heavy at my touch, a low hum escaping him. I love seeing him like this. I love that I'm the one who makes him this way.

Carson rests his hips against mine, his lips moving to my chest. "I was." His kisses move to my collarbone, and he murmurs against my skin, "But today was my last day."

"What?" I pull away to look at him.

"I know," he says, reading my disappointment. "All the work is done, though." Tucking a loose strand of hair behind my ear, he adds, "That's why I need to see you Friday. I'll be working with my dad for the rest of the week."

I nod, but there's a sinking feeling in my gut. He's done working here, summer is almost over, and suddenly, Friday can't come soon enough.

TWENTY-EIGHT

I hate to say it, but I miss waking up to him hammering outside my window.

The only noise that greets me as I walk into the barn this morning is a chorus of soft whinnies from the horses, letting me know they're ready for breakfast. It's been like this all week—Carson's missing presence already making the days long before he even leaves. I knew I loved having him around, but I don't think I realized how much I'd miss his subtle remarks and stolen glances.

It's a taste of what things will be like once he goes back to Tennessee, and I don't want it. I don't want to walk around the barn with no company other than the radio. I don't want the peaceful serenity that comes with an absence of handy work. I don't want to be left here without him.

But we can't always get what we want. Sometimes we have to take what we don't want and make the best of it. I dread that day—the day that he's actually gone. This is only a preview and it's already making my stomach twist.

Mom usually offers to feed the horses, but I told her I'd do it today. I'll need the early start if I want to be ready on time tonight.

For our *date*.

I still can't wrap my head around Carson taking me on a date. The butterflies in my stomach refuse to settle, and my mind only seems to want to think about what he might have planned.

Where he'll take me.

What we'll do.

What I should *wear*.

It's all I can think about as I give the horses their grain and fill the water buckets. After tossing two horses their morning hay, I turn out the others and use the leaf blower to clear the dirt from the aisleway. I get things done more quickly than I normally would and start mucking one of the stalls before I grab Sully for our morning lesson.

Sully and I have been warming up for about ten minutes by the time Lisa pulls up. Stepping out of her SUV, she secures her big, floppy hat and calls out, "How's he feel today?"

"Good!" I answer, circling him to stay within earshot.

"He looks good." She enters the ring and fastens the gate behind her. "Did you get my invitation to the Summer Fest?"

Slowing Sully to a walk, I nod. "Yeah, my mom has it on the fridge."

Lisa makes her way to the center of the ring. "You'll be there, right? I already have mixed feelings about hosting this thing. A lot of the barns are great but I know a certain barn that will compare everything I do to how *they* would have done it… if only they weren't under construction." She gives me a knowing look. "I need my people," she adds with a laugh.

"Of course, I'll be there," I answer with a smile even though a small part of me dreads it. I haven't seen Seth since the horse show, and I'm worried about how he'll act… especially when I show up with Carson.

Lisa's eyes fill with relief. "Good. Now get that boy moving. We've got work to do."

☼   ☼   ☼

Mom pokes her head into my bedroom as I'm finishing getting ready. My blonde hair cascades around my shoulders, and the recent blow-dry is giving it more volume than usual. "You look nice."

"Thanks." I can feel her watching me as I grab my phone from the dresser and tuck it in my back pocket. Taking a seat on my bed, I pull on my shorter cowboy boots. "Why are you staring at me?"

"I thought he was leaving," she says with a smirk.

Stifling a roll of my eyes, I say, "He *is* leaving. We're just…"

I shake my head as I pull on my second boot. "It's nothing. We're just hanging out."

She raises an eyebrow. "Hanging out?"

I force out a breath of laughter. "Yes."

A small frown forms at the corner of her lips. "Just be careful. Relationships and expiration dates are like oil and water. Some things don't mix."

I give myself one last look in the mirror before saying, "What's that other thing you always say? Just because shit happens doesn't mean you should spend your life sitting on the toilet?"

Tossing her head back, she cackles. "I do say that, don't I?" she muses.

A knock at the door tells me Carson is here. My racing heart matches my pounding feet as I bound down the stairs. Over my shoulder, I say to my mother, "Love you, Mom!"

Mom's much slower steps trail behind me, and by the time I've reached the door, yanking it open with too much enthusiasm, she's still halfway up the staircase.

Carson stands in the threshold in his dark jeans, black t-shirt, and matching black hat. The hat might be my favorite part, and I might be smiling too big when I say, "Hi."

"Hi." He gives me an easy grin that makes my heart sing.

"Hello, Carson," Mom says as she leans against the railing.

Ducking around me, Carson gives her a nod and says, "Good evening, Ms. Linley."

Mom smiles to herself at his greeting before continuing down the stairs. "I hope you and my daughter have fun tonight—just not too much fun."

Carson nods again, respectful and unfazed. "Yes, ma'am," at the same time, I say, "Mom," in a warning tone.

She laughs, raising her hands in surrender. "It's my job to say it." Once she's down the steps, she adds, "Oh, and Carson?"

He gives her his full attention.

She smirks. "Thanks for coming to the door."

Carson's eyebrows furrow, but she's already turned and walking towards the kitchen.

"Ignore her," I mutter, practically pushing him through the still-open doorway. Once we're alone and headed toward his truck, I ask, "So, what are we doing tonight?"

He opens the truck door for me, letting me climb inside. Before shutting it, he kisses me and says, "You'll see."

We drive to the outskirts of town, talking over the sound of country music playing on the radio until we pull into the parking lot of a dingy country bar. Between the dirty, beat-up trucks lined up in front despite the burnt-out OPEN sign, I can tell it's a spot where only locals hang out.

"Um, what are we doing here?" I ask, trying and failing to hide my concern.

He puts the truck in park. "What's that look for, Abbie? You don't trust me?"

240

Pointing my thumb over my shoulder, I laugh. "I did up until that last turn."

"Come on. They're about to start."

"Start *what?*" We both hop down from the truck. "Unless you have a fake ID for me, I'm not getting in."

Walking around to my side of the truck, he takes my hand and leads me to the back of the bar, away from the front entrance. "It'll be fine."

"Yeah," I say as I follow him. "That's what everyone says before they walk into a murder den."

He shakes his head as he leads us to the back entrance, knocking on a rusted metal door. It takes a moment, but an older man with a white mustache and a blue flannel shirt answers.

"About time you showed up," the man says with a smile.

Carson shakes his hand. "Thanks for doing this, Neil."

"Of course," the man says happily. "Come on in." He waves for us to follow him.

I've never been in a bar before, and after taking a look around, I can't understand why anyone would come here for fun. It almost looks like someone converted a mobile home into a bar and stuck it out in the middle of nowhere. The dim lighting might hide a lot of things, but it can't mask the smell of sour beer.

Neil goes behind the bar, acknowledging a man who just sat at one of the barstools by putting a cold beer in front of him. He walks back over to us. "How rude of me," he says, looking at me

241

and shaking his head. "You must be Abbie."

"This is my dad's friend, Neil," Carson explains.

"It's nice to meet you." I hold out my hand. "How do you know Ed?"

Neil takes my hand and shakes it with a warm smile, but he doesn't answer my question.

Carson steps in again and says, "Neil is my dad's sponsor."

My eyes jump between the two of them. "As in AA?" I ask, my eyes widening as I look back at Neil. "And you work at a bar?" Clapping a hand over my mouth, I add, "I'm sorry. That was rude."

Neil laughs at that. "It's fine. I didn't always work here. I caught wind that the bartender here was taking AA chips in exchange for free drinks." He shakes his head. "I was roaring mad at that bartender. I told him I'd have his job by morning. That was…" He looks up, trying to remember. "At least ten years ago." Looking back at me, he adds, "I like knowing no one will trade chips for drinks here again, and believe it or not, working in this environment helps to keep me on the straight and narrow." He winks. "I've got a whole town to look out for now."

"Neil agreed to let us join tonight's dance class," Carson says casually.

My mouth falls open. "I'm sorry. What?"

"Couple's dancing!" Neil exclaims. "Looks like they're about to start, too. You kids have fun." Leaning toward us, he adds, "But

242

once the class is over, I'm kicking you both to the curb."

Carson gives him a wave before taking my hand and walking me toward the dance floor.

"I can't dance," I say desperately as he pulls me along.

"That's okay." He squeezes my hand in his. "I can."

TWENTY-NINE

We're easily the only participants under sixty, and I find it adorable. The instructors, a married couple, take turns running through the moves and demonstrating how to two-step.

Carson wasn't lying when he said he knew how to dance. He could lead me all over this dance floor, but my feet struggle to keep up. We take it slow while the elderly couples lap us for the third time.

Carson has one hand clasped with mine and the other on my back when I step on his foot. "I'm sorry… again… Where did you learn to do this?"

If I've hurt him, he hides it well as he spins me and pulls me back to him. "My grandpa made me learn. He said it was an essential skill and a dying art." He laughs. "I hated it when I was younger, but now I think he was right."

I accidentally step the wrong way again, bumping into him. "I'm such a lousy partner."

"Are you kidding?" Carson places both hands on my arms, stopping me before putting us back into position. "You're the best partner I've ever had."

I force a laugh. "I question your taste in dance partners then."

"Abbie," he says, biting back a smile. "Look around. The place I went to in Tennessee wasn't much different than this one."

My lips pull upward. "Did all the old ladies want to dance with you?"

"You have no idea." Leaning in, he whispers in my ear, "I'll take you stomping on my feet any day."

I give him a playful whack on the shoulder. "I am not *stomping* on your feet."

He winces dramatically when our feet inevitably bump again.

I laugh, and his magnetic smile pulls my lips to his.

"Aren't you two just the cutest thing," a woman's voice chimes in, interrupting the kiss. I pull back from Carson, my cheeks flushing, to find a woman with short silver hair, her brace-let-covered arms draped over an elderly man's shoulders. She looks toward her partner. "Aren't they sweet? They remind me of us." She turns back to Carson and me. "A very, *very* long time ago."

The man, in his cowboy hat and flannel shirt, leans in toward us. "She used to step on my toes, too," he says with a wink. "How long have you kids been together?"

Carson and I look at each other briefly before fumbling our way through answers. I go with, "Oh, we're not together," and he says, "It's new."

The man just smiles. "I had to chase this one for six months before she'd even go on a date with me, but I knew by the end of it I'd marry her one day."

His wife rolls her eyes. "Oh, you did not." She turns to us. "He's a liar. Don't listen to a word he says."

The man just laughs as he leads his wife away from us a few steps. "You kids have a good night." Turning so that his wife's back is to us, he whispers, "I knew," over her shoulder, and she calls out to us without looking, "No, he didn't!"

A slow song comes on, forcing everyone else to slow down to my speed, but Carson and I just sway together on the outskirts of the dancefloor. No one seems to mind.

Leaning my head on his chest, I watch the couple as they laugh together and make their way around the dance floor. "I want that one day," I say quietly. I think it's impossible to see something like what they have and not want it, too.

He holds me a little tighter, kissing the top of my hair. "One day, you'll have it."

My stomach tightens knowing, when it comes to Carson and me, *this* is all we'll ever have.

This dance.

246

This night.

This summer.

I close my eyes, soaking in *this* moment for as long as I can.

"Hope you had fun!"

"We did. Thanks again," Carson says as he holds open the metal door for me.

I grin and wave at Neil before leaving. The night air feels warm on my skin. I hurry ahead and turn to face him. "So, what's next?" There's a constant buzzing of energy running through me, and I don't want this night to end.

Carson watches me, a trace of a smile still evident. "Whatever you want."

God, I love the way he looks at me. He's watching me like I'm blossoming before his eyes—and maybe I am. Maybe that's what he does to me.

"Whatever I want?" I mull over all the things I could say. There are plenty of things I want. I want him to kiss me every day. I want to dance with him more than just tonight. I want this feeling—like we're the only two people in the world—to never go away.

He nods. "That's what I said."

Holding back the wants I can't ask for, I say, "French fries?"

He drops his gaze with a faint smile before looking at me again. "French fries."

We get in the truck and hit the nearest drive-through for a large fry, and I hum happily as I pop the first one into my mouth. Then Carson turns down a dirt road.

His headlights eventually shine on a metal gate. I'm about to eat another fry when I stop, my eyes jumping from the gate to him. "Does this lead to another murder den?"

He opens the truck door. "Eat your french fries."

I finish putting the fry in my mouth and smirk at his laughter as he walks toward the gate.

We drive through, and he shuts the gate behind us. A little more driving, and we're in a wide-open field, the only light cast by the moon and countless stars.

Carson parks in the middle of the field and opens his truck door to get out, so I do the same. Hopping down, snack in hand, I look up. "This is beautiful."

"Yeah." Carson opens the tailgate, and the same woven blanket from the horseshow sits rolled in the back. Hoisting himself up into the truck bed, he shakes it open and lays it flat. Holding out a hand to help me climb in, he says, "I used to come out here a lot when I'd visit."

Before taking his hand, I glance over my shoulder at the way we came in. "Are you sure it's okay that we're back here?"

He wraps his fingers around mine, pulling me into the truck

248

bed. "Yeah, this is the back of my dad's property. He used to have cows, but he sold the last of them a few years ago."

I sit, setting the fries between us, and lean back to look at the star-filled sky. "Don't you think it's weird we've never met?" Bringing my eyes back to his, I add, "Since you were here sometimes growing up? I mean, Ed has been shoeing our horses for years."

Carson takes a seat next to me. His back leans against the truck as he rests his elbows on his bent knees. "No. There were plenty of years when I was supposed to come here but didn't want to. And the years I did come, I wasn't exactly happy about being here."

I frown. "When did you and your dad work things out?"

Carson shrugs. "Sometime last year. My grandpa got on my case about it. He and my dad have always stayed in touch."

My lips twitch. "And now you're a farrier, too."

Carson laughs. "Yeah, but I learned from a guy back home. Dad and I sometimes argue about the best way to do things, but I know he's great at what he does." He looks over at me before adding, "Don't worry. Sully is in good hands once I'm gone."

I know Sully is in great hands with Ed, but my smile still falters. It seems like no matter how many times I remind myself that this is temporary, nothing will prepare me for when Carson leaves to go back home. Every time a reminder pops up, I get a sudden rush of dread, like when you think there's one more step, but there isn't.

That's how it feels, sitting here with him. He'll be gone, and I'll still be reaching for that next step with nothing to catch me.

Carson grabs a fry. "Not tonight, Abbie."

"What?"

He points a circling finger my way. "Whatever's going on up there."

An embarrassed smile comes to my lips. "Is it that obvious?"

He leans toward me and kisses me gently. As he pulls away, he keeps his face close to mine. "Only because I catch myself doing the same thing."

"Okay." I sit up straighter and eat another french fry. "Not tonight."

Carson follows my lead and eats another one, too. "What about your dad?"

The question catches me off guard. I've never told Carson about my dad—because I never talk about my dad. "What about him?"

He shrugs. "Your mom would mention him sometimes when she needed work done around your house." He studies me, and I'm suddenly afraid he can see straight through me. "We don't have to talk about him."

"We can talk about him," I say with a nod.

"Okay. So, talk about him."

My mouth opens, but I have nothing to say. I've lived more

of my life with my parents apart than I did with them together, so the topic of their divorce isn't something I think about often.

"You're mom said he lives in Chicago?"

"He does," I say with a nod. Carson's watching me, waiting for more, and I sigh, giving in. "There isn't much to say. That's where he's from originally. They met at a mutual friend's wedding in Georgia. Dad fell hard, moved to Florida to be with my mom, they had me, and then he realized that life here didn't fit. It never felt like home for him, and he needed to go back." I shrug, not knowing what else to say.

Carson looks deep in thought, a crease forming between his eyebrows.

"Home isn't a person. Home is a place," I add. "It isn't fair to expect someone to become your home, anyway. It's too much to ask."

His frown deepens before he focuses on me. "I'm sorry," he says, and I can't help feeling like he isn't apologizing for my dad.

Carson leans in to kiss me, and I close my eyes, trying to commit every last detail to memory.

The way his tongue tastes on mine.

The way having him this close makes me feel perfectly at ease and restless all at once.

The way he puts his hand under my back as he gently lays me down beneath him.

Grabbing his shirt, I kiss him deeper, memorizing how his

body feels against mine. His solid frame somehow molds to me perfectly. My hands find their way under his t-shirt, my fingers raking over him. He presses his hips into me, a low groan dragging from his throat as he kisses my neck. "You've ruined me, you know that?" he murmurs against my ear.

I nod, my breathing shallow. "I know the feeling."

Carson's lips find mine again, his tongue claiming my mouth, and I let him kiss me harder.

I would let this man do anything.

But he pulls away from me, his head snapping up to look out over the truck bed.

I tilt my head to look in the same direction, but all I see is more truck bed. "What are you—"

"Hold on," he says, his jaw set into a hard line.

I listen.

All I hear are crickets. And not in an ironic way. It sounds like they're everywhere. You never even think about them until you're alone, and it's quiet, and you realize you're surrounded.

But then I hear laughter.

THIRTY

A distant yet distinct laughter carries through the trees, and the crease between Carson's eyebrows deepens.

"Is that coming from your dad's house?" I whisper, not sure if it's okay to speak.

He doesn't look at me. He keeps his eyes trained in the direction of the noise. "It sounds like it."

There's a loud crash and more laughter.

"Get in the truck." He jumps down and holds out a hand for me to do the same.

I go to the passenger side as Carson closes the tailgate. By the time I buckle my seatbelt, the truck has started. "What is it?"

Another loud crash sounds in the distance. He barely looks at me before fixing his gaze straight ahead. "I don't know, but I don't think it's good."

He doesn't take us back through the metal gate. Instead, he

tears through the field, then maneuvers through a wide trail in the woods. Grabbing the oh-shit handle overhead, I say, "Is this meant for cars?" as we bump our way through the trees, branches brushing against either side of his truck.

"It's meant for horses." He barely slows the truck before it dips again over the uneven terrain. "And it's a shitty path for them, too."

In the glow of the headlights, I spot a log ahead of us on the left. There's no room for Carson to steer around it, and he doesn't try to. The truck tires roll up and over the log on the left side, putting us at a tilt and leaving me pressed into my passenger window. My hand squeezes around the handle tight enough to make my fingers ache. Once we're level again, he asks, "Are you okay?"

"Uh-huh." I nod and swallow the lump in my throat.

The trail ends, and my eyes land on Ed's barn. Carson races around the barn and down the long driveway. The house is dark in the distance. It almost looks peaceful if it weren't for Phil frantically barking inside.

It takes me a moment to register the car sitting near the front gate with its lights on.

And another moment to realize there are people here.

The familiar silhouettes of three guys stand around Carson's trailer. One tosses back what's left of a beer can before crumpling it and throwing it in the grass, and the other two take turns slamming things against the trailer hard enough to dent the metal.

They're all laughing.

And I think they're throwing his farrier tools.

Seth and his friends don't even notice us until Carson is out of the truck and marching toward them.

Carson yanks one of his metal tools from Seth's hand and tosses it in the grass behind him. Then he shoves Seth up against the trailer, holding him in place.

"*Shit!*" I scramble to run up to them. When Seth looks up and sees me, his mask settles into hard lines of rage, and I stop dead in my tracks. The drunken look he gives me is so much more than just hurt after a breakup—there's a darkness brewing behind those eyes.

In the time Carson has grabbed Seth, both of his friends have stopped destroying the trailer and stumble over. Carson looks at the other two guys before he lets go of Seth and takes a step back. "You've had your fun. Now go."

"Whoa, what's Abbie doing here?" Conner manages to slur his words in a way that is at least comprehendible.

Liam laughs, his eyes jumping to Seth. "Oh… This guy's sti-sticking it to your girl?" He walks over to the truck bed and looks inside. Like vermin rummaging through what isn't theirs. "What were you two doing?" When he sees the blanket in the back, his eyes light up. "Oh, Abbie, you dirty, dirty girl," he says with a shake of his head, his dark hair swaying from left to right.

"Let me guess," I say, trying to hide my anger. "You guys got wasted and mailboxing wasn't good enough? You needed to destroy something bigger?"

My eyes jump to Carson, but he stays still, calculating as he watches them.

"The mailbox is toast, too." Connor does a clumsy sidestep as he takes another sip.

Liam leans against the trailer. "Seth suggested we kick it up a notch."

This seems to pull Seth from his trance. "We were bored." Seth turns to Carson, "Trying to get laid before you leave this weekend?"

I glare at him. "Seth, you don't know what you're talking about." But when I don't hear Carson say anything, I look over at him. He's staring at the dented trailer in front of him, his fists clenched.

When he drops his gaze, staring down at the ground, I say, "Wait. You're leaving *this weekend?*"

"That's what I heard," Seth says.

I blink, my eyes never leaving Carson. "When are you leaving?"

He doesn't look at me. Instead, his hard stare settles on Seth. "Tomorrow."

Seth's gaze jumps between Carson and me, a slow smile forming. "Oh, wait... he didn't tell you?" He unleashes a wicked laugh. "Yeah. The word is out that good ole Ed will take back his

256

clients next week."

Ignoring Seth, I keep my focus on Carson. "You're leaving tomorrow?" I ask, my voice barely audible.

Carson's jaw ticks, but no words come out.

"You're leaving *tomorrow?*" I ask again, this time with a little more force.

He finally looks at me, and his torn expression gives me the answer I'm looking for.

"Tomorrow is the festival," I say quietly. "When exactly did you plan on leaving?"

"I was going to leave after," he says in a low voice.

"Aw," Liam croons from somewhere nearby. I can't take my eyes off Carson to see where he is. "Is this your first lover's spat?"

My brain slows, and our audience fades into the background. I stare at Carson, hoping I misunderstood. "When were you planning on telling me?"

Conner's voice joins him. "Don't worry, Abbie. Seth will probably take you back."

Seth lets out a lazy laugh. "I don't want her." He looks over at Carson. "She's a lousy lay, anyway."

My cheeks burn, but I don't have time to dwell on what he's said because he's not finished.

"How long did it take? Weeks?" Seth asks as he takes a step toward Carson. "Days?" Carson clenches his fist but Seth shrugs. "I know it was less than it took me. I waited seven long months for her to spread her——"

Before I can even think about what I'm doing, I march up to him and shove him as hard as I can. It takes my entire body weight, but he staggers back against the horse trailer with nowhere to go. My open palms beat against his chest. "Shut up! Shut up! Shut up!"

A sharp sting sears into my cheek, and I fall back a step. I clutch the side of my face, not comprehending what just happened.

I blink and see Seth shaking out his hand.

I blink again, and Carson is in front of me.

His lips are moving as his eyes frantically scan over my face, but I don't even hear him. My eyes jump from person to person.

Seth scowling down at his palm.

Connor with a hand clapped over his mouth.

Liam with his eyebrows raised in disbelief.

Carson walking away from me.

I shake my head, and it's like someone unmutes the world. Everything is too loud, and I have to yell to be heard. "Carson! Where are you going?"

Carson glances back at me. "I'm going to hit him now." Anger ripples through him as he closes the space between him and Seth.

I only have half a second to acknowledge the fear in Seth's eyes when he looks up to find Carson in front of him. Before he can even open his mouth to get a word out, Carson's fist collides with the side of Seth's jaw.

The sound is enough to make me flinch.

"What the fuck?" Seth spits, and I peek at the scene as he tries to push Carson back, but Carson shoves him against the trailer again. The back of Seth's head slams against metal.

Carson's fist draws back again, but this time Liam and Conner seem to catch up to the situation. Both guys rush toward him, but not before his fist connects with Seth's face for a second time.

It takes both of them, but Liam and Conner yank Carson away from Seth. Carson staggers backward but catches his footing just in time to block a punch from Liam.

"Stop!" I yell, but it's pointless. Carson is outnumbered and goes from offense to defense, his arms blocking the hits coming his way. I want to help him, but everything's happening so fast, and I'm not sure I'd be able to stop them. When I see Seth get to his feet, I know I have to do *something*.

I grab Seth by the arm. "Seth, just go. You guys need to go," I plead, digging my heels into the ground.

Seth spins around, throwing me off balance and pushing me to the ground. "Get off me."

My tailbone takes the brunt of the hit, but I barely have time to notice before a loud bang rings out.

My eyes frantically scan for the cause of the noise, but they're all looking up with expressions that mirror my own.

"Cops are on their way!" A far-off voice yells. Ed stands with a rifle pointed at the ground.

The three guys curse under their breath, and my heart pounds as I watch Carson press his palm to his cheek, checking for blood.

Seth and his friends glance at each other and start stepping toward the front gate like they're about to make a run for it. I can't let them do that—I can't let them sneak away.

So, I do the only thing I can think of.

I run first.

THIRTY-ONE

The sound of their feet pounding into the earth as they take off after me makes it impossible to slow down. I've never been much of a runner, but I don't let that stop me. Ignoring my screaming muscles, I will my feet to carry me as fast and as hard as they can. Someone yells my name, but the blood pounding in my ears is the only thing I focus on as I close the space between myself and the red Mustang.

I yank open the driver's door, and hands grab at me. I'm barely able to get the keys out of the cupholder before I'm pulled from the car. Seth may not be the person I thought he was in a lot of ways, but he *always* leaves his keys in the cupholder. Turning toward the woods, I throw them as hard as I can. The metal ring barely slips out of my fingers before I'm shoved up against the car. I gasp for breath, but a satisfied smile comes to my lips. Based on the way Liam glares into the woods, I'd say those keys will be hard to find.

"What the hell, Abbie?" Conner growls as he shoves me against the car.

"Take your hands off her." Ed's voice comes from somewhere behind me, steady and even.

Conner's head snaps up, his eyes widening, and he lets go of me immediately. Liam follows his lead, and when I look over my shoulder, Ed stands only a few feet away, pointing the rifle at the two boys.

"Thanks," I say through heaving breaths.

Ed just nods, never taking his eyes off Conner and Liam.

I scan the property for Seth and Carson, and relief washes over me when I see Carson has Seth pinned to the ground, one hand on his throat and a knee on his chest.

By the time I jog up to them, I'm panting. "Carson, are you okay?" He has a gash on his cheek just under his eye, but the rest of him looks fine. I'm sure he'll have a few bruises by morning, but right now, he looks like he blocked most of the blows.

But it's not Carson who answers me, it's Seth. "Abbie, you know my parents will kill me if they find out about this." His eyes frantically jump between Carson and me. "It's a trailer! It's not even a big deal!"

"Assault, trespassing, vandalism…" Carson lists before adding, "being a dick."

"Assault?" Seth sputters at Carson. "You hit me first!"

262

Carson's entire body tenses. He grabs Seth's face and forces him to look toward me. "Her."

My cheek still burns from the slap, but I fight the urge to lift my hand to it. Carson stares down at Seth like he might hit him again, but eventually, he releases his face.

"Are you okay?" Carson asks, turning his attention back to me.

There's a lot I'd like to say to him, but not in front of Seth.

Carson watches me steadily, waiting for me to say something when Seth chimes in again. "I mean, we were just having fun—blowing off steam. You know how that is!" He doesn't mention me or the hit, but the desperation in his voice carries with every syllable.

Carson practically rolls his eyes back to Seth. He gives his throat another shove and groans. "Would you shut the fuck up?"

Seth opens his mouth to speak again, but after seeing the look in Carson's eyes, he seems to decide against it.

"Are you okay?" Carson asks me a second time.

I nod, still catching my breath, and he seems to visibly relax.

My mind wrestles with whether I should say more, but flashing red and blue lights in the distance bring my attention to the front gate. Ed now stands with two officers, his gun at his side.

"I'm sorry, okay?" Seth's eyes are wide. "I'm sorry we came here. We shouldn't have. We were drunk, and we weren't thinking, okay? It was stupid."

Carson stares down at Seth, his expression revealing nothing. Finally, he says, "You should apologize to her, not me."

Seth's eyebrows pull together as he strains his neck to look from Carson to me. My face warms with both of their eyes on me—my past and present colliding. Bitterness laces every word as he says, "I'm *sorry,* Abbie."

Anyone can see he's not, but I don't care. I never needed an apology from him. I don't want one.

He looks back up at Carson with a pleading stare. "There. Can you let me go now?" He says the last word through gritted teeth.

"No."

"But I said I was sorry!"

Carson looks past me to the officers, checking to see how things are going with his dad and the other two guys. "You're still a piece of shit."

"You're an asshole," Seth growls as he struggles against Carson's hold.

Carson adjusts his position, shifting his knee and pressing down. Seth gasps for air, but Carson ignores it. He nods toward the front gate. "Here they come."

I glance over my shoulder to find one of the officers making their way toward us while the other stays by the car with Liam and Conner secured in the back seat.

"Hi, Officer Brewer." I only know who the officers are in this town because we always ride together in the annual 4th of July parade, and Mom went to high school with a few of them.

"Hello, Abbie." He adjusts his belt and assesses the situation. Carson lets go of Seth, and the two of them get to their feet. "Well, what's this about?" he asks Seth as he reaches for a notepad in his pocket.

Seth says nothing.

Officer Brewer lets out a sigh as he tucks the tiny booklet back into his pocket. "Ed hasn't said whether he's pressing charges. He should from the sound of things, but that's up to him." He looks both boys up and down before shaking his head. "Get in the car with the other two, Seth. Officer Foss will take you boys home."

Seth nods, his lips in a thin line as he walks to the car, leaving Carson and me with Officer Brewer. Part of me wants to run over to Ed and ask him why in the world he wouldn't press charges, but my feet feel stuck.

"Do you think you can give me a ride home?" I ask the officer without looking at Carson. Even though Carson not telling me he's leaving isn't the most important thing that happened tonight, it still makes me feel betrayed—it makes me feel like I need to get away.

Carson's eyes burn into me, and in a low voice, he says, "I can take you home, Abbie."

But I don't want him to take me home. We've been dragging this thing out on borrowed time, anyway. By tomorrow night, he'll be gone, so I don't see the point. Maybe this is the perfect excuse to rip off the band-aid.

Officer Brewer raises an eyebrow as he looks between the two of us.

"No, it's okay," I say to Carson. "You should be here with your dad." It's the truth, and we both know it. He drops his gaze, studying the ground in front of him like he's trying to figure out how to fix this.

There's nothing to fix, though.

We knew this would end—maybe not like this, but the end was inevitable. Nothing good would come from us being together.

I hold my breath, waiting for him to say what's on his mind, but he doesn't. There was once a time I'd give anything to know what he was thinking, but right now I'm almost grateful that he keeps his thoughts locked away.

This goodbye feels abrupt and unfinished, but maybe that's what we need. We were never going to finish what we started anyway.

Officer Brewer starts back toward his car, probably to give us some privacy.

My heart thuds in my chest as I look at Carson.

He opens his mouth to say something, but I cut him off. "Don't worry about the Summer Fest." I hug my arms around my torso. "I'm sorry about tonight. I never thought they would come here. Please tell your dad I'm sorry." The words pour out of me.

Fighting back tears, my voice feels thick when I say, "I hope you get home safe."

"Abbie," Carson says to stop me from turning away, but I shake my head.

"Abbie," he says again, this time with a little more conviction. Everything in me is screaming not to face him, but my feet betray me.

"What?" I ask, my arms going limp at my sides.

Carson rubs his palm over his chest, and I'm not sure if he's sore from the blows or if he's hurting the same way I am. "I was going to tell you."

I nod. "I know." It's true. I know Carson wouldn't have left without telling me, but that doesn't change the fact that he's leaving. Nothing will change that. Nothing *should* change that. I'm not angry with him for going home, I just wish he would have told me sooner.

I hold his gaze, waiting for him to say more, but he doesn't. He dips his chin in resignation, his lips pressed in a hard line. A new stab of pain goes to my heart, and I wrap my arms around myself as I rush to catch up with Officer Brewer. The police car with Seth and his friends in the back has already left, and Ed now walks toward Carson.

"Thanks," I say quietly to Officer Brewer as he holds open the car door. I don't waste time fastening my seatbelt so he can take me home.

Back to the life I had before Carson.

THIRTY-TWO

My hands smooth down the soft yellow material of my sundress as I study myself in the mirror. I got little sleep last night, but I think I managed to hide most of the evidence with makeup. I rarely dress up like this, and it's more fun when you're not trying to hide that you've been crying all night.

I twist back and forth, the dress flaring slightly around my knees. It makes me smile. It might be a small, sad smile, but at least it's there.

My shorter cowboy boots pair nicely with the dress. Around here, cowboy boots are an acceptable form of attire for almost any occasion—as long as they aren't covered in mud. It's a good thing too, because I don't own a single pair of heels.

"You look beautiful." Mom peeks through my open doorway. "How are you holding up?"

I had to tell her about last night. She'd find out about it one way or another, so I figured it was best to come clean considering I got a ride home from an officer. I tried to focus on what happened between Carson and Seth, but eventually, through shaking sobs and hot tears, it all came out.

"Fine." I look over my shoulder at her, but with her turned-down smile, I doubt she believes me. "I knew he was leaving," I say as I turn back to the mirror.

"That doesn't mean it hurts any less."

She's right, of course. This hurts more than I want it to. It hurts more than it probably should. How can someone I've known for mere weeks leave such a gaping hole?

This isn't how it's supposed to feel.

This isn't fair.

Frankly, this is *bullshit.*

The most irritating part is when I think about Carson and the memories we created, my heart still flutters. I love the time we had together. I love that he doesn't give out smiles easily. I love the mischievous glint in his eye when he teases me, waiting for my reaction. I love seeing him in that stupid hat.

And then a realization dawns on me, too heavy to bear.

I'll never get to finish falling in love with him.

My eyes burn, and I blink back the threat of tears as I quickly run my fingers through my loose curls.

"Oh, Abbie." She walks toward me, and I spin around.

"I'm fine. Really!" I say too cheerfully. "I told Lisa I'd help her set up, so I need to go, but I'm fine."

I'm afraid to make eye contact with her. I know the care behind her hazel eyes will pull the breakdown right out of me. Giving her a fleeting glance, I try to reassure her. "Mom, I'm fine. Really."

"Is there anything I can do?"

"Nope!" I reach for my phone on the dresser and slip around her before I bound down the stairs. "I won't be out late!" I call out over my shoulder. Then grabbing the keys, I pretend I can't feel her worry and head out the door.

☼　☼　☼

Lisa rests both hands on my shoulders. Her sandy blonde hair falls from her clip, leaving stray pieces to frame her face. "Thanks for getting here early."

"The place looks amazing!" I give her my best smile and hope it doesn't look as forced as it feels. The large, white air-conditioned party tent is filled with scattered round tables, all covered in coordinating white and sage green linens. "It looks like you could host a wedding here."

Worry sparks behind her eyes. "Is it too much?"

"No." I wave my previous comment away. "It's perfect. Really."

She lets out a breath and releases me when the caterer walks in holding a tray of finger foods.

"Where do you want this?" the man asks with a grin.

"Oh! Right over here." Lisa points to a nearby table as she scurries toward him. "Abbie," she adds, looking over her shoulder. "Can you pour the punch into those little glasses and have them lined up?"

"Sure," I say, even though there's no point in answering. She's back to giving the caterer her full attention, and I'm left to my task.

The repetitive work of pouring punch brings the thoughts of last night into the forefront of my mind. Every time I picture Carson standing there, wanting me to stay, my heart aches.

He wanted to drive me home.

He wanted to fix this.

Part of me wishes I would have talked to him. I know he'd never do anything to hurt me on purpose—at least I don't think he would.

But if I would have stayed with him last night, it wouldn't have changed anything. He still would have left today, and I'd still have to put the pieces of myself back together.

Country music plays in the background as guests start to show, and the ache in my chest seems to sink deeper. Being at a party alone amplifies everything. It's like watching everyone else laugh and have fun is just pouring salt on my open wound.

I miss him.

Not because it's been that long since I last saw him, but because I can't stop wondering what it will be like the next time I see him—if that day ever comes. It might be years down the road, but he'll visit Ed again. I imagine coming face to face with him after we're both forced to move on and missing what could have been.

It seems silly to miss something you never had, but we were so close, and I'll always wonder if it could have worked.

I'll wonder if he was almost the one.

I want to know if it was hard for him to decide to go. Before he finalized his plans, did he think of me? Did he hesitate? Or was packing up his life here just the next thing on his list?

The glass of punch I'm pouring overflows, and I curse under my breath. I scan the area for something and find a roll of paper towels. Soaking up the spill, I look up to see Lisa welcoming newcomers at the entrance while more people start to crowd the dance floor.

I've been in denial. I told Carson I would never ask him to stay, and I meant it. But I think a small part of me hoped he would. Even if it was only for an extra day—an extra hour. I hoped he would drag it out.

But he didn't.

We didn't even get a full summer.

He's going back to Tennessee.

He may have left already. It would make sense. I know he was planning on heading out after the Summer Fest, but that was before I told him not to come here—that was before I walked away from him.

Maybe he already left—maybe I'm here, wondering if I'll ever see him again, and he's already moved on from the state of Florida completely.

I look around the tent to force myself back to the present. Someone walks through the entrance, and my breath catches. It isn't until I realize the guy carrying a chair isn't Carson that I can breathe again. I don't even know why I'm looking for him.

Even as I straighten some of the plates on the tables, my eyes jump to the tent entrance every few minutes to check if it's him walking through the opening.

It never is.

Fighting tears, I walk over to the punch table and rotate a few of the cups to keep myself busy.

People from all different riding facilities file in and settle at the tables. The riders from Fox Hill gravitate toward each other, and the same goes for Bridlewood and Spring Oaks.

Seth is here with the rest of the Spring Oaks crew. The only silver lining is that Liam and Conner are nowhere in sight. I do my best to stay busy, but I can feel Seth's eyes on me. As much as I try to ignore him being here, I'm always keenly aware of where he is and what he's doing.

His lip swollen and his eye bruised.

And when he approaches me directly, I can see his eyes are

bloodshot.

He stares down at me and swallows hard. "How's your…" He points to my own face.

My eyes narrow. "How's my cheek after you slapped me?"

His eyes dart around the party. "Can you keep it down?"

"No."

Relationships are a funny thing. A few weeks ago, the guy standing across from me felt like my entire world.

Now, he's practically a stranger, and I'm trying to figure out if it's possible for a person to change that quickly or if I never really knew him at all.

"Listen." He scratches the side of his head. "Things went too far last night. We shouldn't have gone to Ed's—he's a good guy."

I notice he doesn't include Carson, but I don't mention it considering I'm actively trying not to think about him.

"Ed didn't press charges?"

Seth shakes his head, and my mood dips even lower. "No. He just wants us to help fix everything we broke."

"That's generous."

Seth sighs. "Abbie," he says, pulling my eyes to him. "I'm *sorry.*"

This conversation is making me tired, and I can't give him the validation he's looking for. He wants to hear that it's okay. He wants to hear that we all make mistakes. He wants me to understand what he was feeling and somehow justify his actions, but I can't do that for him. I won't.

"Okay, Seth." Turning away, I focus on the party that's now in full swing. Trainers and riders drink small cups of punch as they stand in the white sun-filled tent. A group of kids pretends they're horses, skipping with one leg leading and then doing flying changes in the middle of the dance floor. Lisa has even started to relax with a glass of white wine in her hand as she laughs with one of the other barn owners.

It's all wonderful.

But it's all too much.

I need some air. I can't be around this many people when I'm feeling this fragile. The Summer Fest was supposed to be a distraction, but it's proving to only be a painful reminder.

Exiting the tent, I pace back and forth and force myself to breathe. It's no use, though. I can still hear the shrieks of laughter and the endless chatter. It's deafening, and I want to go home.

Giving up, I turn toward the parked cars where my mom's truck sits somewhere among the rows, and I freeze. The sound of the party fades, replaced by the blood pounding in my ears.

I can't move.

I can't breathe.

I can't tear my eyes away from the guy in the backward hat.

THIRTY-THREE

Carson's gaze makes it impossible for me to focus on anything else.

My heart pounds as his dark eyes lock on me. He's stopped with his arms by his sides, and his keys are still in his hand like he just got here.

A warm summer breeze whisps my hair, and my dress billows. The heat of the day has broken, the sun now hidden between white clouds.

We both just stare at each other, and I'm at a loss for words.

I need to know why he's here. I need to know why he decided to come after I told him not to.

I take a small, hesitant step toward him. Part of me doesn't believe he's actually standing in front of me, but he is. He's wearing dark jeans and a black t-shirt with his black backward hat, and even though he's underdressed for the occasion, he looks perfect.

To me, he's perfect.

As soon as he sees me move toward him, his shoulders relax. My feet pick up their pace, and he meets me in the middle.

I blink up at him, unsure what to say, and that's when I see it. That's when I see through the cracks of his always composed mask and see the heartbreak seeping through.

Smoothing down the front of my dress, I try to gather my thoughts. "You're here."

He rubs the back of his neck. "I'm sorry. I know I shouldn't be. I can go if—,"

I grab his hand, desperate to memorize how it feels to have him this close to me, even if it's painful.

"But why are you?" My heart races as I wait for his answer. He has some bruising under his eye, and it takes everything in me not to reach up and gently touch that spot.

He drops his gaze to the ground. "I should go." He looks like he's at war with himself—like he doesn't know if he should tell me everything or nothing, but I *need* him to tell me.

Because the idea of always wondering terrifies me.

Just when I think he's about to say something, he looks away from me, and it feels like he's giving up.

Frustrated, I run my hands over my hair, pushing it back. "Danm it, Carson. Talk to me."

He stares at me, and his jaw ticks. "I didn't tell you because I kept imagining the look on your face," he blurts. His eyes searching mine. "It broke me, Abbie. Just the thought of disappointing you like that broke me. Then last night..." He shakes his head. "I would have told you last night. That was my plan. And maybe it was a bad plan—to wait that long. I don't know. I just know I wanted to put it off as long as I could because nothing beats seeing you happy. Nothing."

My eyes burn, and it looks like seeing me this way physically pains him.

Gripping the back of his neck, his eyebrows furrow. "I came here because I had to see you." His eyes jump to the tent behind me. "Is Seth here?"

My voice is small when I say, "I wish I could say he wasn't."

Carson nods, his jaw clenching as he runs a hand over his face. "I hate this, Abbie. I hate that he'll be here and I won't. I hate that *you'll* be here and I won't." His stare pins me in place, and I wish I knew what he was looking for as his eyes search mine. "I'm sorry," he says with another shake of his head. "I shouldn't have come here."

"Please don't go." My voice comes out as a quiet plea.

He pauses, looking back at me with a torn expression, and seeing him this way breaks something inside of me. We knew we'd hurt each other. We knew we didn't stand a chance. We knew it was a bad idea.

But we didn't know how deep of a mark we'd leave.

"I don't know what you want from me." His shoulders drop.

My eyes jump back and forth between his, searching for any

sign of what he might be thinking.

"I want you to kiss me."

His eyebrows furrow, and my heart pounds in my chest as I wait for him to say something—*anything.*

Slowly watching me, he says, "Abbie."

I take a step toward him. "Kiss me," I say on the brink of tears.

Carson drops his arms and looks at me like he's seeing me for the first time. We stare at each other, and I've never felt this vulnerable. It's like a vice is tightening around my heart with every passing second.

He paces toward me, and I gasp in a rush of air as his lips crash into mine. His hands are on either side of my face, and my fists clench around the material of his t-shirt. His mouth moves over mine with an urgency I've never felt, and when my lips part, he kisses me deeper. I feel whole again. Even if I know it's a temporary fix—like trying to plug a sinking ship with duct tape.

When he gently lets go of my face, I lean my head against his chest. He doesn't step away from me like I thought he might, and I'm grateful for it.

Because I never want to let go.

His hand cups the back of my neck as his thumb messages small circles into my skin. "So, now what do you want?"

I tilt my head up to look at him. "You tell me," I say as I wrap my arms around his waist. "Make your move."

He pulls back to look at me, his eyes flickering to the tent before settling on me again. "Come on." He takes my hand in his. "Let's get out of here."

THIRTY-FOUR

Carson drives with one hand and he wraps his fingers around mine with the other. His thumb gently brushes the backs of my knuckles. I have no idea where we're going, and I don't care. All I care about is being with him and committing every last detail to memory.

The feeling of his rough hand holding mine.

The comfortable silence between us, accompanied by the soft sound of country music on the radio.

The way I look in the side mirror with the windows rolled down, my hair whipping behind me.

Each piece is a vital component, and together, this simple country drive feels like a unique work of art that I'll never be able to replicate.

And that's okay.

Eventually, my curiosity gets the best of me. "Where are we going?"

Glancing at me, he admits, "I haven't figured that out yet."

I gape at him. "Carson! We've been driving for fifteen minutes."

His lips quirk, but he doesn't crack.

"What?" I ask, mirroring his smile.

"I like the way you say my name," he casually says like it doesn't have the power to undo me. Then, looking over at me, he adds, "And we've been driving for *five.*"

Biting back my smile, I point to the next side street. "Just turn here."

He raises an eyebrow and does as I say. "What's over here?"

"Nothing." I mean it. This road leads to a dead end with a single driveway that the owner of Spring Oaks only uses as a service drive. It's gotten a lot of use lately with the renovations going on. The construction company has large equipment scattered everywhere. But it's Saturday, so no one is working.

Carson parks his truck at the end of the road behind an excavator, and as soon as he looks at me, my mind floods with too many thoughts. "I'm sorry about last night," I blurt. "I shouldn't have left the way I did. I shut down."

"Abbie." Carson tries to interrupt me, but I won't let him.

"No." I shake my head. "I should have stayed and made sure you were alright. I should have helped clean up the mess they made of your dad's property. I don't know what I was thinking. I'm so sorry."

I'm staring down at my hands until Carson puts his over mine.

"Abbie," he says again. "Don't apologize."

"Your dad should have pressed charges," I say quietly, tracing the lines of his palm as my eyes stay trained on our hands.

"Trust me, I wish he could have."

My head snaps up, and I turn toward him. "He absolutely could have!" Just thinking about what happened to Ed's property gets me fired up again, and I feel like I should have said more to Seth at the Summer Fest while I had the chance. "He has every right to take legal action against—"

"Abbie, they're his clients."

My nose crinkles. "No, they're not. Spring Oaks uses their own farrier."

He just shakes his head, his frown deepening. "Geneva is small, and the horse community here is even smaller. He doesn't want what happened last night tied to his name. He's good at what he does, but Seth's family has a lot of say when it comes to things around here. He just wants to keep the peace."

I understand it, but something like this shouldn't come down to money or power. It should come down to what's right and wrong. "I hate that."

A sad smile pulls at his lips, but he doesn't say anything else about Ed or what happened last night. Instead, he studies me, his eyes asking a million questions despite his mouth staying closed.

"What?" I finally ask.

Pulling his hand from mine, he rubs his palms against the dark denim of his jeans. "I went to your house today."

"You did?"

He nods. "Yeah, but you had already left." His frown deepens. "That was hours ago. I could have gone straight to the Summer Fest, but I didn't know if you'd want to see me."

I'm tempted to tell him I wish I could see him every day, but I don't.

Because admitting that wouldn't help either of us.

He grips the back of his neck. "Look, I don't know where you stand, and I need to know."

"Where I stand," I echo.

He nods.

I'm torn. I don't know how much I should say. I don't want to make this harder than it already is. I can't say that I don't want him to go, or that I wish he lived here, or how lonely and quiet this town will feel without him. Instead, I lean over and kiss him. His lips soften against mine before he quietly says, "Abbie."

Kissing him again, I climb over to his side of the truck and straddle him, my legs falling to either side as I move my mouth to his neck.

I know he wants to get our conversation back on track, but it feels like the longer we can put off talking about this, the more time we'll have. This is all we'll ever have, and I just want us to make the most of it.

"We should…" He sucks in a breath when I run my tongue against his skin. "…talk."

I gently suck on his ear.

"Fuck, Abbie." His head falls back against the seat, and I can feel him growing hard beneath me. "We need to talk…" I kiss his lips. "…about me" I reach for the tight bulge in his jeans. "…leaving."

I let my fingers trace over him. "I'd rather do other things."

He groans. "You're making this difficult."

Sitting back, my fingers go to the button of his pants. "I'm making this easy." My lips lightly brush his as I grip him and pump my hand. "I need this, Carson. I need you."

He makes a sound like my words physically unravel him. Our eyes lock, and I silently beg for him to let this go. His pupils are blown, swallowing almost all of the dark mahogany in his eyes.

He lets out a sharp breath. "Damn it, Abbie." Carson crashes his mouth against mine, his tongue claiming my mouth, and I melt into him.

His hand slips under the material of my sundress, and he grips my thighs, pulling me to him, and grinding his hips. I can feel him bare and hard against me and let out a soft moan.

All my pent-up frustration comes boiling to the surface, and the heavy heat between my legs drives me to roll my hips. When his hand slides up my inner thigh, my legs open wider for him. His fingers slip behind the thin cotton, and he teases my opening. I'm slick against his touch, desperate and wanting, and he lets out a low growl when he feels how ready I am for him. "You need this?" he asks, and I nearly collapse at the contact as he circles me. Whatever upper hand I thought I had is completely lost. I grind against his hand, desperate for more.

Gripping the back of my neck, he pulls me closer. "Tell me what else you need."

A whimper leaves my throat as he slips a finger inside me. I roll against his hand as he slowly works in and out of me.

Panting, I struggle to speak.

"Tell me," Carson demands again, and when he pulls his finger out of me, he puts two in its place. I stretch around him as he pumps his hand and my eyes flutter shut.

"I need you inside me," I breathe.

I have no idea where he got a condom from, but he tears it open with his teeth and rolls it on. He slowly pulls his fingers out of me for the last time, and I instantly ache for him. Reaching down, I move my underwear to the side and lower myself onto him. I sink around him, and my head falls back. Being on top of him like this lets me feel all of him, and I don't think I've ever felt this consumed. Catching my breath, I start to move, rolling my hips slowly as I lose myself in him.

His hand rests on my hip, guiding me. Sinking lower, I meet his steady movements, taking him in deeper every time.

Carson's fingertips dig into my hip, stilling me. "If you keep doing that, I'm going to come."

A faint smile comes to my lips as I do it again. "Okay."

Carson thrusts into me harder, and I cry out. He covers my mouth with his, swallowing my moans as he pushes into me again… and again.

We're both frantic and desperate when my legs start to shake. His thumb grazes over my bottom lip as he says in a rough voice, "I need you to come for me."

I nod because I'm too breathless to speak.

Moving his hand to where I need it most, my breathing quickens. He thrusts into me deeper, and I dig my fingertips into his shoulders. His thumb increases pressure, and tension inside me spikes.

Somehow my body feels completely out of control and in control at the same time. I increase my pace, chasing the building heat. The tighter my body coils around him, the harder my fingertips dig into the back of his neck.

"That's it, baby. Come for me," he says through heated breaths, and it's like a switch goes off, short-circuiting throughout my core.

He picks up his pace as I collapse on top of him, my body locking as waves of pleasure take over. Carson curses my name, his head falling back against the seat as he stiffens and comes undone with me.

We stay like that, a tangled mess of limbs clinging to what we can't keep. With my head against his chest, I listen to the steady thud of his heart as he absently runs his fingers through my hair. We don't talk because there's nothing left to say, and by the time I move back to the passenger seat, the sun has started to set.

Carson reaches over and rubs his thumb over my cheek. "You're perfect."

I smile at him, and there's so much I want him to know. I want to tell him how he makes me feel. I want to tell him he's the reason I finally understand so many things about relationships and respect.

But I can't.

Telling him would only make him feel bad that I'm getting attached, and he would apologize. He would tell me again how much he doesn't want to hurt me, and it would cast a shadow over how great this afternoon has been.

So instead, I say, "What time are you leaving?" and the words squeeze around my heart.

Carson sits up straighter. "Later. Why?"

Smoothing down my dress, I try to keep things light. "Because I'd say that's as good of a goodbye as we're going to get."

He nods as he puts the truck in drive. "Okay. I'll take you back."

I wonder if I said something wrong. But as soon as Carson turns on the main road, he takes my hand and brings it to his lips.

He looks deep in thought as he drives, but I force myself not to ask why.

I force myself not to ruin this.

THIRTY-FIVE

The drive back to my mom's truck feels too short. Carson and I don't talk. Our blissful state has been washed away by a heavy dose of reality.

Because this is it.

This is goodbye.

I can barely think. My mind keeps circling through everything that's happened over the past month, and how starting tomorrow, it will be like it never happened. The result of our unspoken agreement to slip back into our old lives looms in the distance. Once he leaves, I'll want to erase all the spellbound moments between us, but right now, I don't want to miss a single detail. I'm doing it even now as I make a mental note of Blake Shelton's "Sangria" playing on the radio.

I watch Carson as he drives in the setting sun. His eyes flicker to me before he takes my hand in his. Looking down, I notice a small scar on his thumb and wonder how he got it. I almost ask but change my mind. There are a lot of things I'll never know about Carson, and I have to accept that.

I don't even realize the truck stops moving until he softly says my name. When my eyes meet his, I quickly look around, remembering where I am—where we are. The Summer Fest is still in full swing, yellow light now shining from the tent opening. There's a roaring bonfire off to the side where people happily make s'mores, drink, and laugh. And everything about the sight in front of me feels wrong. The scene feels out of place, or maybe I just feel out of place in it.

"Are you okay?" Carson squeezes my fingers.

I look at him, and the crease of worry between his brow only makes my chest tighten. I want to run away from this. I want to skip this part entirely. My eyes jump to my mom's truck parked a few feet away.

"Yeah," I say, finally finding my voice. "I'm okay."

"Look," Carson says, taking his hand back from me to adjust his hat like a nervous habit. "This doesn't have to be it. Who knows—"

"Please don't." I know whatever he was about to say next isn't realistic. Long distance doesn't work. Sarah is my best friend, and even our relationship has suffered with her being two hours away. I don't want that to happen with Carson. I don't want this tainted by us gradually drifting apart.

"The only time long-distance is worth trying is when it's temporary, but this..." my voice trails. "There's no end to this."

Which is why we have to end it now.

"I know," he says, those dark eyes burning into me. "I wasn't going to suggest we try long distance."

"Oh." I stare down at my hands in my lap, embarrassed I thought he'd want to go to such lengths to keep me.

He tilts my chin up, forcing me to look at him, his thumb lightly caressing my cheek, and it takes everything in me not to lean into it. "I was going to say this doesn't have to be goodbye forever. Next time I visit my dad, I'll reach out."

Reach out.

Those two words are a cold, fractured piece of what I want, but I have no choice but to take it. "Yeah. Okay."

We lock eyes for a moment, neither of us believing the other's words. I know it won't happen. I don't expect either of us to put our lives on hold, and how long until he visits his dad again? A year? A lot can change in a year.

"And if you're ever in Tennessee—"

I nod. "I'll reach out."

He looks at me with a trace of a frown. "Yeah."

Neither of us says anything, both quietly resigning to our fate. My chest aches, and I know I'm folding in on myself. This is getting to be too much.

"I wish things were different," he says, and even though my

heart breaks a little more at the sound of his voice, a wave of calm washes over me. Knowing we're on the same page helps... I think.

"Me too," I agree, giving him a sad smile. My gaze drifts to the clock on the dashboard. "Shouldn't you be leaving soon?"

Carson eyes the time, nodding. "Yeah." Avoiding my gaze, he adds, "I should probably head back. I still have a few things to pack."

"Of course." My eyes well with the threat of tears. He has things to do—more important things than sitting here with me all night. "I'll go."

"I'll walk you to your truck."

A short laugh leaves my throat. "It's literally right there."

Carson glances at the truck before looking back at me. "So?"

"So, you really don't need to walk me."

He's already opened the driver's side door with a shrug. "I want to."

Carson meets me outside my door and takes my hand as we walk to my mom's truck.

Once we're at the driver's side door, I turn to face him. "So, I guess this is it."

He nods, worry creasing his brow. "I guess it is." He looks like his mind is somewhere else.

I reach up and place my hand on his cheek, careful not to touch his bruise. "It will be okay. I know you have to get going."

"Right," he says with a smile that doesn't reach his eyes.

Grabbing hold of my hand, he moves it to his lips and kisses my palm before pulling me gently toward him and brushing his lips against mine. "Be careful driving home."

My eyes burn, but I refuse to let my tears fall in front of him. The last thing he needs is for me to fall apart.

Carson takes a few steps back, his fingers slipping out of mine. "Goodnight, Abbie Linley."

I want to say something, but my throat is too thick, and I'm afraid if I speak, I'll cry.

He gives me a tight-lipped smile and a nod before turning around and heading for his truck, his hand gripping the back of his neck.

As soon as he's out of sight, I inhale a shuttering breath. Quickly turning to open the driver's side door, I get into the truck, and hot tears roll down my cheeks. One sob breaks out of me after another, each forming a deeper crack in the dam I've been building. The cloak of night is the only comfort I have when I finally break open, clutching the steering wheel like it can somehow save me from this.

But nothing can save me from this.

We knew this would happen.

Wiping my eyes, I grit my teeth and put the truck in drive.

It's time to go home.

Thirty-Six

It's a beautiful morning, and I'm hating every minute of it.

The night dragged. Most of it was either spent lying awake and trying not to cry, or asleep and having restless dreams that drained me. Every time I'd drift off to sleep, my dreams went into overdrive. They weren't always about Carson—although sometimes they were. Other times, it was a dream about Sully, or Mom, or Seth. They all seemed to carry the same anxious pattern. In one dream, Mom decided to sell off the horses without telling me. Or I'd make plans with Carson, only to find that he never shows. I'd go for a ride with Sully and get lost on a trail, unable to find my way home. I'd panic, jolting awake, and think, *What in the world is wrong with me?*

Mom isn't in the kitchen when I head downstairs, and I'm grateful. I saw her last night when I got home, but I kept it brief. I told her I was tired, and even though I know she saw I'd been crying, I was able to play it off like nothing new had happened—like I was still upset for the same reasons as the night before.

Which is partly true.

But if she saw how puffy my eyes are now, all she'd have to do is take one look at me to know something more is wrong. She'd insist the barn work can wait, and then she'd cook me breakfast as she slowly tore down my wall brick by brick. She'd pull it out of me like she always does, and we'd talk about how I'm feeling.

But I don't want to talk.

I want to patch up the hole in my heart, and until it heals, I'll distract myself with the one thing I can count on—the horses.

When I open the door to the back porch, the sun shines too brightly for my tired eyes. Squinting, I close it behind me and pull the brim of my hat down as I peer out over the barn. It's a morning like any other. The hot sun sticks to my skin, and I glance up to find a vibrant red cardinal perched on our roof. I watch before it takes flight, and the sight makes my mouth turn upward ever so slightly. This is my home—the place I love more than anywhere else, but my shadow of a smile only lasts a few steps before I'm hit with a sinking feeling.

Because I'm not who I was a few weeks ago, and I know I'll never be that girl again. As I look out over the place I call home, I can't help feeling like something is missing.

He is missing.

Even after Carson stopped working here, I was comforted

knowing he was only a five-minute drive down the road. He might not be hammering outside my window first thing in the morning, but I always knew I could see him.

Now it doesn't matter how fast I get the barn work done. Tennessee is still too far.

Sighing at the thought, I pull on my boots and try to ignite a spark of motivation. I've always had a flame in me when it comes to riding, but this morning even that feels dim. Hopefully taking Sully out will undo that.

My feet are clunky as I head down the wooden steps. My body feels sluggish, and my usual walk in Florida's sandy soil taking more effort than it should. I bite the inside of my cheek to keep the tears at bay. Everything will take more effort today. I wonder how many days will be like this before thinking of Carson and his stupid hat won't make my eyes well with tears.

A couple of the horses are out already, so I'm assuming Mom did turnout when she fed this morning. I wonder if Ed called her. Maybe she knows everything that happened and she's trying to help any way she can.

Stepping into the barn, I make a kissing noise and say, "Good morning, boy."

Then, I stop.

My brain shuffles through fragments of thoughts and emotions before grasping what I'm seeing in front of me.

Carson.

Carson is here.

Not in Tennessee.

He's *here*, and he's standing outside Sully's stall like this is the most normal place for him to be on a Sunday morning. All I can do is stare at him wide-eyed and clueless.

He turns to face me, and he looks as tired as I feel. He looks like he was up all night battling his own demons. "Hey."

"Hi." I shake my head and continue toward him. "Wait. How are you here?"

"Are you happy to see me?"

I blink. "Of course. But I don't understand."

Carson reaches out to Sully again, giving him a pat before resting his forearms on the door of the stall. Looking over at me, he says, "I told my grandpa about you."

"You did?"

He nods.

"And?" I can't stop staring at him. The bruise on his cheek has faded since last night, and his shirt is wrinkled—like it might have spent the last twelve hours in a suitcase.

Part of me wants to hug him and kiss him and celebrate because he's *here,* but another part of me can't help worrying. Because he shouldn't be. He should be on his way back to Tennessee where his life waits for him.

Carson gives me a small smile as he gently kicks the bottom of the stall door. "Well, first, he called me a dumbass."

I laugh, and the feeling is so strange after last night, but I welcome it. I welcome whatever this is. "And then?"

"And then," he says, pausing to study me, "he asked if there was a chance I would regret coming back to Tennessee right now."

Something squeezes around my heart as I wait for him to say more. It's a happy feeling, but a scary feeling, too. This isn't what we agreed on. This isn't supposed to happen.

Watching for my reaction, he continues, "I told him I might."

"Carson…" I feel the pressure of his decision on my shoulders. I can't be the reason he stays here. What if I let him down? What if he regrets *this?*

With a shake of his head, he cuts me off and walks up to me. "I know what you're thinking, but you're wrong."

The corners of my mouth dip, not sure what to think or say. All I know is that I don't want to be the reason he's unhappy. I don't want him to sacrifice anything for me.

"Do you want to know why he called me a dumbass?" he asks.

"Because you're giving up your life for someone you met a month ago?"

He shakes his head and his eyebrows furrow like he's still considering what he should say. "I told him Tennessee is my home, but that there's a girl in Florida who feels a lot like home, too."

I smile, but it's a sad one.

He stares at me. "Do you want to know what he said?"

"Okay." I practically sigh out the word, my shoulders dropping. There's a sinking feeling in my chest at the thought of having to say goodbye to him again. The first time was painful enough.

"He said he'd like to meet the girl who rivals Tennessee, and he can't do that when I'm sulking on his couch." There's absolute clarity behind those brown eyes—a determination behind them I haven't seen before. "The thing is, Abbie, home isn't just a place." His touch is feather light as his fingers graze the back of my arm, pulling me toward him, but I feel it from my spine to my toes. I feel his touch everywhere, and if I'm going to keep my bearings during this conversation, I need space.

"No," I say with conviction as I take a step back. "You'll resent me, and then you'll leave. That's what happens." Hugging myself, I shake my head. "I'm not doing that with you."

He stares at me the way he always does. It's the way that puts me on edge. Because he's not just looking at me.

He's analyzing me.

He's studying me.

He's trying to understand me in a way that no one else has, and it makes me want to hide.

"I can't speak for your dad, Abbie. I don't know him, but I know I'm not him." He takes a slow step toward me like he's trying not to spook a wild horse. "There are a lot of things that make a place a home, and family is one of them." He pauses, his eyes burning into me. "*You're* one of them."

A tear rolls down my cheek, and Carson catches it with his thumb, brushing it away. I want to believe him. His words are trying to mend a broken piece of me, but I'm afraid if that piece breaks again, it'll shatter. The remaining shards will be too small to put back together.

His thumb lingers on my cheek. I can't help leaning into his touch as the familiar fog starts to muffle my worries and concerns. I'm hanging on by a thread when I look up at him and softly say, "You'll resent me."

His hand drops from my cheek. "I won't."

"What about proving them wrong?" I ask, and the question helps me refocus. I step away from him again. "You want to show people in Tennessee you're not like your dad."

Taking off his hat, he runs a hand over his hair before putting it back in place. "You're right. That's what I wanted."

I raise my eyebrows. "Well, it's not like you can do that from here." Crossing my arms, I add, "If you stay here, they'll never know who you really are. That will be the lasting impression you leave."

He doesn't try to close the space between us again. He stands firmly where I left him. "I know."

I scoff. "And you're just suddenly okay with that?"

He's still watching me like he thinks I may bolt any second, but he's so calm. "Yeah, I guess I am."

"Bullshit," I snap.

302

He runs a hand over his face. "Damn it, Abbie. It's not bull-shit." He steps towards me, catching my face between his hands. "I want you. I want you more than all of that."

Resting his forehead against mine, he seems to collect his thoughts. When he finally pulls away to look at me, still holding me in place, that clarity and determination shines through his eyes again. "I won't resent you."

I want to believe him. I want to lean into everything he's saying. "And if it doesn't work?"

He shrugs, his eyes never leaving mine. "Then at least we tried." Tucking a strand of hair behind my ear, he tips my hat upward so he can look me in the eyes. "I want to try, Abbie. Let me."

My heart pounds in my chest. Not because Carson has ever given me a reason to doubt him—Carson has never given me a reason to doubt anything.

He isn't careless.

He doesn't make rash decisions.

He's thought about this. He's calculated his options, and this is what he wants.

He wants to stay.

He wants to stay because it's what will make him happiest. My teeth sink into my bottom lip, but before I can spiral back into my fears, I say, "Okay."

His mouth quirks, making my heart flutter. "I'm going to kiss you now, and if you'll let me, I'd like to kiss you tomorrow, too—and the next day."

Another tear falls, but I can't fight the breath of laughter that comes out with it. I look up at him. "And the day after that?"

Leaning toward me, he rests his forehead against mine. "And the day after that."

Six Months Later

"I can't believe you left for Tennessee as soon as I came home for break." Sarah's voice carries through the phone along with a huff.

Holding the phone to my ear, I glance at Carson as he drives. He must hear her because he shakes his head, a tight-lipped smile forming on his lips. "We should have gotten together before Christmas. Your school is only two hours away from Geneva. It isn't that far."

"I know," Sarah groans. "But I don't even know what we'd do if we met halfway. Hang out in Lakeland?" She says it like I'm crazy for even suggesting such a thing.

"What's wrong with Lakeland?" I ask with a laugh. "All we need is a place to meet for dinner or something."

"I'm not sitting in an Applebee's the first time I meet your boyfriend, Abbie."

"And meeting him at my house is better?" I glance at Carson, but he has no reaction to our conversation. He's used to hearing us talk about him at this point.

Sarah sighs. "Yes. Your house is a million times better than an Applebee's."

"We'll be back by New Year's," I reassure her. "You'll meet him then."

"I better." She perks up. "Is he excited to meet me?"

Looking over at Carson, I relay the question. "Are you excited to meet her?"

He doesn't pull his eyes away from the road. "Very."

His dry response makes my lips twist into a smile. "He's very excited to meet you." The car turns down a narrow road with a mailbox, and I add, "I think we're here. I'll call you later, okay?"

Her response is delayed, and the TV plays in the background. "Fine. Have fun, but I'm coming over as soon as you get back."

"As soon as we get back," I confirm.

I hang up as Carson parks our rental car in front of a quaint farmhouse at the top of the long, winding driveway. The only other building in sight is an old barn with faded red paint in the distance.

It's a chilly December evening, but the first snow of the season hasn't fallen yet. The trees are bare, and a steady plume of smoke streams from the chimney—the only sign of life for miles. "How many acres does he have?"

Carson takes the key out of the ignition, and even though I'm not looking at him, I can feel his eyes on me.

Catching him looking at me, full of love, has become my new

favorite superpower. It usually only lasts a moment, vanishing once I look his way, but those moments let me know how he feels about me.

I've thought about saying those three words more times than I can count, but I always chicken out. So, for now, I sneak glances.

He eyes the house as he answers. "A little over eighty."

"*Eighty acres?*" I gape at him. "As in eight-zero?"

His lips twitch like he finds me amusing. "A lot of people out here have a few hundred."

A man, who doesn't look old enough to be Carson's grandpa, opens the screen door and steps out onto the front porch. In a way, he's how I expected him to look: worn Wranglers, flannel shirt, cowboy boots.

Just about twenty years younger.

Carson opens the door to the rental car before looking over at me. "I hope you're ready."

I've heard a lot of stories about Carson's grandpa at this point, so when the man immediately comes down the front porch steps and says, "What the hell did they give you? A damn Prius?" it makes me grin.

The two men shake hands before pulling each other in for a hug. "Long time no see," Carson says, still hugging him.

Looking over Carson's shoulder, his grandpa smiles at me. "Is he treating you good? Because if he's not, I could take him down. Right now." His hug turns into a headlock, and I laugh.

"He's treating me just fine."

Carson's grandpa still holds Carson in place when he says, "Alright, if you say so." He finally releases him, and Carson shakes his head with a hand rubbing the back of his neck.

"That was a close one," Carson mutters as he walks around the back of the car and pops the trunk open.

"I know. You're lucky I didn't roughen you up in front of this nice young lady." His grandpa winks at me.

Carson's eyebrows furrow as he lifts our suitcases from the trunk. "No. I was worried you might break a hip."

His grandpa looks at me with wide eyes. "No respect." Then reaching out a hand, he introduces himself. "Jerry, and you must be Miss Abigail."

Laughter bubbles in my throat. "Just Abbie is fine. It's nice to meet you."

"Well, 'Just Abbie,' it's a pleasure to meet you." Releasing my hand, he walks over to help Carson with one of the suitcases. "Here, let me take one. Don't hurt yourself."

Jerry grabs a bag and leads us back toward the house. "Come on in, you two. Let's get you out of the cold. I've got chili on the stove."

I look over at Carson with wide eyes, and he lets out a breath of laughter that clouds from the cold.

Everything about the house screams we're in the Smokey Mountains. Wood paneling accents most of the rooms along with a considerable amount of bear décor. I'm not sure how many bear-themed items are supposed to be in the average household, but I'd say Jerry has them beat.

We eat, we talk, we laugh, and Jerry even makes Carson blush a few times which I have *never* seen, and it's rapidly becoming my new favorite thing. Once we're warm and full of the most delicious chili I've ever eaten, we move from the kitchen to the family room.

Everything about the living room feels comforting. Large bookshelves take up one of the walls while a huge fireplace takes up the other. The crackling flames cast a flickering glow over the large leather couch.

After a round of coffee and some cheesecake, Carson's grandpa retires into his bedroom for the night, but not without reminding Carson he'll have him up at the crack of dawn to help with the horses tomorrow morning.

Then we're alone, the dying fire casting shadows over the quiet room. My back rests against his chest as we lie on the couch, Carson's fingers smoothing down my hair.

"I like having you here." He kisses the top of my head.

Shifting to look up at him, I grin. "I like being here." Letting out a laugh, I say, "And your grandpa is hysterical."

Carson claps a hand over my mouth. "Shh. If he hears you, it will only encourage him."

My laugh meets the inside of his palm and pulls a smile to his lips. I love when he smiles at me. Carson's hand moves to cup my face, and he leans down to kiss me.

As he pulls away, he says, "I want to show you something."

I push myself off the couch and take his hand, loving the way his fingers wrap around mine. We do our best to keep our footsteps quiet as we make our way up the old, wooden steps, but they still creek anyway.

"Where are you taking me?" I whisper behind him.

Carson looks over his shoulder at me, his eyes widening slightly as he presses a finger to his lips.

I clamp my lips tighter together to keep my laugh from escaping.

Turning at the top of the stairs, we walk into a small bedroom. Our bags rest near the doorway where he must have set them earlier. I'm pretty sure this used to be Carson's bedroom, and I'm tempted to stop and stare at everything, but he keeps walking us toward a glass door on the far wall.

Carson opens the door onto a large balcony. The view overlooks the mountains, and it's beautiful enough to take my breath away. Letting go of his hand, I walk to the edge of the wood railing and gaze up at the stars. It's just past 11 p.m., but the moon casts enough natural light for the view to be stunning.

"Wow," I say. "Florida certainly doesn't have this."

Wrapping his arms around me, Carson takes in the view. "No, it doesn't."

"Why don't you live here again?" I ask in a playful tone even though my question is serious.

Turning me to face him, my back leaning against the railing, Carson hooks a finger under my chin. "Because Tennessee doesn't have this." He presses his lips to mine. It's a short and sweet kiss, but it's enough for me to lift myself onto my toes, wanting to make it last just a little bit longer.

"I love it here." I tilt my head up toward the moon and stars.

"Wait until you see it in the morning." He stands next to me and rests his elbows on the railing.

"Don't you miss it?" I ask, looking over at him. He's happy in Florida—I know because I've asked him about a million times. But as I stand here, staring out over this gorgeous moonlit view, I can't help feeling like *I'm* going to miss Tennessee, and I've only been here for a few hours.

He nods, taking in the view before looking back at me. "Yeah. I love it here." His words make me frown, but when he catches my expression, he nudges me softly. "But I love Florida, too."

I scoff. "What is there to love about Florida?"

"You," he says with all seriousness like the answer should be obvious.

I stare at him, my voice barely above a whisper. "Me?"

Carson leans over, kissing the side of my temple. When he pulls back, he says, "I love you, Abbie. So much. You have to know that."

He said it like he's said it countless times before. "What?"

He laughs, and it's the best sound. "I love you."

Okay, maybe his laugh is the second best sound.

"You've never said that before."

"I know." His lips pull into an easy smile. "When I thought about saying it, I always pictured us here."

"You love me." I try to let it sink in.

"I do," he says with a nod.

He just said the words I've wanted to hear for months, and it makes my whole body feel light. The happiness swelling my chest might as well lift me into the air.

"It's okay if you don't want to say it back." He gives me a sideways glance, his eyes teasing.

"Oh, my god!" I clap a hand over my mouth. "I love you!" I practically squeal and throw my arms around his neck. "I love you. I love you. I love you!"

He kisses me, and it somehow beats all the kisses he's given me before. We laugh against each other's lips, and the warmth radiating from us conquers the chill of winter.

"When did you know?" I can't wipe the stupid grin off my face.

Carson smooths my hair back and kisses my forehead. He wraps his arms around me, tucking my head under his chin, and says, "When I decided to make my move."

THE END

Bonus Chapter

Carson and Sarah come face to face on New Year's Eve.
Read the bonus chapter by scanning the code below!

OTHER BOOKS

Want to keep reading? Scan the code below to check out other books by Heather Garvin.

ACKNOWLEDGMENTS

It never ceases to amaze me how many people I get to thank at the end of these books. The list is ever growing, and so is my appreciation for each and every one of you.

While working on Abbie and Carson's story, I was lucky enough to have more than a few familiar friends help me improve the story. Cat Broomell, Katie Moye, Corey Wys, and Gabby Spiller have all helped me with multiple books, and I love getting their take on things. Thank you all for reading the worst versions of my words, helping me clean them up, and then hyping the book for everyone else. I have probably said this a million times, but when I bring the story to each of you, it is only ever a shell of what it could be. It takes a village to write a book, and I am truly grateful to have you on my side!

My long-time friend (and future author), Courtney Grifo, helped bring this story to life as well. Your many reactions and "pterodactyl noises" made the editing process way more fun than it should have been. Anyone who hates editing needs to find themselves a Courtney.

Fellow Authors! I was lucky enough to have not one, not two, but THREE authors help me brainstorm and pick apart Make Your Move. Dani Keen, Tisa Matthews, and Sarah Hill all helped polish this story. The feedback I gained from each of you not only enhanced the story but also enhanced my skills as an author. Thank you for caring about this story as much as I do.

And finally, I have to thank my ultimate proofreader, Ava Rogers. Even though romance isn't your genre of choice, you always step up to the plate when I need another set of eyes. Thank you!

We all have busy lives, and the fact that each of you took time out of your day to read my made-up love story makes me happier than you will ever know. I can't imagine doing this without you.

THANK YOU.

About the Author

Heather Garvin works as a nationally certified sign language interpreter by day and writes a variety of romances in her spare time.

Aside from working and writing, she's also a wife, mom, and a fur mama to two dogs, two cats, and Tuskan: the horse who inspired the logo and name for her publishing company, Tuskan Publishhing LLC.

There's nothing Heather loves more than hearing from readers. Connect with her on Instagram!

heathergarvinbooks

Printed in Great Britain
by Amazon

27549545R00189